KINN PORSCHE

NOVEL 04

WRITTEN BY
Daemi

TRANSLATION BY
Frigga, Onyx, Linarii

INTERIOR ILLUSTRATIONS BY
Avaritia

Seven Seas Entertainment

Published originally under the title of รักโคตรร้ายสุดท้ายโคตรรัก (KinnPorsche)
Author©Daemi
English edition rights under license granted by Daemi House Limited Partnership
English edition copyright©2025 Seven Seas Entertainment, Inc.
Arranged through JS Agency Co., Ltd.
All rights reserved

Cover illustrations by ビリー・バリバリ

Illustrations, design and text design are granted under license by Reve Books Co., Ltd.
(Pinsin Publishing)
Interior illustrations by Avaritia

No portion of this book may be reproduced or transmitted in any form without written permission from the copyright holders. This is a work of fiction. Names, characters, places, and incidents are the products of the author's imagination or are used fictitiously. Any resemblance to actual events, locales, or persons, living or dead, is entirely coincidental. Any information or opinions expressed by the creators of this book belong to those individual creators and do not necessarily reflect the views of Seven Seas Entertainment or its employees.

Seven Seas press and purchase enquiries can be sent to
Marketing Manager Lauren Hill at press@gomanga.com.
Information regarding the distribution and purchase of
digital editions is available from Digital Operations Manager CK Russell
at digital@gomanga.com.

Seven Seas and the Seven Seas logo are trademarks of
Seven Seas Entertainment. All rights reserved.

Follow Seven Seas Entertainment online at
sevenseasentertainment.com.

TRANSLATION: Frigga, Onyx, Linarii
ADAPTATION: Abigail Clark
LOGO & COVER DESIGN: G. A. Slight
INTERIOR DESIGN: Clay Gardner
INTERIOR LAYOUT: Sheenly S.
COPY EDITOR: Kim E.
PROOFREADER: Ami Leh, Adrian Mayall
EDITOR: Hardleigh Hewmann
PREPRESS TECHNICIAN: Salvador Chan Jr., April Malig, Jules Valera
MANAGING EDITOR: Alyssa Scavetta
EDITOR-IN-CHIEF: Julie Davis
PUBLISHER: Lianne Sentar
VICE PRESIDENT: Adam Arnold
PRESIDENT: Jason DeAngelis

ISBN: 979-8-89160-080-5
Printed in Canada
First Printing: August 2025
10 9 8 7 6 5 4 3 2 1

CONTENTS

SS	Vegas × Pete 5	7
SS	Vegas × Pete 6	33
SS	Vegas × Pete 7	65
VIP	VEGAS × PETE 1	93
36	Parting	105
SS	Vegas × Pete 8	151
SS	Vegas × Pete 9	191
37	Topsy-Turvy	233
SS	Vegas × Pete 10	275
•	Character & Name Guide	291

Vegas × Pete 5

PETE

THE MOMENT VEGAS LEFT the room, I tried to break free. No matter how much I wanted to jump out the window, the chains held my wrists in place. I banged my wrists against the wall over and over, but the shackles showed no sign of budging. It was stupid to try, wasn't it? But I had to test every idea that came to mind.

I had nothing I could use to unlock the cuffs. Anything to pierce it, break it—nothing. I could only come up with stupid methods like struggling to yank my hands free. Which fucking hurt.

Even as day bled into night, I refused to give up. I searched in every nook and cranny of the room—even under the bed and inside the drawers—but found nothing that could help me.

I opened the big wardrobe to search for a hard object I could use to pick the lock, but couldn't find a single fucking thing. Not to mention that, after searching, I had to fold the bastard's clothes back into their original arrangement. Damn, why did his wardrobe have to be so fucking tidy? If he came back and noticed that something was off, he'd tie me down to the bed again. *Ugh!*

"And what the fuck is this?" I muttered quietly to myself as I pulled open a drawer.

"Shit! You pervert!" I cursed. I couldn't believe my eyes. "Damn you and all your ancestors, Vegas! You sick, degenerate fuck!"

I picked through the items in disgust. There was plenty of stuff: ropes, whips, handcuffs, sex toys, and much more. There was so much perverted crap in there that I cringed, goosebumps forming on my skin.

"You sick little freak! Your head's full of nothing but filth! Fuckin' sex-crazed pervert!" I tossed the paraphernalia back into the drawer and rubbed my arms in horror. Fucking hell. I didn't want to be here a moment longer!

Click.

I heard the door unlock. I hurried over to the bed, lay down on my side, and pretended to be asleep, throwing the blanket over myself for the finishing touch.

Not long after that, the door swung open, and the smell of alcohol permeated the room. I could sense Vegas slowly approaching the bed. My heart pounded in my chest—I was terrified. Fuck, just knowing he was nearby sent my pulse through the roof.

Something dropped next to me on the bed with a *thud*, startling me. I squeezed my eyes shut and frantically prayed in silence. I almost forgot to breathe when I realized Vegas was lying there next to me. But...why was he being so quiet and calm? I let out the breath I was holding in a big huff, then slowly cracked my eyes open and peeked behind me.

Vegas was splayed out on his stomach, looking exhausted. I could make out the faded outlines of red handprints on his face and a few bruises on his lips. They'd probably come from Mr. Kant—he and Vegas had a big fight today.

I lifted myself up from the bed and watched Vegas quietly. His eyes remained closed. From the outside, he seemed like a regular guy.

Even though he had a bit of a cunning expression, every time I'd met him in the past, he'd sported a kind and friendly smile. I'd always thought of him as a normal person. Even though I'd heard a bunch of horrible things about him from Mr. Kinn and Mr. Tankhun, I'd never seen him act that way myself, so I never believed them.

But now, I believed them with all my heart. There was much more to this man than met the eye. I'd never imagined he could be like this. It was as if he was suppressing another identity entirely. It was frightening to find out that an incomprehensible evil lurked behind his friendly facade.

His eyes opened, and he shot me a stern glare. "Still awake?" he asked in a slurred voice. I flinched and jumped back against the headrest.

"Huh... Why are you so afraid of me?" he asked, chuckling. He was still on his stomach.

"Imagine if someone was trying to kill *you*, huh?" I said as I pulled my knees up, hugging them tightly.

"But I haven't killed you, have I?" he deadpanned.

I averted my eyes. I didn't want to see his face. The more I looked at him, the more uneasy I became.

"You hate me that bad, huh?" he asked, glaring at me. He clearly had no intention of backing down.

I turned to snarl at him, "Yeah, I do! I fucking hate you!" But all I got in return was a chuckle and a smirk.

"Hah! Of course. It's always like that. Everybody hates me," Vegas said. His voice lowering to a murmur, he continued, "Even my dad."

I looked down, then stared into the distance.

"Do you know? That my dad... Fuck! Do you know how much he hurts me? He's been kicking the shit out of me my whole life. Even when I was a little kid."

I glanced at him out of the corner of my eye. It looked like he was zoning out. His eyes were blank, but I could see the instability and weakness flickering behind his stare.

I bit my lip and said nothing in response. Vegas's behavior made me so uneasy that I could barely move. I couldn't figure out what was going through his head.

"Some days, he compares me to Kinn, says I'm good for nothing. Why is he so obsessed with the Major Clan? Hah! What can I do? We're called the fucking Minor Clan—we've been the underdogs from the start! That asshole blames us, but it's his damn fault for being Agong's second child!"

I was beginning to connect the dots. All the love the Minor Clan family members showed each other was just a front—Vegas and Macau were nothing more than Mr. Kant's pawns.

"Hmph! Yeah, Kinn is so good at everything." Vegas kept spilling his guts. "He's so fucking lucky. Lucky from the day he was born. He has the privilege of being from the Major Clan—he doesn't have to suffer in this shitty Minor Clan like I do!"

Vegas didn't seem to get along with his father at all. He'd probably been slapped around like this many times before. Maybe none of this would have happened if Mr. Kant gave his kids a shred of love and affection.

"I can't think of a single area where the Minor Clan can surpass the Major Clan. Their sons are all better than me. Be is smarter, and his business has soared to such great heights. Then look at the Minor Clan—we can't get a single thing right."

Then he chuckled. "I guess there *is* one thing: pretending. Right, Pete? You can see how good my father is at showing his love for Macau and me, but that's all it is—a show. In the eyes of the public, we're his precious sons. But behind the curtain? We're just his puppets. If he steers us left, we go left. If he steers us right, we go right. When we can't do that, he blames it all on us."

Under normal circumstances, I would have felt sorry for Vegas, but he had no right to use his frustrations with his father as an excuse to hurt other people. He needed to be reasonable. He shouldn't have behaved like a brat who didn't get enough attention, putting his emotions above his reasoning—otherwise, he wasn't much different from his father.

I stayed silent and let Vegas continue.

"Be is always so kind to his sons. Whether it's Khun, Kinn, or Kim... They can screw up their lives however the hell they want, but Be doesn't mind. And he wouldn't trample on their feelings by marrying a new wife. Don't you agree?" Vegas shifted his gaze toward me expectantly.

"...Mm-hmm." I hummed my agreement just to get by.

"The Minor Clan fucking sucks! Just me being gay is enough to drive my father crazy! He despises me, acts like I'm a freak! Why? I *hate* women! All they want is money. They're gold diggers!"

Everyone had their own reasoning behind their opinions. Vegas was no different—but his opinion was all wrong.

"...But not *all* of them are, right?" I blurted out my thoughts, then quickly pressed my lips together. I shouldn't have shared that out loud.

"All the women I've seen are like that... They're repulsive. Shameless," Vegas continued, emotion tinging his voice.

"...It depends! There are both good and bad people out there—men *and* women. Your logic is wrong." I didn't want to save him from whatever hellhole he was wallowing in, but if he stayed on this train of thought, he'd be stuck on the wrong path for the rest of his life.

"Oh? So are you telling me that I'm wrong for preferring men?"

"No..." I started to speak, but then I shut my mouth, stopping myself from lecturing him further. If he wanted to stay mired in his misery, then so be it. I'd find pleasure in his pain. I wouldn't let this asshole drag me into his bullshit.

"Hah. I get that it depends on the person. But I hate, *hate* those bitches. For as long as I can remember, I saw them make my mother cry. Saw it more times than I can count," Vegas ranted. "I hate them. I fucking hate them. I hate all of them! Hate them like I hate the Major Clan! I hate everyone who turned my life into this mess!"

Hearing that, I couldn't help but ask, "What did the Major Clan do to you?"

"They framed my mother for crimes she didn't commit. They drove her to suicide."

"But...you gotta be reasonable. That was your elders' doings, and it happened a long time ago!" I shot back. Shit, did this guy grow up on mother's milk or *donkey's* milk? Why couldn't he grasp an easy concept like this?

Well, have fun dwelling on your dark and miserable life, Vegas.

"Hmph... So loyal to the Major Clan, huh?" Vegas scoffed. "Seriously, are you Kinn's butt buddy or something?"

"Only you could come to such a fucked-up conclusion." I wanted to kick him in the teeth. *Mr. Kinn is a far better man than you think, Vegas.*

"Hmph! I'm so jealous of Kinn! He's fucking better than me at everything! No matter how hard I try, all I can ever be is second best. Always second best! Fitting for the Minor Clan, huh? Think about it. Even Porsche doesn't love me. I treated him well from the start, but no matter how nice I was, he ended up choosing that fucker Kinn over me!"

Oh, Vegas! What a sore loser. He sounded like a man-child.

"...If you don't want people to compare you to Mr. Kinn, why do *you* keep doing it?" I asked.

"Right? Why am I comparing myself to that bastard? Hah!" Vegas laughed. His vacant eyes shifted to focus on me. I gulped nervously. What did this suspicious motherfucker want now?

I watched Vegas in silent paranoia as he slowly lifted himself up off the bed and crept toward me.

"What about you? You've compared me to Kinn too."

I wanted to dodge him, but as I attempted to block his approach with my foot, he trapped me within the bracket of his arms.

"Fuck you, Vegas!" I snarled at him, thrashing around. He was starting to scare me—his eyes were terrifying.

He cackled. "Come to think of it, you're kinda cute," he slurred. His breath reeked of alcohol—had he been drinking booze or *drowning* in it?

"Back off!" I yelled as I pushed him. He fell on his back into the same spot as earlier. When he started to move again, I got up from the bed, tightly holding a pillow against me as a shield in case he tried to do unspeakable things to me again.

However, all I was met with was stillness. Vegas stayed sprawled out on the bed, his face turned away from me. He lay entirely still, not budging a bit. That was strange.

"V-Vegas..." I called his name in dread. "Vegas... V-Vegas?"

I lifted my foot and poked his arm with it, but it elicited no response. "Are you dead? You... Hah! You'd better be!" I snapped, unintentionally raising my voice. Vegas twitched in his stupor.

I jolted in surprise, throwing my back against the wall. I didn't think he'd still be awake! *Shhhhhh, Pete! Be quiet!* I was scared shitless. *Damn it, I'm such a pussy!*

"Fuck! Should I just suffocate him with a pillow?" I mused. "No...if I kill him, his henchmen will find out. They'll catch me red-handed. I'm screwed... Wait, maybe I can do it and blame it on alcohol poisoning."

I sighed. "I can't. His dad wouldn't let me walk away with my life. What do I do? I want to kill you—I want to fucking kill you! But I don't want to be a murderer!"

I dwelled on it for ages before collapsing back onto the bed. As I looked at Vegas's prone form in frustration, I realized something: Vegas must have his phone with him. I could use it to contact someone.

I slowly crept toward Vegas, poking at both of his pockets. They were empty. I got out of the bed and went to check his expensive designer bag as quietly as I could. But I still came up with nothing. *Hmph! Why do you have to be so careful, huh?!* He must have left his phone on his desk, outside this room.

"Son of a bitch!" I cursed in exasperation and sat back down on the bed. "You're a piece of shit. You affection-starved son of a bitch!" I kicked him off the bed with both of my feet. I couldn't stand seeing his face.

His body rolled off the bed and fell to the floor with a *thud*. That was satisfying. I'd take it; I'd take any form of revenge, no matter how petty.

"Oops! I didn't do anything, you just fell. Serves you right, motherfucker!" I spat. "Ugh, I'm just gonna go to bed."

With that, I crawled under the blanket and reached over the headboard to switch off the lights. *Nice!* I'd take this as a victory.

I needed to encourage Vegas to drink more often—when he was drunk, I could kick him off the bed. If I kicked him off the bed every night, he might just get a fatal contusion. *Heh, and I won't feel guilty either...* Wait, what kind of a stupid plan was this? Had I spent too much time with Mr. Tankhun? I mean, I *was* scared out of my mind. That was probably why I'd come up with such a stupid plan. I must have been going crazy!

I cracked my eyes open the next morning, woken by my aching body. I barely got any damn sleep, but who would under these circumstances?

I'd spent the whole night concocting plans to kill Vegas. I could strangle him with these chains, but I'd still be stuck here. Fuck. It was useless. Even if I managed to take Vegas out, the Minor Clan would kill me. I had to remember my grandma. I had to stay alive for her sake, even if I wanted to finish Vegas once and for all.

"So, you let the big fish swim away?!" I heard a voice shout. "Couldn't clean up your own mess, and you still have the gall to show up here?!"

Thud! Crash!

The sound of stuff breaking prompted me to sit up on the bed and look out through the frosted glass.

Vegas was on a rampage again. This time, he was scolding two of his men, pointing his finger at them as they stood there with their heads hung low.

"But this was Big's responsibility, sir," one of his men said timidly. "I took over at the end, but they'd already refused to sign a contract with us."

"Idiot! And where the hell is Big, anyway?!" Vegas shouted. "Get out of my sight, both of you! Go!"

Vegas's men left the room. As soon as I saw Vegas heading back to the bedroom, I quickly dropped down on the bed and pretended to be asleep.

The door opened with a *creak*.

"Quit the act, Pete! I know you heard all of that."

As I hid under the blanket, I curled my hands into fists and took a deep breath. I could tell Vegas was furious, but I didn't say a word.

"Get up!" Vegas shouted, yanking the blanket off of my body. My foot reflexively shot out, accidentally kicking him in the chest.

"Pete, you little shit! How dare you?!" Vegas sputtered, his gaze full of wrath.

All the blood drained from my face. I hadn't meant to add fuel to the flames. I knew that when Vegas got angry, nobody could calm him down. He would take out his anger on anyone and anything within reach. But what could I have done? Vegas had startled me, and my body had reacted on its own!

Frightened, I lifted myself up on my elbow and told him, "I-I didn't mean to do that."

Vegas breathed deeply, on the verge of erupting in anger again. "Do you know what happens when I get mad?" he asked as he pinned both of my arms against the headboard.

I thrashed against his hold in an attempt to free myself, but it was useless. "Let me go!"

"When I'm angry, nobody gets in my way. And what did you do, huh?" Vegas taunted me. His grip was so strong that I couldn't fight back. This demon wearing Vegas's face had come back to torment me once again.

"I told you, I didn't mean to kick you!" I shut my eyes tightly, trying to break free.

"And another thing—why was I on the floor last night, hmm? What did you do?" Vegas leaned over me, his face inching closer to mine. He pressed against me with all his weight, immobilizing my legs.

"I have no idea! You were drunk!"

"You tried to kill me, didn't you? Let me tell you something, Pete—as long as I'm still breathing, you will live. You will live, and you will *suffer*. Do you know what that's going to be like?" Vegas buried his face into the crook of my neck, sending a shiver down my spine.

"Get the fuck off of me, Vegas!" I used all my strength to struggle against him. I didn't even register any pain as I tried to break free.

"Stop struggling! The more you fight me, the more it turns me on," Vegas hissed quietly into my ear. "All right, consider this helping me blow off some steam—I just can't contain myself."

I was disgusted. "Let go of me! You can't use me like that!" I refused to back down. No matter what happened, I wouldn't let him assault me again!

"Heh," Vegas giggled.

"You're a fucking scumbag! That's why nobody loves you! You're just an asshole starved for affection! Let me go, you son of a bitch!" I frantically fought back in every way I could.

"The fuck did you say, Pete?!" he spat. He released his grip on my wrists so he could press my head against the bed instead.

"Motherfucker! Get off me, Vegas!" I tried to hit his arms, but he pinned my head down with one hand and gripped my throat with the other.

"Say that again! What did you call me?! Say it!" he snarled, his iron grip growing tighter and tighter with each word.

I gasped for breath. "L-let me go..." My hands went weak from lack of oxygen. It felt like I was drowning. I was in so much agony that I started to lose consciousness.

"A guy like you is better off dead!" Vegas growled.

I cracked my eyes open. Vegas became a blurry image as my eyes brimmed with tears of pain. His eyes blazed like a predator going in for the kill.

Knock, knock!

"Mr. Vegas, we have a problem!" one of Vegas's underlings shouted from outside. "Mr. Macau got into a fight with Mr. Kant again, sir!"

Vegas instantly let go of my throat. I lay on the bed and gasped a big gulp of air into my lungs.

"Wha-what are you—?" I spoke hoarsely, coughing. My body was limp on the bed, my chest rising and falling with my labored breaths. Vegas went over to the drawer and fetched the other handcuffs. He yanked my wrists and forcefully bound them to the bedpost.

"Vegas... No... Let me go," I pleaded, my eyes widening. Both of my wrists were shackled together.

"That's what you get for having a smart mouth," he said. "Don't go anywhere!"

With that, he left the room.

"Vegas, you monster! I hope you fucking *die*!" I screamed curses at him as I tried in vain to break free from my shackles. I was back to being completely bound—I couldn't walk; I couldn't even lie down. All I could do was sit there on the bed.

"Let me go!"

I was left shouting into the empty room for some time. I was starting to lose my mind. I'd had the freedom to roam around, if only for a short moment, and now I'd been pulled back into this excruciating state once again. Damn it!

I didn't know how much time passed, but Vegas eventually returned. He changed into his university uniform, grabbed his bag, then left.

"Let me go, Vegas!" I demanded. No matter how loudly I yelled, he didn't even bat an eye. I kicked the bedpost and yanked my wrists, but it was no use. My body was in rough shape, and my strength hadn't recovered—not to mention I'd been raped over and over again. If things kept going like this, I was likely to end up a dead man.

The sound of the glass door sliding open made my eyes sparkle with hope. A guy walked in with a food tray—I knew him pretty well.

"Nop... Help me!" I called out as soon as he stepped inside. Nop used to be a bodyguard for the Major Clan before he turned coat and became a Minor Clan lapdog instead. "Help!"

Even though the clans hated each other, Nop and I had never had personal beef. I hoped he would have at least a scrap of sympathy for me.

"Here's your food. Eat up." Nop put the tray on the bedside table.

I watched him sorrowfully and pleaded for his help. "Nop, let me go. Help me, please. I'm begging you."

I looked at him with imploring eyes. I watched as he took in my appearance: bare save for a pair of sweatpants. He turned away, shaking his head as if he couldn't bear the sight.

"Pete... I can't believe I'm seeing you like this," he said, dismayed.

"Then you've got to help me. I won't cause you any trouble, I promise," I said hastily, making an empty promise just to survive.

"I can't help you, Pete. You...should stop trying to escape. Just accept it."

"Fuck you! Don't you see what he's done to me? You've gotta help me out here!" I refused to give up. Nop was a spark of hope, a light at the end of the tunnel. Even though that light looked dim, at least I might have a chance.

"The only way out of this house is in a body bag," Nop said. "I'm sure you're well aware."

I bit down hard on my lip. Unlike the Major Clan, the Minor Clan was ruthlessly cruel. Mr. Kant was no stranger to murder. I knew precisely what Nop was implying.

"Then tell him to finish me off already!" I said hopelessly. *If you're saying I have zero chance of survival, then please...please just put me out of my misery.*

"...He will. He won't let you get away."

"And you're not gonna do anything? You're just gonna let me sit here and wait for death?"

"I can give you this advice: Do what he wants you to do. Vegas gets bored easily. When he's tired of you, he might take pity on you and let you go. Consider it a way to buy time. That's all I can say to help you..."

With that, Nop was gone, and my glimmer of hope left with him.

"Hey! Come back! At least untie me! How am I supposed to eat like this? Huh?!"

Nop, you shithead! You only had one job—feeding me! What am I supposed to do, eat with my eyes?! Are you crazy?! Didn't you just tell me to buy time? Then at least let me eat or drink something first! I'm dying of thirst here!

I gazed gloomily at the tray. Even though my brain was a chaotic mess of racing thoughts, I knew that I needed to stay alive and keep my hopes up. I had to get back so I could see my grandma. I wouldn't let myself die here! Fuck, it was so close, yet so far—the glass was right there in front of me, but I couldn't drink from it. Did Nop think I was a ghost?! Just add some incense to that tray, and you'd have a spirit offering.

Nop was gone for the rest of the day. I was completely parched; my throat was as dry as sandpaper. I was so exhausted that I couldn't stay sitting up. I rested my head on the headboard and dozed off.

I jolted awake at the sound of Vegas opening the door. Terrified, I shuffled around a bit before pressing my forehead against the bedpost. I was so fucking hungry that my stomach was beginning to ache. I really needed to take a leak too...but I was too afraid to tell Vegas. Just the sight of his face scared me to death, even though his expression was neutral right now. It was a far cry from this morning's fury. He changed out of his university uniform, then ambled around the room, acting as if I wasn't even there. What an asshole.

"Have you finally learned how to shut up?" he said at last, breaking the silence.

I didn't reply.

"If you disobey me again, your punishment will be much worse," he added, his voice softening. That aggressive aura from earlier had vanished entirely. Was this bastard bipolar or what? He was so unpredictable. Fuck, it was such a pain in the ass figuring out his moods!

He laughed quietly. "Come on. I'm not *that* unreasonable."

"Yeah?" I shot back in a hoarse voice. I tried to hold back my words, afraid of provoking him into another argument.

"If you behave, I won't punish you," he said, his voice coming closer and closer behind me.

"Mm."

"And why the fuck haven't you eaten anything? Are you gonna just fucking sit around and look at it?! Watched too many soap operas with Tankhun, huh? Going on a hunger strike? Damn, you're a melodramatic little bitch." Vegas came up next to me, his hands resting loosely on his hips as he stared me down.

I weakly turned my head toward him. "If you want me to eat, stop bitching and get me out of these shackles first."

"Oh, Nop didn't let you out?" Vegas asked, surprised.

"No! Brought me the food and left."

"Hah! Is he nuts?" Vegas laughed and shook his head. He really was in a better mood—I couldn't see a trace of the Vegas from this morning.

"*You're* nuts," I muttered.

"Ugh! Come here." Vegas procured a key from his pocket and uncuffed me. I pulled my wrists away and rubbed at them; they really hurt.

"And remember—from now on, don't get smart with me," he warned me.

I barely paid attention to what he was saying as I poured myself some water and gulped it down. Then I shot up from the bed and ran over to the toilet to relieve myself. I'd been holding my bladder since that morning. Was I going to get a kidney stone from all this?

I washed my face and took the time to mentally prepare myself before going out to face Vegas. I was starving, though, so I mustered up my courage and went back into the room. I grabbed the plate and went to eat on the bed without so much as a flinch.

Vegas, who was on his phone on the bed, shot me a scolding glare. "Not on the bed. Go eat on the sofa."

I was too tired to argue, so I obediently went over to the sofa. I used to think that if I could put up with Tankhun, I could put up with anyone on earth—but that wasn't true at all. I knew for sure that I couldn't put up with Vegas's shit at all.

Once I finished eating, I made a beeline to the bathroom again. I was sweating bullets. I couldn't stand breathing the same air as Vegas for too long.

I spent almost two hours in there: pacing around, sitting, showering, doing whatever I could to delay returning to that bedroom. The bathroom was the only safe zone in my life right now, and I wanted to spend as much time in there as possible.

Once I got out of the bathroom, I was relieved to find the bedroom empty. But then I shifted my gaze to the glass door and saw Vegas diligently studying at the desk in his office. Well, that was good. I had the chance to breathe a little.

I dropped down on the bed, and fear crept into my head. Would he tie me up like that again tonight? I wanted to hit myself with something so I could just black out. I was too tired to face anything.

As I paced and randomly explored the room, I heard the *click* of a door opening—someone was here to see Vegas.

"Hiaaa..." A small figure ran up and tearfully hugged Vegas. I watched the scene with hopeful eyes.

Mr. Macau...

"Help me! Mr. Macau! Help!" I yelled loudly, trying to drag myself over to the door. I couldn't get there, however; the chain held my arm back.

I had no idea if Mr. Macau heard me or not, but Vegas pulled his brother into a tight embrace against his chest before they both left the room. Vegas smirked and gave me a taunting glance before the door closed.

"Damn it!" I cursed. "Is this room soundproofed?"

I paced the room in frustration. *Shit!* None of my attempts had worked. And Vegas was likely going to come back and punish me for this one. I looked left and right, searching for something I could use to defend myself with and finding nothing. Even the bed lamps were fixed to the wall; I couldn't just yank one of them out. I grabbed a pillow and held it tightly. *What am I gonna do?!*

I heard the door open. I quickly hopped onto the sofa and assumed a fighting stance, preparing to kick out as soon as Vegas reached me. Even though my body was worn out, I wouldn't give in!

Vegas sighed. "You love to get yourself into trouble, don't you?" he said, cracking a manic grin. He slid the glass door shut and slowly crept toward me.

"Come any closer, and I'll strangle you!" I threw the pillow at him and picked up the chain, wrapping it around my hands.

Vegas ignored my threat and continued to close in on me. "Hah... Do you know how many times you've pissed me off? Just today alone?"

"Don't come any closer," I said. My eyes darted left and right, looking for an escape.

"Do you think you're in any position to make demands, Pete? Huh?!"

Vegas reached me with a quick lunge. I raised my leg to kick him, but his hands managed to catch my foot. He grabbed and pulled it, immediately knocking me off-balance, and I fell heavily onto the sofa.

"Heh," Vegas laughed.

Now that I'd lost the upper hand, Vegas was quick to claim it, climbing on top of me and pinning my arms down.

I thrashed against his hold. "Get off me!"

"Hmm? Where's the man who planned to strangle me? Come on. Show me." Vegas burst into a fit of crazed giggles. It sounded so insane that my heart pounded in fear.

"Let me go!" I fought back with everything I had, trying to free myself from him. He held my wrists above my head and bound them with the chain. Even though he did it sloppily, the chain was heavy enough to hold my wrists in place.

"Scream as loud as you want. Do it. See if anyone comes to save you!" Vegas pulled my pants down to my knees before turning away to open the bedside drawer. I used the opportunity to kick him in the chest with all my might and tried to struggle free.

Vegas lost his balance and fell off the sofa. "Pete, you little shit!" he snarled, his eyes flashing with fury. He got off the floor, held his hand up, then swung at my face with full force.

The sound of his slap rang through the room. The tang of iron lingered in my mouth, and my head began to spin. Before I could collect myself, Vegas dragged me away from the sofa and forcefully tossed me onto the bed.

"You're such a... I don't know how to get it through your thick skull—but I already told you not to disobey me!" Vegas climbed on top of me and pointed a finger in my face, furious. "What do you think your life's gonna be like after this?!"

"Let me go, Vegas... Leave me alone." I trembled with fear, shaking like a leaf in the wind. My heart shattered as the painful memories of Vegas's assault trampled upon it once again.

"How many times do I need to punish you before you get it, huh?!" he snarled at me, landing a sucker punch to my stomach. I writhed on the bed, biting down hard on my lip to distract myself from the pain. Vegas wasted no time spreading my legs and forcing himself between them.

"D-don't!" I tried to beg as loudly as I could, but that punch to the gut had slowed my movements.

"Hah... You always test my patience, Pete. Do you refuse to learn, or do you just like getting punished?" Vegas asked. I narrowed my eyes at him in hatred.

Once again, my heart was forced to endure bitterness and pain. Vegas tore open a condom wrapper, then uncapped a bottle of lube. I shut my eyes tightly and tensed up in fear. He had never been gentle, never bothered with foreplay—nothing. The only gift he gave me was torment.

It didn't take long for the pain to shoot up my spine. That bastard shoved his cock inside me, ignoring how much I writhed in agony. He took his time as he forced himself into me; I felt fullness and numbness in equal measure. He thrust in a short rhythm, and then he sped up without warning.

I couldn't feel a thing. I was far beyond the point of pain already. All I could feel was that deep bitterness that never faded away. It would always be with me.

"Ahhh... Mmm."

Every time I heard Vegas moan, it cast the atrocity he was committing into starker relief. I cracked my eyes open to give him a spiteful glare.

Vegas tilted his face up, basking in bliss on top of me. Even though there were a few moments where he hit a spot inside me that sent strange tingles through my body, I never took it as pleasure.

"Ngh..." I bit my lip to hold back my cries. Vegas kept slamming his pelvis into mine without any sign of stopping.

"Ahh... So good... Feels so good inside of you." The more Vegas described his pleasure, the more disgusted I became.

But my body was starting to catch up with Vegas's actions. The numbness in my ass started to dissipate, and I slowly grew attuned to the feeling of his cock thrusting in and out of me.

"E-enough... You...you monster!" I tried to scream at him, but all I could manage was a quiet plea.

"You're getting turned on, aren't you?" Vegas said, leering down at my dick. Whenever he hit the right spot inside me, my traitorous body would react.

"I-I hate you!" I growled, biting down hard on my lip. Vegas moved faster and faster until my body started to sway with the force of it.

Vegas smirked triumphantly. "Are you gonna come...? I can wait for you."

"I'll never come for a bastard like you!" I spat at him, but it only seemed to provoke him further. He kept thrusting, controlling the pace as he pleased.

"*Ahhh*. Watch your mouth," Vegas said, his voice echoing through the room. I didn't have the energy to argue back. I had no idea what was going to happen next, but my body seemed to be accepting the situation. I was certain that my hatred for him was stronger than my physical reactions—my body wouldn't betray my feelings like that.

It took a while, but Vegas eventually found his release. I didn't have time to collect myself, though, before he flipped me over onto my belly: Tonight wouldn't end with a single round. I could only clutch the sheets in pain and anger. I didn't feel a thing except for the tears brimming in the corners of my eyes.

I could no longer bear Vegas's intrusion. My heart pounded as I panted in exhaustion, attempting to endure the onslaught. I refused to reach orgasm, no matter how many rounds Vegas went—I never would!

You scumbag! One day, I'll bring you to your knees and make you beg for my mercy, motherfucker!

At some point, I must have passed out. My body was so battered, I couldn't bear it. Just slowly shifting my position was enough to make the pain in my backside shoot all throughout my body. I could feel it in my bones.

I lay under the blanket, wearing a new pair of pants that Vegas must have put on me. I couldn't remember how many rounds it had taken for him to satisfy his lust; all I knew was that I eventually couldn't take it any longer and passed out.

Creeeak.

Startled, I whipped my head around to face the glass door. I was relieved when I saw it was Nop, bringing in a tray of food. I was lucky Vegas hadn't tied me down like the day before—he'd only shackled me with a single chain today.

"Oh, Pete... What did you do to piss him off this time?" Nop wondered aloud as he studied my face. *Guess that slap last night left a bruise.*

I coughed weakly. "Help me, Nop... Please." I gently pushed myself up and leaned against the headboard.

Nop poured some water and handed the glass to me. His face showed genuine sympathy. "Pete... I feel bad, I really do. I've never had a problem with you, but you've got to understand my situation—I fear for my life."

I gulped the water down in my thirst, then scanned the room. "Where is he?"

"At university, of course. He has exams this entire week. I guess it's stressing him out, so he's taking it out on you." Nop took the glass from me and put it back on the tray.

I held on to Nop's arm and shook him gently. "You...you don't have to help me yourself, Nop. But please, call the Major Clan—Arm or Pol. Maybe even Nont will help me. I'm begging you."

"There's a new set of sheets at the end of the bed. Vegas wants you to change them once you get up," Nop said, changing the subject and ignoring my pleas.

"Nop... *Please*," I begged.

Nop let out a sigh, then gently pried my hand off him. "Pete... A guy like Vegas treats everyone like shit, except for the few people he loves. Just deal with it, man."

With that, Nop left the room.

I was left sitting on the floor, watching sadly as he walked away. *Vegas treats everyone like shit, except for the few people he loves?* I replayed Nop's words in my head. He was right, I guess, because look at how well Vegas treated Porsche!

Speaking of Porsche...if he were in this situation, what would he do? He was really lucky that he'd met Mr. Kinn. He loved Mr. Kinn, and Mr. Kinn loved him in return. So, there was no chance Mr. Kinn would have done these kinds of vile things to Porsche...right?

Vegas couldn't possibly be human; he was the devil incarnate. Everyone was someone's child, a person who was loved and cherished—he couldn't just trample on someone's labor of love like that! No! People had feelings. *I can't wait for the day karma catches up to you, Vegas. By then, no one you care about will be left in your life!*

Vegas was no different from any other spoiled rich kid, but he was deeper and more calculating than most. He was full of horrible thoughts that had been building up since childhood. It was probably from the lack of love he received from his father. Vegas must have put up walls in his heart and locked his demons in there.

Whenever he met someone weaker than him, he'd let those demons out one by one. If I kept playing his game, how long would it take for it to end? But what if...?

"Hah. Just go, Porsche. Mr. Kinn's already in a bad mood today, and I don't want to get in trouble."

"Fucking hell! What the fuck does he want from me?!"

"Just go with the flow."

"What do you mean, go with the flow?!"

"Spoiled people like Kinn... If you go along with them for a while, then they'll get bored and stop. If you keep resisting, it'll only rile them up."

The advice I'd given to Porsche a while back bubbled up in my brain. What if I refused to entertain Vegas? What if I didn't play along with his twisted game? What would happen if I made him get bored with me?

I had taught Porsche this strategy so he could deal with Mr. Kinn bossing him around. Vegas seemed to be cut from the same cloth. That was how you defeated these damned attention-seekers who didn't know when to stop.

All right. I'd survive this situation, in case there was a way out. The worst thing that could happen was Vegas killing me—I had nothing to lose.

Come on, Pete! Give it a shot!

KINN
PORSCHE

Vegas × Pete 6

PETE

I GOT OUT OF BED and struggled toward the bathroom. I didn't think it was possible, but the pain was even more excruciating than before. How long would I have to live through this hell?

Reliving the same torture again and again had left me exhausted and distraught. The Major Clan probably thought I was dead. Had Mr. Kinn really forgotten about me? Was Mr. Tankhun going about his day like nothing was out of the ordinary? Suddenly, I felt betrayed.

But maybe they were looking for a way to rescue me. I was sure that Porsche, Pol, and Arm would remember me. They had to be trying to find me. *Please hurry up and save me. I don't know how much longer I can bear this pain.*

I was so weak, so utterly powerless. I'd never felt this way before—like all the life had been drained out of me. *Damn it!*

I decided to take a shower. Luckily, Vegas had left all his toiletries in here. I didn't know what he'd allow me to use, so I just picked one at random.

Or...maybe I shouldn't clean myself? If I stayed filthy, Vegas wouldn't want to come near me. But the stains he'd left all over my body disgusted me. The thought of the vile acts he'd committed made me want to scrub my skin raw. No, it was a stupid idea to stay dirty—I couldn't stand myself in that state.

After I showered, I turned up the AC. It was cold, but I couldn't put on a shirt, thanks to the chains. The only thing I had on was a pair of pants I dug out from Vegas's closet. Luckily, we were about the same height and build. I didn't want to touch his stuff, but I had no choice.

I went to eat the breakfast Nop had brought for me and sighed heavily when I saw what was on the plate: sausages, a fried egg, and a single piece of bread. How could this satisfy anyone's hunger? But I couldn't blame these rich bastards; they all ate like birds, apart from Mr. Tankhun, who ate anything and everything. I felt wistful at the thought of Mr. Tankhun—I'd rather endure his childishness than be tortured like this...

The difference between the Major Clan and the Minor Clan was stark. Even though the atmosphere was thick with expectations and responsibility, the Major Clan's house felt like a home. Everyone respected each other, and under Mr. Korn's nurturing love and kindness, the family remained as strong as a deep-rooted tree.

The Minor Clan's house, on the other hand, was entrenched in flames. Everyone struggled to survive, like withering plants in desperate need of water. The two brothers' love for each other wasn't enough to make up for the lack of affection from their father; the family languished as a result.

I'd been following Mr. Vegas for weeks before my capture, and I knew that he barely came home. Mr. Macau was the same. I was surprised at first, but I eventually noticed the cracks in the Minor Clan's foundation.

After I'd finished my breakfast, I got up from the sofa and turned to glare at the dark-blue sheet folded on the foot of the bed. I was absolutely furious that I had to act like a slave for the Minor Clan, but I tamped down my rage and hastily changed the sheets before Vegas could get angry with me again—I wanted to avoid that at all costs.

It wasn't exactly a surprise that he'd grown up to become like this, since he'd had these problems since he was a child...

After haphazardly throwing the sheet over the bed, I focused on replacing the pillowcases. At that moment, Nop returned to the room; I quickly dropped everything and approached him.

"Nop..."

"I'm here to take the food tray," Nop said without looking at me. It seemed like he was trying to walk away from me, but I followed him until the chain holding my wrist went taut.

"Nop, please help me," I begged. I knew my chances were slim, but I needed to try everything I could.

"Don't forget to use the air freshener spray," he added. "Mr. Vegas is a clean freak, and he doesn't like the smell of food in his bedroom. And look at the way you put on the bedsheet! Do you want him to hit you again? This room needs to be pristine!" Then he slammed the door in my face.

"Damn it!" I cursed. With my hands on my hips, I glared at the bed—the sheet was tucked in at all the corners.

"How is this not neat?" I grumbled. "Do I need to iron it too, you son of a bitch?!"

I collapsed on the bed, questioning what the hell I was doing. Did that asshole Vegas have anything good in his life? Well, he had good looks, but everything else about him was utter garbage.

I looked around the room, cursing Vegas under my breath. Everything in this room was very tidy indeed. What a perfectionist. Should I try driving him crazy? I bet he'd go batshit if anything in this room was out of order. The thought made me chuckle.

I started rearranging the books on his desk, making them lay in a zigzag pattern. I turned everything upside down, putting things the opposite of how they should be. I rummaged through his clothes until his wardrobe was a total disaster.

I smiled broadly at my masterpiece: Vegas's room was a total wreck. His clothes were strewn across the floor, no longer organized by color, and the bedsheets were wrinkled. Vegas would lose his shit when he got home. He'd glare at me hard, and a vein would pop out on his forehead like it was about to burst. Then, he'd start going on a rampage...

Shit! What the fuck did I just do?! Why did I *want* to rile Vegas up? I was gonna be in deep shit! *Why are you so stupid, Pete?!*

Twenty minutes after I'd started making a mess of things, I set about putting everything back in its place. I cursed myself for spending so much effort tidying up his room. I told myself that I needed to do as he pleased until he got tired of me. The angrier that man got, the more he wanted to control me. I couldn't get caught up in his mind games.

I spent almost the entire rest of the day putting everything back in its exact spot. If I'd had a ruler right then, I'd have arranged things down to the inch!

Finally done, I flopped restlessly on the bed. It had been so easy to mess up Vegas's room; why was it so difficult to put it back in order?

Creak.

I started at the sound of the bedroom door opening. I immediately sat up and put my back flush against the headboard.

"Yeah... I'll send my part to you tonight. Don't come over. It's not convenient for me. Leave it for tomorrow." Vegas spoke into his phone as he came in with my dinner. He carelessly dropped the food tray near the sofa while my eyes darted around nervously. I was so hypervigilant, my body reacted automatically; I couldn't control my anxiety.

"Ugh, I have more exams to take and reports to do," Vegas said wearily once he'd hung up. "I'm fed up with all of it."

I remained silent, staring at him fearfully.

He glanced at me. "Come eat. I brought you dinner."

Vegas's demeanor sent a cold sweat down my spine. I was afraid to move; my body tensed up so tightly that my muscles practically spasmed.

"Eat!" he snapped.

I did as I'd planned to do: I would not argue with him, resist him, or talk to him. I would do as he said without argument. I would keep my emotions as neutral as possible, even if I felt reluctant to follow his orders.

I dropped onto the sofa, frowning at what I saw on the food tray—a fish fillet and some salad. *Fucking hell! How is this supposed to fill me up?* I was going to lose a lot of weight staying here. The portions they served were for ants!

"So obedient," Vegas said flatly as he watched me. "Good."

I ignored him and ate my food. I sighed with relief when Vegas finally grabbed a towel and headed to the bathroom. Thankfully, he wasn't in a bad mood today—I'd be dead otherwise.

I put the empty plate on the desk and remembered to spray the room with air freshener. I'd do everything I could to prevent Vegas from getting angry. I was tired of taking his beatings.

Vegas returned from the bathroom. He got dressed, and then he watched me as he leisurely dried his hair. I sat on the bed, still ignoring him, and tried to look for something to read from the collection of books in his room. *Oh, hell! Why are most of these in English?*

I wouldn't be able to read them. The only books in Thai were on philosophy. *Great, that'll be exciting...*

"Do you like to read?" Vegas asked.

"Mm-hmm," I replied, hoping he'd stop talking. I didn't really care about reading, but there was nothing to do in this room besides lie around. I was starting to understand what people in prison must feel like.

Vegas went to retrieve his laptop from outside the bedroom. He sat on the sofa before arranging some books on the coffee table and turning on his computer. I didn't know what he was doing with it.

"Pete, come here."

I put down the book and obediently walked toward him. I stood over him with my eyebrow raised, silently asking him what he wanted.

"You're acting weird. Did you eat something strange? Are you sick? Do you have a fever?" Vegas asked, pulling me down to sit next to him. I cursed and tensed up when he pressed the back of his hand to my forehead. I kept telling myself not to resist him, but he was making the hair on my arms stand on end.

"No fever. Why aren't you throwing a fit today?" Vegas asked, frowning. I pretended to be interested in the items on the coffee table, still not answering him. He looked surprised. "What's the matter? Cat got your tongue?" he said, leaning closer. He stared at me like I was some kind of freak.

I turned and gave him a small smile. "Yes?" I asked, trying to sound casual. I cursed at him internally but didn't dare say anything else. What if he didn't like what I said and decided to beat me?

"What's wrong with you, Pete?"

"I'm fine," I said, my voice a pitch higher than usual before I lowered it back to its normal tone. "Nothing's wrong."

"All right. I'm glad you're cooperating. I'm exhausted from today's exam, but I still have to finish my report. Why don't you help me?" he suggested.

I paled. "H...how?" *Shit!* I wasn't sure if his definition of 'help' was the same as mine. The ambiguity of his words worried me.

"Do you know how to type with a computer?"

"Hey! I went to school," I protested—and then snapped my mouth shut. Shit, I'd blurted that out before I could stop myself. I didn't want him to think I was arguing with him. *Argh!*

I was frustrated that he'd asked for my help, but at the same time, it was a relief. The help he was asking for wasn't something vile like I'd first thought.

"Ah...that's good. Can you help type my report? The part I highlighted—type those words in."

I gritted my teeth, wondering why he couldn't just ask one of his men instead. Why did he have to ask me?

"Of course," I replied cheerfully. Vegas kept staring at me in disbelief.

I looked at the computer in front of me, lighting up when I realized I might be able to sneak onto Facebook and DM someone to ask them to rescue me.

"Pfft! Don't look so optimistic," Vegas said. "I already disconnected the internet. Nice try."

I sighed, disheartened. Why did he have to be such a smart-ass? I sat on the floor, resting my back against the sofa so I could type on the laptop comfortably.

Copying his report was difficult because everything was in English. I silently swore, wondering if Vegas would beat me up if I made any mistakes. I needed to say something so he wouldn't blow up at me.

"English isn't my strong suit. You better check everything—I might make a mistake," I said, tilting my head to look at him. He was already staring at me, and our eyes locked briefly. For a moment, I was stunned. I couldn't tell what was going on in Vegas's head. I quickly averted my gaze and went back to typing his report, trying to focus on the text in front of me instead of Vegas's stare.

Vegas seemed very busy today. He kept switching between reading books and highlighting the parts he wanted me to type. And that wasn't all—he also talked to his friend on the phone every ten minutes.

Mr. Kinn and Mr. Tankhun had been busy studying like this during their midterms too. When Mr. Tankhun had his exams, Arm, Pol, and I had to take turns reading his textbook out loud for him all day. It didn't matter if he was sleeping, eating, or showering; I had to shout each sentence from his textbook until the subject was drilled into his brain cells. Luckily, Mr. Tankhun had already been in his fourth year of university when I'd started working for him. Otherwise, I'd still be reading textbooks to him.

"How's it going?" Vegas asked, leaning over from behind me and bracketing me between his arms. I jumped.

Vegas pressed the touch pad to scroll down through the document. I glanced at the side of his face, my heart racing with fear as I inhaled his familiar scent.

"Did...did I do it correctly?" I asked, shifting slightly away from him. He nodded before moving back to his spot on the couch.

"You did fine," he said casually, before returning his attention to the book in his hand.

I sighed. He wasn't acting like a maniac today. He was acting almost like the old Vegas—the one I knew before he took me prisoner. Somehow, it only made me more uneasy.

Time passed, and the room fell silent save for the sound of my fingers against the keyboard and Vegas turning the pages of his book. I concentrated on the screen, trying to repeat the words in my head before I typed them so I wouldn't make any mistakes. I concentrated on the task at hand, relieved that Vegas had stopped threatening me like before.

Abruptly, Vegas's fingertip touched the corner of my mouth. I flinched and snapped my head around to stare at him.

Vegas was lying down on the sofa with his eyes fixed on me. "Does it hurt?" he whispered, his finger brushing my mouth again before moving to my cheek.

I wanted to yell at him, *Yes, it fucking hurts!* The cut near my lips burned, and on my cheek still bloomed a bruise in the shape of his hand.

"Mm-hmm," I hummed, not daring to say more. I didn't know what he was trying to get at. He might hit me again if I said something that annoyed him.

"Never resist me again," Vegas said. "I'll be nice to you if you behave...and you won't get hurt." He removed his hand from my face and propped it behind his head. His eyes went back to his book.

I was shocked. *Who the hell are you, and what have you done with that evil bastard Vegas?! Spit him out, now!*

I paused that train of thought. Why did I want that horrible monster to return? *Please swallow that demon and never let him out ever again. Amen!*

It took a while before I could concentrate on typing again. I didn't really understand why, but my decision not to fight Vegas seemed to have worked. From now on, whatever he told me to do, I'd immediately comply! I'd obey him until he stopped abusing me for his own amusement.

I was absorbed in typing the highlighted words, but as the night wore on, I started to feel hungry. The food here was no good; it was pretty much all vegetables. I didn't have a single grain of rice in my stomach!

I contemplated telling Vegas I was hungry, wondering if he'd take pity on me. How should I phrase it? *'Do you have anything for me to eat?'* No, that wouldn't work. *'Don't you want a late-night snack?'* No... Ugh.

I kept debating with myself until I finally built up the courage to turn to Vegas and ask about some food.

"Oh..."

Vegas was asleep, with his book lying flat on his chest. He breathed steadily, faintly snoring. He was probably exhausted. Good! I had two more sentences to type, and then I could sleep.

I felt relieved that I had survived another day. I quickly typed the last highlighted passage, then closed the laptop screen. I got onto the bed and crawled under the blanket. It was so cold in here—it felt more like a refrigerated morgue than a bedroom.

I reached for the light switch next to the headboard when another thought struck me: Would Vegas get cold? My gaze shifted to the sofa. Vegas, dressed in black silk pajamas, was still in the same position, fast asleep. He didn't have a blanket.

Good! I wanted to let him freeze to death. I even thought about turning down the thermostat even further...but I only let myself imagine it for a moment.

I turned off the light and searched for a comfortable sleeping position. I closed my eyes, ready to go to bed without sparing another thought for Vegas.

"Mom... Mom...don't leave me," he mumbled in his sleep. "Please, Mom, I don't want to be alone."

I opened my eyes and fumbled for the light switch. I'd assumed that Vegas was lonely and wanted someone to protect him; he acted like an unloved child desperate for affection. That didn't make me feel bad for him, though—I still hated his guts!

I contemplated walking over to the sofa and pretending to be his father, menacingly whispering in his ear. That'd give him a nightmare frightening enough to scare him to death. *Oh, hell, I spend way too much time with Mr. Tankhun. What a stupid idea.*

Pushing myself up from the bed, I took a moment to consider my next course of action. Right now, I needed to stay on his good side. It might be a good idea to get Vegas a blanket, so he'd thank me when he woke up instead of yelling at me.

Since it was only the two of us in this room, he would know it was me. He'd feel grateful and think that I cared about him. He would realize that I was a good person and say, "You're too good to be locked up, Pete. I'll let you live your life."

Yes! That's it, Pete. Remember, you're a good person! I chanted in my head as I retrieved an extra blanket from the wardrobe. I draped the blanket over him, feeling very proud of myself. Then, I returned to bed and turned off the light once more.

Sweet dreams, Pete. You didn't have anything to be stressed about today. How nice!

The following day, my routine remained the same. I woke up to find that Vegas had already left; his blanket was folded neatly on the bed. He was probably already at the university, taking his exam.

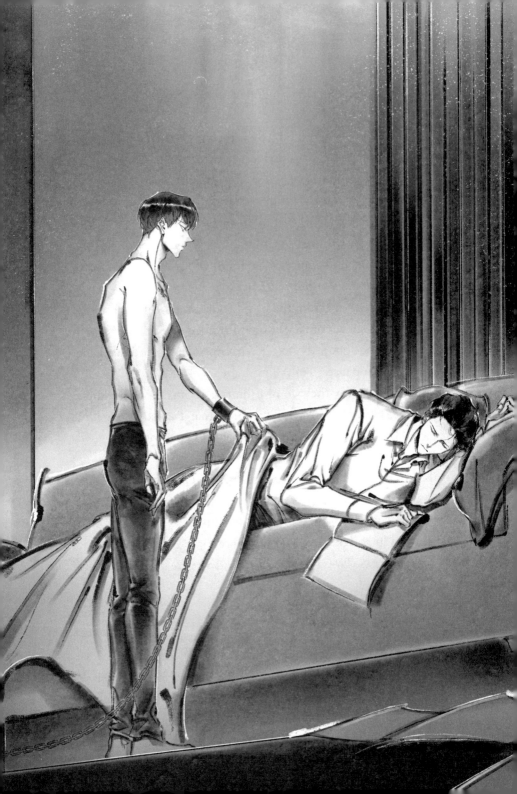

Good riddance! I didn't want to see him when I woke up. He was infuriating!

I took a shower, made the bed, and resumed trying to figure out how to get this goddamn chain off my wrist. *I won't give up, you piece of shit!* I cursed at the chain. I tried prying it open and using soap to help slip it off, but it wouldn't budge. *What kind of chain is this, anyway? Why is it so damn sturdy?*

"Nop," I said, rolling my eyes when I saw what he'd brought me for breakfast. It was still the same as always: some sausage, an egg, and a piece of bread.

"Don't bother asking me for help, Pete," he said.

"That's not it," I told him. "I'm still hungry. Can I get more food? What do you usually eat here?"

"Just ordinary rice and curry. Why?"

"I want that too! I don't want fucking bread or salad. Do I look like a Westerner?"

"You can't. I'm under Mr. Vegas's orders."

"What? Did he tell you to feed me only bland vegetables and creamy Western food?"

"Just eat it and stop being picky!" Nop snapped, slamming the door in my face with a loud bang.

"Hey! Nop!" I shouted after him. "I'm not eating this!"

Well, who was I kidding? I had to eat this crap eventually. The food here was unbelievable. I was glad Mr. Tankhun liked eating delicious spicy food, not the flavorless garbage I was getting served here.

I spent the rest of the day looking for a way out, napping, walking in a circle, and exercising. I was bored out of my mind. I had the sudden desire to watch TV or sing karaoke. Fucking hell, I really missed Mr. Tankhun.

Nop returned at dinnertime. When I saw the food, I wanted to die for the millionth time.

"Spaghetti carbonara? Where the hell are we, Italy?"

Nop didn't wait to hear me complain; he left immediately.

The sons of the Major Clan were half European, but they never ate spaghetti. Why would the Minor Clan, who were Chinks through and through, be so obsessed with this kind of creamy, buttery food? I was a Southern Thai guy. I wanted to eat something seasoned and satisfying. These assholes could at least give me a Thai-style omelet!

I was constantly hungry in this place, and it was making me agitated. I was used to eating rice; spaghetti and bread didn't fill my stomach in the same way. Not to mention Nop only brought me two meals per day: It was either breakfast or lunch—never both—and then dinner. How could I stay alive like this? Was Vegas's plan to keep me barely fed so I wouldn't have enough energy to fight him? *That conniving bastard!*

Crash!

I was startled from my thoughts by the sound of something shattering. I could faintly hear Mr. Kant and Vegas arguing, but I couldn't make out what they were saying. It sounded like they were fighting somewhere far away. *Shit, looks like father and son are at odds again.* Vegas would be pissed off today, and he'd take it out on me for sure. *Think, Pete! Quick, think of something!*

The door opened before I could come up with a plan. Vegas stomped into the room, fuming. My life was on the line again. I wished someone would perform a Buddhist life-extension ritual for me—I was knocking on death's door too often these days. I took a deep breath, bracing myself to face him.

"That motherfucking bastard!" Vegas cursed as he furiously threw everything in his path onto the floor.

I stared at him, petrified. He ripped the sheets off of the bed, his eyes burning with rage. He'd completely snapped, unable to control himself at all. The faded bruise on his face had regained its prominence.

"What the hell are you looking at?" he snarled.

Of course, that was meant for the only soul in this room apart from him: me. I tried to focus and not show him how scared and nervous I was as he glared daggers at me. I didn't know if it was working or not because Vegas kept coming closer. My heart hammered so hard, I felt like it was about to jump out of my chest.

"Why are you looking at me like that? You think I deserve this?" Vegas hissed, his hand poised to hit me.

I stepped forward swiftly and touched his bruised face with a gentle hand. "Does it hurt?" I whispered.

Vegas was stunned. His anger seemed to waver.

I stood in silence as I looked into his eyes, scared shitless. I wanted to yell at him to stop acting like a thug—but I felt pity for him, too. Every single time he came home, his father screamed at him.

I carefully caressed his bruised cheek, comforting him. "It hurts, doesn't it? Shh, it's okay. Everything will be all right."

After a while, Vegas visibly calmed down. His eyes softened, and he kept them on me as he gently pulled my hand away.

Then he turned around and slammed his fist into the nearest wall to release the rest of his anger.

"Fuck you, you bastard!"

"Vegas, calm down." I pulled his hand away from the wall, trying to stop him. His knuckles had already turned black and blue.

"Damn it!" Vegas shook me off and slumped on the sofa. "Everything I do is wrong! Have you *ever* listened to me?"

I watched as Vegas poured out his emotions. It seemed like words weren't enough to ease his anguish; I'd just made him act out physically. I stood in silence and let him continue to fume.

"Our business is about to fail, and he's blaming it all on me. It's going bankrupt because it was corrupt from the start. I never wanted to do it, but he kept forcing me to. He said I was useless and ungrateful for not wanting to help the family. Then when the business went bad, he said it was my fault. I fucking hate it! I hate it all!"

"He must expect a lot from you," I said in a neutral voice. "You're his eldest son."

Vegas looked at me for a moment, then turned away. "Just because I'm his eldest son?" he hissed. "He never asks me about school. He never asks if I'm okay or about what I've been through. Not even once. Not even when I was a kid. You know why? He's never seen me as his son!"

Vegas still looked furious. His eyes had turned red around the rims, and his hands were clenched so tightly that his veins were starting to bulge. Although I despised him with all my heart, I felt sorry for him. Everyone wanted a loving, accepting family. We all wanted to make our families proud, and the essential things that helped us achieve that were the love, support, and protection from our families. But from what Vegas had told me, he'd never had any of that.

"Well...you still have Macau," I pointed out. "He loves you a whole lot, right?"

"I don't want him to grow up to be like me," Vegas said. "Right now, I'm his only sanctuary."

Why was there no love for the children in this family? There was no one to support these two brothers while they were growing up. All they had was each other.

"I don't know what's going on between you and your father," I said. "But I believe that, deep down, he doesn't hate you."

"He doesn't hate me? Bullshit!" Vegas's voice shook. "How would you know? He never shows me that he loves me. My mom died when I was young, and I grew up raised by a nanny. Then, my father fired her. It felt like I was alone in this world."

Vegas gritted his teeth. Every time he mentioned his father, his eyes burned with rage. I could sense a lot of anguish hidden inside him—the motherless child with a father who'd never cared for him. His nanny, who was closest to him, was also taken away when he was young. If I could overlook his own cruelty, I'd have felt incredibly sorry for Vegas.

"I didn't have a mother either," I said. I wasn't sure why I was suddenly mentioning my family. But somehow, I understood his feelings, even if I didn't want to. "She died when I was young. I never knew who my father was. I don't even know if he's still alive. I don't know why he abandoned us—I never had the chance to ask him. You're lucky that your father is still alive and provides for you. I never knew my father, and I hardly remember my mother—and I'm an only child too. When I was young, my friends used to make fun of me for being an orphan. But I didn't care. I still have my grandparents, and I love them with all my heart. You have Macau, who loves you deeply. You love him too, right?"

Vegas was silent. Maybe he was contemplating what I'd said. Then, he asked me, "Did you grow up with your grandparents?"

"Yeah. My childhood was tough. We were poor, unlike you. I had to work to pay for my education and to come to Bangkok. I was fortunate enough to finish high school. There are a lot of people who struggle more than you do, Vegas."

"And...are you happy?" he asked.

"Yes. Everything is as good as it gets. As long as it doesn't hurt anyone, I can do whatever I want with my life."

"Pfft. You're lucky to be happy with such trivial shit."

"Isn't that what life is about?" I said. "Being happy with what we have?"

"Do you read too much philosophy or what?" Vegas scoffed. He got up from the sofa and headed to the bathroom.

"Well, those are the books you have lying around in your room! Have *you* read any of them?" I yelled after him.

When the bathroom door clicked shut, I let out a sigh. Exhausted, I slouched on the sofa and took several deep breaths. My heart had practically given out in fear. I was terrified, but I had to look as calm as possible. Thank fuck Mr. Tankhun kept making me stay up all night to watch all those soap operas—I'd learned my acting skills from them.

Vegas showered and changed into his pajamas before stretching out on the sofa with a pile of books, just like last night. He put me to work again, typing out highlighted paragraphs in a language I didn't understand. I stayed focused on typing, acting like I didn't know Vegas was watching me the entire time. I pretended to be oblivious, behaving as normally as possible. I didn't want to look at him; I was paranoid!

Then, I felt Vegas's hand stroke my hair. My body tensed up, a lump forming in my throat, and a shiver ran down my spine.

"You're a good person, Pete," Vegas said.

I straightened up and quickly turned to face him. Was he about to remove the chain because he'd seen my strong morals?

"And?" I urged, my heart blooming with hope.

"And that's it," Vegas said, looking at me. He took his hand away from my hair and touched his own head instead.

"Oh... Do you appreciate it, though?" I babbled nervously.

Vegas frowned. "What? You're as crazy as Tankhun. You probably spend too much time with him." He chuckled. His demeanor had returned to normal; he wasn't acting like a raging demon anymore.

I sighed, disappointed that I hadn't gotten the answer I wanted.

"Hey, wait!" Vegas tilted my head with his other hand to make me face him again. I didn't resist.

"What?" I asked.

"Why are you such an obedient dog lately?" he said, brushing the hair out of my face.

"I'm not a dog," I muttered.

"You are." He leaned closer, snickering when he saw how annoyed I was.

Don't fall for his game, Pete! He's baiting you. Remember, Pete, you're a good person! "Fine, whatever," I mumbled.

Vegas raised his eyebrows at me. "You... How did you learn to make such a pleading face?"

I frowned. Was I really making a pleading face? I bit my lip to stop myself from cursing at him and tried not to get riled up. *Do you know I'm suppressing all this cursing? It's frustrating!*

Vegas lightly pushed at my head before lying down on the sofa again. "Hey, is Tankhun nice to you?" he asked, gazing blankly at the ceiling.

"Of course Mr. Tankhun is nice to me!" Except when he was bossy.

"You seem to like Tankhun and Kinn a lot."

"I like Mr. Kim too, but I don't see him that often," I said.

Vegas sighed. "And why do you like those guys so much?"

I stared at him in confusion. I didn't know why he was acting so sentimental all of a sudden. "Well, I'm...no, *everyone* from my island is indebted to the Major Clan," I explained.

"Your hometown is an island?"

"Yup. It's a small island in the south," I said. "Back when I was a kid, a tycoon bought the island and banished all the residents who used to live there. He banned people from harvesting the bird nests there, which was the main source of income on our island, and let his men take over our businesses.

"Then, Mr. Korn acquired the island's bird-nest business. He allowed the local islanders to resume harvesting the bird nests and bought our harvests without skimping out on the price. Anyone who couldn't find a job could work for Mr. Korn's company. Everyone on the island adored him.

"I wanted to work for someone as kind as Mr. Korn when I grew up. So, when I finally came looking for a job in Bangkok, I approached his company. I was still young, though, and I got scared when I saw how huge his business was. I ran away and worked odd jobs here and there for a year until I built up the courage to apply for a job in Mr. Korn's company.

"When he learned where my grandparents were from, he immediately accepted my application, no questions asked. His men even look after my grandparents when they need to visit the hospital. The Major Clan takes really good care of us, especially Mr. Tankhun. When my grandparents visit, he welcomes them with open arms, as if they're his family too. My grandma probably loves Mr. Tankhun more than me. Whenever Mr. Tankhun goes to the island on vacation, my grandparents pamper him and completely ignore me."

I recounted it all with a smile. I couldn't help but think about the time my grandma had to be brought to the hospital for some illness that was common in the elderly. Mr. Tankhun had taken care of everything. I'd never forget the times Mr. Tankhun cared for my family like they were his own grandparents.

Hold on, though—was this really the right time to be reminiscing about my past? I took a quick glance at Vegas. I forgot he might get angry if I praised the Major Clan. I cursed at myself for failing to read the situation. *And I thought I might escape a beating today...*

"Have you ever considered that those stories were just a lie?" Vegas asked, propping up to rest his chin on his hand.

"Why would my grandparents lie?"

"I don't know... My dad and Be aren't that different, I guess. They look like good people on the outside, but they're rotten on the inside."

I knew that Mr. Korn had a dark side. But I also knew he always had a reason for everything he did.

"You're pessimistic," I told him.

"And you're naive."

"That's none of your business."

"And what do you think about me?" Vegas asked, his eyes boring into mine.

"You're a fucking asshole, stup—" I blurted out without thinking. *Fuck! Why did I say that?* I quickly swallowed the rest of my curses and tried to backpedal. "Well, actually, you have reasons for doing what you do." I wanted to slap my mouth. *Pete, you idiot! You can't slip up like that!*

Vegas sneered at me. His eyes roamed all over my body, leering like he was coming up with some wicked plan.

"That's right, I have my reasons. Now, I want..." Vegas paused, clasping his fingers around my neck and slowly pulling me toward him.

"Wh...what are you doing?" I asked nervously. I contemplated whether or not to resist him. I didn't know what would give me a better chance at escaping this situation: resistance or compliance.

"I want sex..."

I squeezed my eyes shut and pushed my head back against the force of his hand. Warm breath ghosted closer to my face. *No! Stop it, you bastard! What should I do?*

"My reason is because I'm horn—"

My stomach growled loudly. Vegas paused mid-sentence.

"Are you hungry?" he asked.

I quickly pulled his hand away from my neck and nodded. My stomach had saved my life! "Yes! Do you have anything to eat?" I said, eager for the chance to change the subject.

Vegas sat up and looked at me in confusion. "Didn't you eat dinner?"

"I did!" I seized the opportunity to complain about the shitty food I'd been served. "But the sausage, eggs, and spaghetti you feed me are insufficient! I want rice!"

Vegas chuckled. "We're an upper-class family. We only eat Western food and American-style breakfasts."

I frowned. "I'm hungry."

"Suck it up! It's going to be morning soon."

"I don't want to eat bread and salad anymore," I whined. I couldn't believe I was saying all this, but I was so hungry that it was pissing me off.

"Just deal with it," Vegas said with a laugh. "My dad's new wife only eats that kind of food. She'll throw a tantrum if we serve the regular stuff."

He was smiling as he spoke, but his eyes showed annoyance.

The situation looked like it was taking a turn, so I decided to stop nagging him about food. I accepted my fate. I pretended to focus on typing again and kept my hunger to myself.

After a stretch of silence, Vegas suddenly swore, "Damn it!" He stood up from the sofa with a sigh, put on his slippers, and left the room.

What the hell was that about? I wondered what had gotten into him this time. I only hoped he wouldn't be mad when he returned. I was sick of his shit!

Vegas was gone for a long time. I hurried my typing, hoping to finish his report before he returned so I could pretend to be already asleep. I didn't want to face his wrath again.

However, the door slid open, and Vegas returned before I reached the last highlighted paragraph. A mouthwatering smell suddenly hit my nose.

"This is all we've got," Vegas said, putting down a bowl of instant noodles in front of me. It was overfull, the broth almost reaching the brim.

I looked between him and the bowl.

"Is this for me?" I gasped, pointing at myself in surprise.

"Yes! I couldn't find any other food. The maid probably put dinner away already." He sat down on the sofa and fumbled around for a book to read.

"Why is there so much soup?" I asked, looking at the enormous bowl. It had far too much liquid for only one packet of instant noodles.

Vegas put down the book and glared sharply at me. "Stop being picky!" he said, sounding mildly irritated. "You should be thankful I made it for you at all."

"You made this?" I asked, taken aback.

"I just added the hot water."

"Why didn't you ask one of your subordinates to do it?"

He lifted the open book until it covered his face. "We don't have men patrolling the inside of our house like the Major Clan does. They're all outside. I didn't bother to call one of them in."

"So, you added the hot water without looking?" I grumbled, tasting the soup with a spoon. "Mmm, it's pork flavored. You added too much water, though. It's so watered down, I can barely taste it. I'd rather eat cardboard—" I immediately shut up when I realized what I'd said. *You blurted shit out without thinking again. Don't be a dumbass, Pete!*

Why was I such a blabbermouth? Had I become like Porsche? I froze on the spot and didn't dare look at Vegas. What if he got angry and flipped the hot bowl of soup over my head? *Shit, I hate my big mouth!*

"Argh, you're so damn picky!" Vegas exclaimed. He rose from the sofa, snatching the bowl back before he left.

Great. Now I didn't have anything to eat. Although that bowl of noodles was tasteless, it still could've filled my stomach. Now I had to go back to being hungry. I was so stupid!

Vegas was gone for some time. I was lucky he hadn't poured the hot soup on me. I kept berating myself for my stupidity. I braced myself for the consequences of my actions.

The door slid open, and Vegas returned once more. I didn't dare look up at him, but I noticed that the soup had a more robust aroma this time. He placed a bowl of instant noodles in front of me—it had about half the amount of broth this time.

"Happy now?" he asked. He lay back down on the sofa to continue reading his book without sparing another glance in my direction.

I didn't dare utter another word to him. *You did it, Pete! See what happened after you put the blanket on him last night?* Being obedient was working out better than I thought it would. I told myself to continue with this plan—I might be able to get out of here somehow.

I mixed the noodles with the soup before slurping it all up. I smiled at my brilliant plan as I chewed, still unable to believe that there was a light at the end of the tunnel now. *Vegas made you a bowl of noodles because he was thankful for what you did. You're so smart, Pete!*

Vegas took the bowl out of his bedroom once I'd finished. He even sprayed copious amounts of air freshener until its scent permeated the room. *What a neat freak.*

I ignored him and went back to typing up his report. The next time I turned to look at him, Vegas was already asleep. I'd completed my task by then, so I went to the bathroom to brush my teeth—and this time, I didn't hesitate to get the extra blanket from the cupboard for Vegas. *Should I give him two blankets tonight? He might feel twice as thankful.*

I dropped that thought in the end, though; I didn't want him to think I was doing anything to annoy him. *Just go to bed, Pete!*

The next morning, Vegas left very early again. I woke up to see him walking around the bedroom, but I pretended to be asleep I didn't want to face him. It was so frustrating having to tamp down on my emotions and reactions around him.

I went about my day as usual: I showered, made the bed, and tried to remove the chain. Repeating these tedious tasks was all there was for me to do.

When Nop brought me food, I had no choice but to eat it. It was still the same Western crap: bread, cream of mushroom soup, and a salad. My muscles would wither if I had to eat this every day. But what could I do? Even though I was practically a prisoner on death row, I should have had the right to eat the food I liked!

After I ate, I made another once-over of the room, searching for sharp objects. Although my hope was wearing thin, I still needed to try, because succeeding would be everything.

It was late in the afternoon. I was lying on my stomach on the floor, stretching my arm to reach under the bed. I hoped Vegas might have dropped something—a pair of scissors, a knife, some other blunt object—and kicked it under the bed. I was going to continue searching without giving up.

I was startled by the sound of the glass bedroom door sliding open; I turned sharply.

"What the hell are you doing?" Vegas barked.

Shit! My life was over. Why had he come home so early? It was still the afternoon!

"Umm…" I gulped nervously and started pushing myself up and down. "I'm doing push-ups!" I answered, trying to stay calm.

"Push-ups?" Vegas raised his eyebrows, confused.

"Yes!" I kept doing push-ups vigorously. "You lock me up in here all day. There's nothing to do besides eat and sleep. I'll lose all my muscles!"

"Sheesh, all right!" Vegas headed to his closet to change out of his university uniform.

I couldn't help but ask, "How come you're home early?" I wasn't really interested, but he usually didn't come home until it was dark.

"I only had one test in the morning. I came home after it was finished. What's your problem?"

"Nothing," I said, silently lamenting that the time I had to myself was getting shorter each day.

Vegas finished changing and came to crouch down next to me. I ignored him and kept doing push-ups.

"Oh, my friends are coming over to work on our report. If you make any noise or do anything you shouldn't...I. Will. Kill. You!" Stressing the last words, he pushed my back so hard, I almost hit my face on the floor.

I turned to glare at him. "All right!" I replied tersely. Why couldn't he have said it nicely? I would have understood!

So, his friends were coming over. It'd be interesting to know how they'd react if they saw my bruised body chained up in his room. They might call the police, and Vegas could be charged with sexual assault and false imprisonment. That would give him several years in jail!

I got off the floor when he left for his desk in the other room, and I hopped onto the bed to think about how I could let his friends know I was here. The glass door was a one-way mirror, so they couldn't see inside. The room also seemed to be somewhat soundproofed. *What should I do?*

"Hey, man! Why did you ditch us after the exam?"

Two of his friends had entered the next room. I was glad to see some new faces. They could be my salvation!

"Go check his room, Jay. Let's see if he's hiding someone in there. He always goes straight home after class lately—it's suspicious."

One of his friends walked around Vegas's office before heading straight to the bedroom. *Yes! Come in! I'm in here!*

"Cut that shit out!" snapped Vegas. "Are you going to work on the report or not? If you aren't going to do it, then fuck off!"

His friends immediately quit their antics and headed toward him. "Hey! You're always so cruel!"

Yikes, what a control freak. Vegas even ordered his friends around like they were his subordinates. He'd never get far in life acting so entitled all the time.

I was disappointed. His friends had almost found me! I paced around the room, trying to concoct another plan.

Then I caught sight of the tray with the empty plates. An idea suddenly popped into my head...

Crash!

I pushed the tray off the table, and the plates fell to the floor with a loud clatter. The reaction from Vegas's friends was immediate.

"What the hell was that sound?"

I heard some commotion, and then everything went quiet. I knew it wouldn't be long until someone opened the door. I started counting down the seconds in my head, hoping one of his friends would come in.

Creak...

The door opened and closed. I quickly pretended to be startled by the broken plates on the floor.

"Damn it, Pete!" Vegas stood with his hands on his hips. His eyes were fiery with rage.

Fuck! It was just Vegas. There was no sign of any of his friends.

I gulped. "Wh-what? They just fell. I didn't do anything," I said, quickly crouching to pick up the broken plates. Suddenly, it became difficult to breathe. *If my plan fails, I'm dead!*

"Did you really think that stupid stunt would help you get out of here?" Vegas demanded, his voice harsh.

"I didn't do it," I flatly lied, trying to dodge the blame. I wondered why his friends weren't curious about the noise. Didn't they want to come in and check?

"Don't do it again!" Vegas warned, pointing his finger at my face. "Clean this up!"

"I got it!" I grumbled. He glared at me once more before he left. I sighed in relief. I'd expected him to be angrier than that.

With that escape plan down the drain, I was back to square one. I thought about giving up—the possibility of escaping Vegas seemed like a delusion at this point. But you guys get it, right? I was desperate to escape, so I was willing to try anything, no matter how impossible it sounded. Even if my plans failed, I'd know I had tried my hardest.

After cleaning up the broken shards, I went to wash my hands. I splashed water on my face to freshen up, muttering to myself that I had to find a way out of here, no matter what.

As I returned from the bathroom, the glass door to Vegas's bedroom suddenly slid open, and I was confronted with an unfamiliar face.

"What the hell?!"

We both jumped. Vegas's friend, still in his university uniform, stared at me from head to toe.

"Who the fuck are you?" he asked.

"Help... Please help me," I begged. I grabbed his arm, afraid to let this opportunity go.

"Thew! Hey, Thew!" the guy yelled.

I craned my neck and saw another man—Thew, presumably—coming over. Vegas was nowhere in sight.

I shook his arm and continued begging, "Please, you have to help me."

"Shit, Jay! What the hell are you doing?" I heard Vegas yell. He rushed in and yanked his friend away from me.

His two friends hesitated. "What is this, Vegas?"

"Why did you come in here?!" Vegas screamed at his friends.

"I needed to use the bathroom," Jay replied, sounding nervous.

This was finally my chance to escape. I sidled up to Jay. "Sir, please help me!"

Jay stared at me in silence, as if he was pondering something. Then, he shifted his gaze to Vegas.

"Well, well... Now I know why you've been so eager to go home when you usually like to stay at my condo," Jay said, crossing his arms over his chest and circling me. His eyes were unreadable.

"Yeah, yeah, whatever. Get out, both of you!" Vegas brushed off his friends and tried to push them out of his bedroom.

"Help..." I whispered, looking between his two friends.

The three of them exchanged looks in silence; Vegas was clearly trying to tell them something. Then, Jay's gaze shifted from curiosity to leering.

"Mmm... He looks delicious. Why didn't you tell us you were hiding the good stuff?"

My heart sank. My chance at an escape had met another dead end. Fear began to creep in; I backed away one step at a time.

"He's got a decent face and a nice body," Thew said, stalking toward me. "Vegas, you selfish bastard! You're keeping him all to yourself?"

The situation suddenly felt dangerous. Somehow, I instinctively moved to hide behind Vegas's back. I was afraid to look his friends in the eye.

Vegas craned his neck and looked sharply at me. I stared in horror, my hands tightly grasping the hem of his shirt. Then, Vegas turned back and sneered at his friends.

"You want him?" Vegas asked. "He's a great piece of ass."

Jay raised his eyebrows provocatively. "Can I?"

"No! Don't..." I shook my head frantically, squeezing Vegas's shirt tighter. I knew what Jay meant; I was terrified.

"So, can I fuck him?" Jay insisted.

"No! Get out!" Vegas yelled harshly, pushing his friends out of his bedroom.

I heard them laugh and shout back, "Protective bastard! Fine, we'll leave. You'd better have a good explanation for us!"

My knees gave out. I crumpled on the bed, hyperventilating from the shock. I couldn't believe Vegas was friends with such vile men. He surrounded himself with horrible people—it was no surprise he'd turned out to be such an evil bastard himself.

"So, do you still want someone to help you?" Vegas asked as he returned to the bedroom. He slapped my shoulder and grabbed it hard. It hurt a lot, but I kept my head down and accepted my fate. I was both scared and disappointed.

"Why do you always rile me up? You like making me angry, don't you? Answer me!" Vegas pushed me against the bed and pinned me down with his body.

"Vegas, please let me go," I begged, hoping he might finally take pity on me. My body trembled in fear.

Vegas huffed. "You never learn, do you?" he said, pinning my arms down.

I thrashed against his hold. "Vegas... Don't..."

"You don't want me. Do you want them instead? Should I call them back in?" he hissed, leaning his face in closer until our noses almost touched.

"Vegas!"

"Stop fighting back, or I'll hurt you! I'll make sure it hurts more than last time!"

I froze and bit my lip hard, trying to keep myself from crying. A terrifying realization slowly dawned on me:

There was no way out.

Do I really have to let him humiliate me again? Will it hurt less if I stop resisting him?

Perhaps I simply had to endure what was to come.

"Can you let me go?" I asked. I knew he'd turn a deaf ear to my pleading, but I needed to say it; I had to do *something*.

"It's your choice—either them or me." Vegas gave me an ultimatum. I squeezed my eyes shut as he pressed his body harder into mine. I couldn't see any other way to escape this situation...

So, I surrendered.

"You... Only you."

Vegas × Pete 7

PETE

"**Y**OU... ONLY YOU."

I just blindly said it. In my heart, I didn't mean it. I wanted to run away from this place, but as Vegas often pointed out, I was trapped here—so I had to swallow my pride and let Vegas do vile things to my body over and over again.

There was mockery in Vegas's predatory eyes, as if he'd already won; his smile slowly widened as he gradually bent down to nuzzle my neck.

I closed my eyes, my body stiffening and my skin crawling. Vegas made me disgusted with every part of my body, so much so that I almost wanted to die instead of living on in this defiled flesh.

"I love it when you're obedient like this," Vegas whispered breathily as he nibbled at my earlobe, sending chills down my spine. I swallowed thickly, knowing full well the torture I would soon face.

"Let me go..." Even though I knew I had no way out, and even though I'd stopped struggling, my mouth still begged him to stop. I wanted to resist. I wanted to fight. I wanted to use all my strength to push him away, but if I did that, I'd only make the inevitable agony worse.

Vegas sucked and bit as he pleased, his warm breath and wet lips tainting my skin. The more he touched me, the faster my heart hammered in fear. His hand slowly dragged along my body, pausing to squeeze my chest.

"Vegas... Please, I'm begging you," I pleaded.

"Beg, then... I like to hear it," he murmured, nosing along my collarbone and then moving down. As soon as his tongue grazed my nipple, a strange sensation shot through me. My whole body shivered, and my stomach flipped upside down.

I bit my lip hard when Vegas began to suck. It wasn't painful like before; instead, it elicited a feeling I couldn't quite describe. But even if it didn't hurt, bitterness still welled up within me. I was so tense that my body trembled, and in my panic, wetness began to form at the corners of my eyes. I didn't want to admit how weak I was. I wasn't in pain, but it felt like I was suffocating—a torment that I couldn't withstand.

I didn't know how much of my fear showed on my face. My hands clutched and pulled at the sheets until they were a rumpled mess. I closed my eyes and let the tears fall; in that moment, Vegas, who had been busy licking my chest, suddenly stopped.

I was trying to hide my face in the mattress, so I couldn't see Vegas's expression. He let go of my hands, the weight pinning me down disappearing in an instant. I squinted at Vegas warily as he pushed himself off of me, running his hand through his hair and heaving a heavy sigh.

"I'm not in the mood anymore," he snapped. "Why are you crying like a pussy?!"

I immediately scooted backward until my back hit the headboard. I roughly wiped at my tears with the back of my hand, not responding to his question.

"Why?! Do I disgust you that much?" he demanded, staring at me. I turned my face away from him.

I didn't know what Vegas was going to do next. He was acting annoyed, and he really did look like he wasn't "in the mood," but I still didn't trust him.

"Fuck! What is wrong with me?" he cursed to himself, pulling at his hair.

I didn't want to look at his face right now. I was terrified, and it was getting harder and harder to hide it.

At that moment, a voice echoed through the wall: "Hia!"

I recognized Macau's voice, even if it was a bit muffled. I was certain it was Macau because Vegas reacted immediately, marching out of the room without hesitation.

I poked my head past the glass doors to see one of the bodyguards frantically running toward Vegas. "Mr. Vegas! Ms. Pim and Mr. Macau are arguing!"

I felt a rush of relief when Vegas finally left the room. I dove for the bathroom, shucking off my pants and quickly washing Vegas's filth from my body. I scrubbed and scrubbed until my skin went red, the smell of soap calming my racing heart. I finally had a chance to calm down and collect my thoughts. What had happened with Vegas just now?

Little by little, my fear began to fade, along with my wariness. Right now, only questions filled my head: Had it really worked? Was Vegas finally getting bored? I had acted like I'd given up, not talking back or fighting him. I'd refused to let him have his fun or feel like he was winning. Now that I was no longer resisting his attacks, I was boring to him. *Hey! The plan really worked!*

I'd managed to escape an assault without really knowing how. I could finally see the faint, flickering light at the end of the tunnel again. *Shit, Pete, you're on the right track!*

I stayed in the bathroom for about an hour, trying to come back to my senses and get my emotions under control. I couldn't show Vegas any defiance, otherwise he'd beat me up again. I had to go along with it—it was the only way!

I toweled myself dry and put on the same pair of pants, not wanting to come out in just a towel in case Vegas had returned. As soon as I walked out... *Shit! That bastard is back already!* I tried to act natural, toweling my hair dry without paying attention to him.

Vegas stood there like a statue, his expression troubled and his eyes unfocused. He grabbed a pack of cigarettes and headed for the balcony, sliding the door open. He leaned against the railing and began to smoke.

Bastard! What are you smoking for? I wanted one, too—how long had I gone without a cigarette? I wanted to grab a whole bunch, light them all up, and fill my lungs with smoke. *Fucking hell!*

I wiped my hair and gingerly made my way over to the balcony, breathing in the scent of the cigarette on the breeze. *Jonesing for secondhand smoke? How pathetic can I get? Fuck my life!*

I weighed my options, wondering if I should ask him for a cig or not, but I was afraid of getting roughed up for my insolence. In the end, I just stood there and took deep breaths. I'd hid in the bathroom for so long that my fear toward Vegas had subsided a little. Especially seeing him like this—it gave me confidence. *Heh. Go on, get bored of me. I won't fight. I'll be as uninteresting as possible.*

"Is it so wrong that I'm like this?"

I startled when Vegas started talking. *Ugh...I'm so jumpy lately.*

"Is it so wrong that I'm gay? He doesn't even see me and Macau as his children." Vegas blew the cigarette smoke from his mouth and stared into the distance. I looked left and right, checking to make sure that he was really talking to me. It was only us in this room, so he must have been talking to me.

I stood there and listened to him talk. I wasn't sure if I should offer my opinion. *Is he asking me or just telling me?*

"That bitch, Pim... How dare she try to discipline Macau? She acts all dignified in front of our father, but when he turns his back, she's one snide bitch."

My curiosity got the better of me. "Who's Pim?" I blurted out, silently cursing myself as soon as the words left my mouth. *Who wants to know about this bastard's problems? Pete, you dumbass!*

"My father's new wife, that's who. This one is pretty shrewd, baby-trapping him like that. She's got him wrapped around her little finger—he says he's putting all his hopes on the kid in her belly. He says Pim will raise the kid well, make sure it doesn't grow up to be a faggot like me and Macau..."

Yeah, that sentence would bring anyone up short. For his own father to say that... If I were in Vegas's shoes, I'd be hurt too.

I saw the corners of Vegas's eyes turn red as he clenched his fists. Oddly enough, I was starting to pity him more than I hated him—in this moment, at least. I should've felt triumphant, should have felt that he'd had it coming, but I didn't feel that way at all. Although I was still disgusted by the vile things Vegas had done to me, seeing him like this... It was kind of sad.

"He can pin all his hopes on that baby if he wants to, but he can't pass over me and Macau like this. He could at least listen to us and not blindly side with his new wife!" Vegas tossed his cigarette butt to the ground, then started stalking toward me.

For some absurd reason, in that moment, I felt brave, able to stand there and face him. My fear had completely melted away, leaving something strange and new in its wake.

"Am I so disgusting, Pete?" Vegas rasped. So many emotions flitted across his face, from sadness to disappointment. He was being vulnerable in a way I'd never witnessed before.

Vegas bit his lip like he was trying to hold everything in. I didn't know how to respond. Vegas was less intense as of late—even when he'd gone back to being cruel earlier, it'd only been for a moment.

"No..." I started to speak, but before I could add anything like "It's all right," Vegas slumped his head onto my shoulder and stayed there.

"I'm so tired," he mumbled, sliding his forehead to rest against my shoulder. Both his hands fell to his sides as he leaned his weight against me, betraying how vulnerable he was right now.

"I don't want to stay in this house anymore," he continued, a slight tremor shaking his voice. I wanted to tell him that I didn't want to be in this damned house either, but I could only reach out and gently pat his arm. Hopefully, this small offering of comfort would stop him from getting angry and taking it out on me.

"It's all right...it's all right," I repeated.

I stood there with Vegas for a long while. He didn't say anything else; I could only keep patting his arm.

How was I supposed to feel about this motherfucker? I despised him, but sometimes I felt sorry for the bastard. I was all fucked up about it; my emotions couldn't keep up with all these sudden changes. *Staying with Vegas is gonna make me go crazy!*

Vegas lifted his head from my shoulder. "You're quite adaptable," he said evenly. "A couple of hours ago, you were acting so scared of me."

I didn't want to say that I was just as confused as he was. But I had to survive somehow.

"You're just so relaxed, like you don't care," Vegas said. "Don't you hate me at all?"

I said nothing, but I might've unconsciously pulled a face at that last sentence. What I felt for Vegas was far beyond simple hatred. But I was putting on an act to keep living another day!

"Heh." He lifted an eyebrow at me. "You must be gloating deep down inside. Afraid I'll take it out on you?"

Ding, ding, ding! We've got a smart one here.

"Did you know?" Vegas said. "There's just something about you... I'm at ease when you're near me." Then, he immediately backed away, grabbed a towel, and disappeared into the bathroom.

The hell was that? "At ease?" *Huh...* And Vegas wasn't the first one to say that. Mr. Tankhun used to say he liked me the most because I was fun to be around. Was that the same thing? Probably. But how was I *fun*? I was trying to be boring! *Don't look at me like that! I have to be the most boring guy ever!*

The day had passed in a confusing blur. I hurriedly put a pillow in the middle of the bed and willed myself to sleep before Vegas came out of the bathroom.

I was drifting off when Vegas emerged, bustling about the room for a while before collapsing onto the bed next to me. What was up with him? Why did he seem different these days? Had he gotten a hold of his madness, or was he finally taking his meds? Maybe the merit I'd made was finally taking effect—I'd been taking refuge in the Triple Gem. Was that what had allowed me to survive up until now? *Ah, forget it!*

In the morning, I woke up and went through the same routine as usual, although I did manage to catch a glimpse of Vegas getting dressed in casual clothes before leaving the room. I was happy every time he left; when he was here, the atmosphere was stifling.

Nop brought me a tray of food, like always. What the fuck did he bring me today—macaroni soup and bread? What a joke! *When*

I get out of here, my grandma won't be able to recognize me! My eyes are going to turn blue at this rate!

I passed the day in boredom, pacing in circles like a prisoner. At least actual prisoners had entertainment! I had nothing to do, nothing to occupy myself with. I was like a madman, pacing the room, exercising, trying to break open my chain, then finally just putting everything away and lying around, reading. There was really nothing I could do. I wanted to escape, but I really couldn't think of a single way that would work.

Later in the afternoon, the sound of the door sliding open made me tear my eyes away from my book and frown. Vegas walked in with a heaping armful of shopping bags. He dumped everything on the sofa and sat down, one hand dramatically tugging at his collar.

"Turn up the AC. It's too hot in here," Vegas complained.

I didn't really want to—this room was fucking freezing already—but I could only obediently reach out and grab the thermostat's remote.

Vegas got up and grabbed the shopping bags, throwing them down on the bed in front of me. "Here. I bought you these."

"What?" I said as I opened them and peered inside.

It was mostly everyday items. There were plain pajama shorts and long pants in different colors, all tagged with some pricey brand's logo. Other bags contained toiletries like face wash, soap, and shampoo. I rummaged through everything, hoping that something like a shaving razor might've made its way in, but it was a futile search.

Vegas rested his hands loosely on his hips as he watched me inspect the bags. "I went to campus to turn in my report, so I dropped by the mall and got you these," he said expressionlessly. "Take a look and see if there's anything else you want."

I frowned as I pulled out a big gold box, then my mouth dropped open in shock. "What the hell is wrong with you?!" I snapped, forgetting myself. I held up the box of condoms in disbelief.

Vegas smirked at me. "What, have you never seen a condom? That's impossible... I use them every time."

"'Every time,' your ass!" I flung the box at him, but he only laughed in response.

I slipped up and reacted in front of him again. Ugh...I really should have better control.

"Heh. If you don't want to use them, I'm okay with that too." He smiled widely, looking far too pleased with himself. Where had this cheerful version of Vegas come from?

"Of course *you're* okay with that, you scumbag," I muttered, quietly enough for only me to hear.

I grabbed a different bag to distract myself from Vegas's perverted bullshit. It was full of books. "What is this? *The Light to Guide Your Life's Path...? Change Your Life Through the Power of Happiness? You Like Him, But I Like You?*" I read each title out loud. "What is up with you?" I asked him curiously.

"I saw that you like to read, so I bought you some books," he said, turning away.

I sighed at the books in surrender. "I don't like to read, but there's nothing else for me to do here." I'd read more books while cooped up in this room than back when I was studying for exams, for fuck's sake.

Vegas chuckled. "Then what else do you want?" he asked. He knew damn well what I wanted, but he continued to screw with me.

"I want a TV. I want a phone. I want anything that'll offer me some relief!" I said, testing the waters. *If you won't let me go, Vegas, then at least let me have some color in my life! As for the phone...that'd just be a bonus!*

"Heh. Do I really look *that* stupid to you?"

"I want some entertainment! I've been stuck pacing this tiny box of a room with nothing to look at but philosophy and dharma books—at this rate, I might just reach enlightenment!" I gathered all my courage to bargain with him. I knew I had zero chance of success, but I had to ask. I had to be going crazy to start rambling at Vegas this much, but I was really starting to miss the nonstop TV marathons and the karaoke machine in Mr. Tankhun's room.

"Fine. I'll find something to entertain you."

I swallowed nervously. What did he mean by "entertain"? Was it the same thing I meant? *Don't you dare try anything perverted with me in the middle of the day, Vegas. Otherwise, I'm back to being boring. Try me, bastard!*

But I was worried over nothing. Vegas went to his office and came back with a guitar. He sat down on the sofa and put his feet up on the coffee table. He settled into the cushions, casually tuning the strings. *Don't tell me he's going to entertain me by playing that thing.*

I sighed and rolled my eyes. "I don't want to listen to music," I muttered.

"Just go along with it... I've got a good singing voice," he insisted.

I made a face. "Who told you that?" *Vegas? Sing?* It wasn't like I'd never heard him sing, though. Back when I was tailing him, I had seen him gathering around with his friends to play the guitar and sing sometimes. *But isn't this kinda awkward? What does he think he's doing?!*

"Everyone. Are you going to listen or not? If not, I can entertain you in other ways." Vegas leered at me, slowly dragging his eyes up my body. I had to grab a pillow and hold it in front of me.

"Fine. If you want to sing, then sing." It wasn't like I could say no. *Let's go with his first offer—that should be safe.* He was getting weirder every day, suddenly so damned cheerful. It was freaking me out.

Vegas began to strum out a slow melody. The song felt familiar, but I couldn't quite place it. As soon as he opened his mouth to sing, though, I scowled.

"It's been two weeks since you left me in the cold,
I heard Kinn took you away to be sold.
My heart is broken and bruised,
But I have to endure when being poor means I can't choose."[1]

Vegas was clearly trying to get on my nerves. The bastard stared at me with a shit-eating grin.

"Asshole," I mouthed silently.

"Which province did you come from?" he asked me.

I had a weird feeling about this, but what would happen if I refused to answer? "Chumphon," I answered curtly.

"...From Chumphon to sell yourself in Su-ngai Kolok."[2] Vegas continued to strum and sing his modified lyrics.

"Fuck you!" I mouthed another curse.

"I'll wait for you to come back to me,
I might have no TV or anything fancy,
But that's fine, we don't care what people say,
We can work the land, and we'll be okay."

Vegas laughed as he sang, his eyes never leaving mine. I wanted to slug him. What had put him in this mood? Did he eat something weird today? Why was he changing the lyrics to piss me off like this?

"Only been in this world for..." Vegas paused and turned to me. "How old are you?"

---

1   Modified lyrics to Redeem You Back (Tai Ter Keun Maa) by Pu Pongsit Kampee.
2   A large town on the Thai-Malaysian border and one of the main economic hubs in the area.

"Motherfucker... I'm twenty-one," I said through gritted teeth.
"Only been in this world for twenty-one years,
But the world has been so cruel,
Been through the hands of hundreds of men,
But you have to swallow your pride,
Save up money to send home
And redeem yourself to come back to my side. Ha ha ha!"

I couldn't take it anymore. I threw the pillow at him, but he dodged it. *Bastard! Scumbag! Asshole!*

Vegas howled with laughter like I'd never heard from him before. He was clearly elated to have gotten a reaction out of me. Even though I wanted to keep a straight face and say it was all fine, tell him to keep singing, I couldn't. *"Been through the hands of hundreds of men?" Really? Fuck, he's such an asshole.*

"*Been through the hands of hundreds of men.*" Vegas repeated the same verse. I saw red.

"What do you mean, 'been through the hands of hundreds of men'? There's only been y—" *Shit!* I snapped my mouth closed—I'd accidentally blurted out something I shouldn't have. *Shit, Pete! You've done it again! What the fuck did you say that for?*

Vegas smiled widely and set his guitar down. He stood up with a satisfied smirk and threw a towel over his shoulder before turning to me.

"Okay, I believe you," he said. "There's only been me."

Vegas went into the bathroom, whistling all the while. I pulled at my hair in frustration. *What the hell did I just do?!* I'd been under too much pressure for too long, so stressed out that I'd run my mouth without thinking. *Damn it!*

When Vegas came out of the bathroom, I couldn't look him in the eye. He ordered me to put away the things he'd bought while he went to sit in his office. I saw two or three of his men come in to help him. He glanced into the bedroom every now and then, but I acted indifferent to his attention. I knew he couldn't see anything through the one-way glass, anyway, so I found things to occupy myself with—like trying to pry open my chain.

Vegas worked through the afternoon, up until the evening. He then disappeared for several hours—my guess was that he took Macau out to dinner. As for me, Nop brought me my meal tray. No need to think about what weird European slop it was; I'd just eat and be done with it.

It was late when Vegas returned. Today, it looked like he'd been working hard on a huge pile of paperwork. He went to wash his face and immediately collapsed onto the bed.

I congratulated myself, proud that my genius strategy was still working. Vegas hadn't done anything to me for a while now; it wouldn't be long before he got tired of my face and told me to scram. I couldn't wait for that day to come—I got excited just thinking about it.

I turned the bedside lights off and tossed and turned. We slept so far apart that we were basically on opposite edges of the bed, with a pillow between us. I refused to sleep on the sofa or the floor. If this was my life now, I wanted to at least be comfortable when I closed my eyes.

I couldn't fall asleep tonight, though. Dinner had been some dumb salad, so my stomach still growled and ached. My body really wasn't used to this "organic" crap. I couldn't digest it—it was just too different from what I was used to. I flipped onto my side, so wrapped up in thinking about all my favorite foods that I hadn't noticed Vegas was still awake.

"Can't sleep?" he asked, his arm reaching over to hug my waist from behind. His warm hand, brushing against my body under the covers, was enough to make me jump. When had he removed the pillow between us? I whipped around to stare at him in shock, flailing and toppling off the bed.

"Ow!" I yelped.

"Ah?" Vegas poked his head over the edge to peer at me on the floor as I rubbed my back in pain. A faint light filtering in from the balcony illuminated the room enough for me to see Vegas smirk and slowly shake his head. *I really have been jumpy lately. What the hell is he doing?!*

"Shit... That hurt," I cursed under my breath.

"Do you have to be so scared of me?" Vegas asked.

"You surprised me. I thought you were a ghost," I lied. In truth, Vegas terrified me.

"Hah! What ghost? Scaredy-cat."

Of course I'm scared! Put yourself in my shoes!

Vegas propped his chin on his hands and stared at me through the darkness. "Can't sleep? You keep tossing and turning."

"...I'm hungry," I answered hesitantly.

"Again?" Vegas let out a sigh. "The food at my house never makes you full, does it?"

"Yes, *again*. Since I've been locked up here, I haven't touched a single grain of rice. Not even boiled rice!" I complained, my stomach protesting even harder.

Vegas flopped back onto the bed and let out a long sigh.

"Get back to your side already. Move!" I grumbled, getting up from the floor and nudging Vegas back to his side of the bed. He rolled back without resistance.

No matter how scared I was of getting punished for daring to order Vegas around, I was too cranky from hunger to care.

"Damn it!" Vegas got up from the bed and slid his feet into his slippers. His hands fumbled for the light switch by the headboard. With that, he walked out of the room, grumbling under his breath.

"Where are you going?" I shouted after him. *Has he finally had enough of me? Is he going to sleep somewhere else? Is he going to get the key to unlock the chain...? Hey, it could happen!*

But if he's feeling really vicious, he might be summoning his men to come beat me up.

What is he going to do?

Vegas was gone for a long time. I sat there, biting my nails, my heart hammering in anticipation. Was I going to be free sooner than expected? How should I celebrate my newfound freedom?

Before I could lose myself in my fantasies, Vegas came back into the bedroom with a bowl of instant noodles, like last time, the delicious smell filling the room. My eyes lit up, and I completely forgot what I'd been hoping for earlier.

"Come eat on the sofa," Vegas said. He set the bowl down on the coffee table and plopped himself onto the couch.

"That's for me?" I asked, just to be sure. I got up, following the spicy aroma.

"Who else would it be for?" Vegas said. "You've given me a lot of trouble."

I sank down next to Vegas, picking up the bowl of noodles and giving it a stir. There was just the right amount of broth in the bowl this time around. I wasted no time picking up my fork and digging in. *Holy shit! I'm in heaven. It's Tom Yum Kung-flavored too! I finally get to eat something spicy!*

"Don't slurp it so fast, you'll burn your mouth," Vegas reprimanded me. He poured water from a pitcher into a glass and handed it over.

I took the glass from him and drank the water. I didn't pay attention to anything else, even when I noticed that Vegas had swung his legs up onto the sofa and squeezed into my space. He put both his hands behind his head and stared at me without blinking.

I scooted over so Vegas could fully stretch out his legs and tried to focus on eating my noodles, savoring the taste. But it was awkward to have someone staring at me while I ate; I could feel the pressure and slowed down. *Why the fuck is he staring at me?!*

Not knowing what else to do, I held up the bowl toward him. "You want some?"

"Nah. My nanny used to say you'll die young if you eat that kind of junk."

I was twirling the noodles into my mouth just then, and Vegas's words nearly made me choke. As I coughed, I saw Vegas failing to hide a smile. *Bastard! It might not be the healthiest, but at least it fills my stomach!*

"Slow down and eat properly," he said evenly. I took another sip of water, trying to swallow my mouthful of noodles.

"You can go to sleep," I told him. "I'll spray some air freshener after."

"Nah, I'll wait for you to finish first," Vegas said, smiling slightly. I nearly choked again—what was he waiting for?

"Then get back on the bed," I said as I ate. "I can't sit properly with you crowding me like this. And what are you looking at me for if you're not hungry?" The atmosphere was so stifling that I had to ask.

"It's my house, I can sit wherever I want. And they're my eyes, so I can look at whatever I want."

I pulled a face at Vegas and spun around with my bowl, eating with my back to him. I didn't listen, didn't look, didn't pay any attention to him. I ate the whole bowl and chased it down with two more glasses of water. I wasn't completely full—it was only one packet of instant noodles, after all—but what could I do? If I made any more of a fuss, Vegas would lose his temper.

"If you're done, go brush your teeth," Vegas said. He took the soup bowl and water glass outside, and I obediently went into the bathroom to brush my teeth.

When I came back into the room, Vegas had already sprayed air freshener everywhere. He blocked me from lying down straight away, ordering me to sit up against the headboard for a while so I wouldn't choke on any acid reflux. Then he turned off all the lights, burrowed under the blankets, and was fast asleep in no time.

"Fuckin' tyrant," I cursed under my breath. Why was Vegas being so nice these days? It was weird. This version of Vegas was better to have around, though: I wasn't getting beat up, and I was no longer the target of his anger. *Please keep this up. I'll take it as the merit I accumulated in my past lives.*

It was a new day of being locked up. I wondered if there was chalk or charcoal somewhere in this room so I could mark the days on the wall like a prisoner. *How did Sirius Black avoid the Dementors when he escaped from Azkaban?* I didn't know what else I could say—my life was exactly the same!

Vegas went to work in his office in the late hours of the morning. In the afternoon, he was called to work at the company by his father, judging from the snippets I heard from his men. Vegas was swamped with work, and it was stressing him out.

I was pretty sure Vegas and his father were getting ready to run, or at least they must be planning a way to deny the evidence I had sent to Mr. Kinn. But what was the Major Clan doing right now? I knew that Mr. Kinn, Mr. Korn, and even P'Chan must already have had some sort of grand plan. However, for a fraction of a moment, I just wanted to know…did they ever think about me? Did they miss Pete at all?

The glass door slid open with a *creak*, pulling me from my thoughts. I stopped doing sit-ups and craned my neck to see what was going on.

It was Nop. "Pete, Mr. Vegas wants to talk to you," he said, handing me a phone. I couldn't contain my excitement. "Don't look so pleased," he added. "Mr. Vegas told me to stand guard. If you do anything suspicious, I'll shoot." He lifted his suit jacket to show me the gun at his hip. I scowled at him and held the phone up to my ear.

"What?" I said into the phone.

"What do you want to eat?" Vegas asked. It sounded like he was laughing—he'd probably heard Nop threatening to shoot me just now.

"Hmm? What was that?" I must've misheard, so I had to check.

"I said, what do you want to eat? So I can buy it for you."

Was this the real Vegas? Why was he acting so out of character? I looked at the phone in confusion, but the name on the screen was correct, and so was the voice. It was him. *What sort of spirit is possessing him now? It weirds me out when he's this…nice.*

"I can choose?" I asked, surprised.

"I'm too lazy to keep boiling noodles for you at night," he said impatiently. "What do you want to eat? Tell me, and make it quick."

"Uh..."

"I'm at a Japanese restaurant with Macau. Sushi, sashimi, you want something like that?"

"Ugh... Nah. I just want some rice and curry. The spicier, the better—especially if it's Southern." My brain was already dreaming up an endless stream of food.

"Where am I supposed to find that? Choose something easier."

"What?! How hard can it be to find a khao kaeng place? Don't you know what that is?"

"Such a pain. Fine, fine. Pass the phone back to Nop—I want to speak with him."

I handed the phone to Nop without protest. I was in a much better mood now, even if I was still angry at Vegas, deep down. *Curry is a pain to find, my ass! Curry-and-rice shops are everywhere, you dipshit!*

"Yes, Mr. Vegas. Understood," Nop said, and hung up. He turned to stare at my face, and my smile vanished. I didn't even know when I'd started making such a gleeful expression in the first place.

"I think you're on the right path, Pete," said Nop. "You might just survive this. Keep it up, man." With that, he walked out of the room.

Nop thinks I'm on the right path? I do too. That's the nicest thing you've ever said to me, Nop. I could feel that glimmer of hope shining even brighter. It wouldn't be long before Vegas wanted to get rid of me—he couldn't put up with this for long! I'd just keep my head down and continue to act as uninteresting as possible. *Vegas must've complained to Nop that I was starting to bore him. Heh.*

I eagerly awaited my food. I was so engrossed in anticipation that...I. Forgot. About. Everything. Else! Why was I such a glutton?!

Instead of trying to figure out how to escape, waiting for the day Vegas would get bored and throw me out seemed more appealing. I must've been numb to the situation already, but I had to learn to adapt and not dwell on the same thing. If the chain wouldn't come off, I should forget trying to pry it open—my new escape route was full of hope.

The door sliding open made me jump in my seat. I spun around, hoping to see...*Vegas? Why would I want to see him?*

But, to my disappointment, it was Nop. He handed the phone to me again. "Here! Mr. Vegas wants to talk to you again."

I took it from him wearily and sighed into the receiver, "What's up?"

"I'm at a khao kaeng place," Vegas asked. "What do you want?"

"What do they have?"

"I don't know what you want to eat. Just tell me."

"What?! How am I supposed to know what to order when I don't know what they've got?" *Are you stupid?!*

"Phi, what's the spiciest thing you've got?"

I couldn't help but smile when I overheard Vegas talking to the vendor. *Has he ever eaten at one of these places in his life?*

"Khua kling[3]...and..."

"That one, that one, that one!" I cut in when I heard my favorite food being mentioned.

"I'll take that, Phi," Vegas said.

"Is there sweet pork belly?" I said. "I want sweet pork belly, too."

"Do you have sweet pork belly...? Then I'll take that as well. Do you want anything else, Pete?"

"I want kaeng lueang[4] with shrimp and coconut shoots."

---

3 Meat dry-fried in red curry paste.
4 An extremely spicy Southern-style sour curry made with fresh turmeric, which gives it a distinctive deep-yellow color.

"Argh, fine! I'll take some kaeng lueang with shrimp and coconut shoots too. You've got that, right? What else do you want?"

"You know what? Just get everything they have. I can get Nop to microwave it for me."

"Fine, fucking hell," Vegas grumbled. "Pass the phone back to Nop."

I gave the phone back to Nop and went to sit back down on the sofa like before, grinning to myself. My beloved Southern food! At last, I was getting the chance to eat something good. I finally had something to be happy about since getting stuck in this hellhole!

I lazed around on the sofa, having found some books to pass the time with. I'd always been able to find happiness in the little things, so everyone saw me as chill and easygoing. I really was like that, though. Take what happened just now, for example—such a simple thing had erased so many days' worth of stress. Even if I was awaiting my own execution, at least I got to eat my favorite foods as a last meal.

Just over an hour passed before Vegas came in with my food, followed by Nop, who brought plates to set on the coffee table. I was probably grinning like an idiot, but I didn't care. I chose two dishes to eat right then, along with two portions of rice. I got Nop to put the rest in the fridge for me while I poured everything else out onto the plates.

I ate slowly, savoring my meal and letting the flavors seep into my taste buds as Vegas paced the room. He went to the balcony door and threw it open, as if afraid the smell would stink up his room. I chewed as I watched his antics, both my cheeks bulging with food.

"Aren't you being a bit overdramatic? It's just curry. Are you going to die from having it in your room?" *Ah, shit! I don't know where that came from!* Why did I forget myself? I must've caught that cocky habit from Porsche.

"Don't talk with your mouth full," Vegas said, setting a glass of water next to my plate as he sat down next to me on the couch.

I pulled a face and cursed under my breath. "Bratty fucking rich kid."

Vegas threw his arm over the backrest and settled onto the couch. "Is it good? I was going to get you some Japanese food, but you didn't want any."

"Yes! Good! I've had enough of the bland stuff! This is where it's at," I said, exulting in the taste of the sweet pork belly and khua kling. *These are the flavors of life!*

Vegas looked at my face, then at my plate. "That color's insane. Isn't it too spicy?"

"Nope. Sweet pork belly and khua kling go great together."

Vegas shook his head. I was afraid he wouldn't believe me if he'd never tasted Southern food, so with my spoon, I scooped up some rice, sweet pork belly, and a little bit of khua kling to give it a kick.

I held the spoonful up to his mouth. "Have some," I said. I did it without thinking—I was just proud of the food I grew up with.

Vegas looked at my face and froze. "I...I already ate dinner with Macau," he said, looking stunned.

"Try it! Just try some," I insisted, shoving the spoon at him.

"I don't do spicy."

"I know. That's why I made sure you got lots of sweet pork belly. Here, come on, try it."

Vegas hesitated before slowly opening his mouth.

I stared at him eagerly as he chewed. "How is it?" *Shit! Why do I have to be so excited? It really must be as they say: Southern blood runs deep.*

"It's okay." Vegas swallowed and immediately reached for my glass, gulping all the water down in one go.

"You'll get addicted to it soon enough," I said. I turned back to my plate, buzzing with joy. *How long has it been since I felt this content?*

"I'm already addicted. What should I do?" He said it in a whisper—but I managed to overhear him.

I moved my plate out of his reach and turned to glare at him. "Then go buy more. This is mine." I bent down to eat faster.

Vegas chuckled. "Give me more of that sweet pork belly. I'm going to go work."

I frowned, feeling protective of my dinner. I didn't want to drag it out, though, so I just did as he said: I scooped up some rice and sweet pork belly, holding it up to his mouth, and Vegas ate it with a smile. Once he was done, he drank more water and refilled my glass before getting up and going to his office.

"Hmph! Can't you buy your own, motherfucker?" I muttered after he'd left.

I enjoyed my meal until I was full. Damn, I'd eaten so much, I was about to burst. I sat there digesting, then went into the bathroom to take care of my business. I washed up and brushed my teeth, planning to go to sleep early. I'd eaten too much, and now my eyelids were drooping.

I put on a pair of pajama bottoms and stood at the sink, splashing water onto my face. The situation I was stuck in shouldn't have made me happy or allowed me to smile, but since I couldn't escape, I had to do everything I could to find the strength to keep fighting. At least if my brain was releasing endorphins, my thoughts could clear up. I might be able to hatch a new escape plan.

I was about to turn around and leave the bathroom, but Vegas pushed past me before I could react.

"What are you coming in here for?" I asked him, alarmed. It was a good thing I was already dressed. *Don't tell me something provoked him, and he wants to take it out on me again... Huh?*

In his hand, he held something I couldn't quite see. I stood still, tense with anxiety, then slowly backed away as Vegas advanced toward me.

"Heh." Vegas smirked and kept creeping closer. I backed up until my back hit the wall, my heart hammering wildly.

This lunatic! Fine for three days, crazy for four! Did I accidentally offend him somehow?! I squeezed my eyes shut as Vegas leaned in. His face was so close to mine that I could feel his warm breath against my cheek.

"V-Vegas," I called his name, my voice shaking. In that moment, something cold tickled my jaw, then my chin and around my lips. I opened my eyes just a sliver to find Vegas spraying shaving cream onto my face. I heard the sound of an electric razor starting up.

"Stay still," Vegas instructed, using one hand to hold my head in place. His eyes focused on my jaw as he slowly began to shave me.

"I...I can do that myself," I said, utterly dumbfounded and unprepared for what was happening.

"Pfft. You think I'm stupid enough to let you have a weapon? What if you slit my throat?" Vegas said, his hand continuing to shave off my scruff.

"Don't be crazy! Why would I do that? I'm...I'm just nervous." My heart skipped a beat every time the razor made a pass across my jaw. No one else had ever shaved me before. Who in their right mind would shave another person, unless they were a barber?

"Stop talking and stay still," Vegas scolded. I could only stand there, frozen in fear.

"Careful. You're scaring me stiff," I said without thinking.

"Heh." Vegas smiled. "I've made you *stiff* before. There's nothing to be afraid of." I wanted to kick him away from me, but if I did that, I could guarantee I'd get a new cut on my face.

I stood there in silence, nervously watching Vegas. He did everything so skillfully and confidently that I let go of my fear. When I saw that everything had gone smoothly, I relaxed.

"Clean the foam off," Vegas ordered, and I did as he said. Once I'd washed off the shaving cream, I lifted my head and stared at him.

"There's still a little bit here," he said. Holding my head in place, he leaned in close and carefully made a second pass. I stared, weirded out by his serious demeanor. *If you take out the craziness, he isn't so bad. Even thoughtful and kind at times... I can't believe this is the same guy.*

I didn't know how long I stared at him, but the next thing I knew, Vegas's eyes were boring into mine. His sharp gaze was mysterious and stormy, filled with so many emotions, yet somehow unwavering.

My heart pounded in my chest, a strange feeling running through me. I wasn't sure how or why, but those eyes were pinning me in place. The next thing I knew, I felt the warmth of Vegas's breath and the softness of his lips against my own.

I closed my eyes, staying still to receive his gentle touch. He didn't deepen the kiss, didn't invade my mouth with his tongue; it was just the barest press of lips, lingering until I began to feel uneasy. My brain soon caught up with the situation: What the fuck was I doing?

I pushed Vegas off in shock. Vegas seemed equally stunned. I turned away, unable to look him in the eye.

"All done," Vegas said. "I'll be outside."

Why the hell did he need to tell me that?

Vegas picked up his can of shaving cream and the electric razor before spinning around and marching out of the bathroom. I clutched at my chest, cursing at myself.

What the fuck am I doing?!

KINN
 PORSCHE

VEGAS × PETE 1

VEGAS

I STARED BLANKLY at the pen rocking between my fingers, an old habit of mine. The chatter of the people in the meeting room didn't interest me enough to pull me out of my thoughts.

What's he doing now?
What kind of face is he making?
Has he eaten yet?
Does he like today's food?
Was he relieved when he woke up and didn't see me this morning?

I chuckled. I hadn't thought Tankhun's head bodyguard would be so much fun. He was just as eccentric as his boss, but Pete was less annoying. He was mindful and cautious and more reasonable. He was not someone you'd call weak.

It was pretty shocking to have become interested in a person I thought I'd never care about. I'd never imagined someone like Pete even existed...

I felt content just being close to Pete. We didn't need to talk or touch; the mere thought of having him around put me at ease. It was a reassuring feeling that I'd never thought I'd get to experience.

My life had been filled with stressful situations. For example, when I was with my father, I felt so frustrated that I wanted to run away. And then there was the social pressure—people expected me to conform to their expectations. They wanted me to act how my social status dictated, to carry myself as they deemed appropriate. I almost didn't have a place where I could be myself. Nowadays, I barely even knew who I was.

"Mr. Justin, you can ask my son if you have any questions. He's very meticulous and reliable. Right, Vegas? Vegas!"

I was abruptly pulled out of my thoughts by the sound of my father's voice. I glanced over to find him staring at me. He kicked my shin under the table, hard.

I looked blankly at my father until he signaled me toward the man sitting next to him—Mr. Justin, an important client of ours.

I gave a fake smile that didn't reflect my current mood. "Yes, sir."

"I've been giving him a lot of responsibilities lately. That's why he seems so sluggish," my father explained. He turned to me. "Do you want another coffee? I can order one for you."

I didn't reply to him. I didn't even want to look at him right now. Although he sounded kind and polite in public, his hateful, accusatory stare was the same as in private.

He thinks I'm disgusting because I'm gay, because I'm not as good as the sons of the Major Clan.

He pretended to love me only to ensure the stability of his business. He used me as a puppet so the power would remain in his hands. But, hey, at least now our clients knew I could continue the family business.

"Take Mr. Justin to dinner. You were rude to him earlier, and I don't want to see that again!" my father hissed to me as we walked out of the meeting room. His voice was quiet, but he was clearly angry.

"I'm not free this evening," I said, without looking at him.

"Then rearrange your schedule," he ordered, walking past me. "Do as I say!"

I closed my eyes, took a deep breath to quell my fury, and returned to my office.

"Argh! That bastard!" I screamed once the door was closed. I pounded my fist against the wall to release the anger, sadness, and disappointment inside me, venting every pent-up emotion I'd felt during that meeting. No, not just in that meeting—it was all the pent-up emotions I experienced whenever I was around my father.

I hated myself for never being able to do anything my way. It was because of my father that I'd started to question why I did those vile things; why I'd been so ruthless that I'd almost killed someone. I had to let it all out. I hadn't known I was capable of such atrocities until I was under constant pressure. I'd become a total stranger—an unfamiliar entity, a man I'd never wanted to know.

However, sometimes, being that person gave me satisfaction. My father wanted me to defeat the Major Clan, so I did as he wished. I wanted the people my father always compared me to, especially Kinn, to feel the same pain I did.

I only needed to glance at Kinn to know his weakness. He seemed stoic, but he let his emotions guide him. It wasn't a surprise that love was his fatal flaw. That was why I'd drugged the man he loved—anyone with eyes could see how infatuated Kinn was with his new bodyguard.

Unfortunately, my plan had failed. It seemed like luck was still on Kinn's side. Still, I'd kept trying to get closer to Porsche, the person Kinn so ardently desired. That should've knocked him off-balance, like when he went out with Tawan. I would've been incredibly satisfied if that was the case—and maybe my father would stop comparing me to Kinn.

While I stood there obsessing over defeating Kinn and falling further into my hateful persona, a face popped up in my thoughts: *Pete.*

I stopped hitting the wall where the cracks had spread, day by day.

What was so good about Pete?

I'd always thought Pete was just some dumb Major Clan bodyguard. But now, my mind kept wandering to his face and his spontaneous smile; the images instantly calmed me.

Any little thing could make Pete smile. I reflected on the time I'd been spending with him. When I made instant noodle soup for him, his eyes lit up like he'd discovered buried treasure. When I talked about food, his expression changed to one of pure bliss.

Aren't you suffering from everything I've done to you, Pete? How can you still be so lively when you're living in hell?

I don't understand...

"Mr. Vegas, Mr. Justin's waiting for you downstairs," one of my subordinates announced as he entered my office. He kept his head low, afraid to face me. He'd probably heard me punching the wall. He didn't seem surprised, though. I was sure he was used to it at this point—I did this whenever I got angry.

"I got it," I sighed and calmly straightened my clothes. Yet again, I had to obey my father. *Damn it!*

A thought popped into my head, telling me to destroy anyone who dared to force me to obey. I didn't want to feel this way anymore, but there was nothing I could do. I could only live through each day and try to find a way to release these dark thoughts.

I drove off with Mr. Justin. It was just the two of us in the car; I'd instructed my bodyguards not to follow me. Mr. Justin had said the same to his bodyguards. I already knew his intentions just from the way he looked at me; I'd known it since our eyes met in the meeting room.

Do you want to sign a deal with this client, Father? Do you want him to be our business partner that bad? Will you be satisfied if I satisfy him? Fine! I'll do it! I'll do whatever you fucking want!

I pushed the slender man until he lay on his back in the back seat of my BMW. Then, I crossed his arms over his head and used my belt to tightly bind his wrists together.

"This is what you're into, Mr. Vegas?" Justin asked.

"Yeah. That all right with you?" I asked, pushing myself between his spread legs. I'd only met Justin three or four hours ago. He seemed to be half white and half Thai, with a flawless face and perfect, pale skin like an aristocrat's. You could call him cute, even. He wasn't exactly my type, but his looks were enough to arouse me.

"It's okay with me," he said, "but please be gentle."

That ticked me off a little, but I put it aside. I pressed my face into the crook of his pale neck and bit hard enough to make him jump.

"Ow! That hurts!" Justin jerked his head away, his eyes full of pain and fear.

I didn't pay attention to his reaction. I kept nuzzling his body, inhaling the scent of his cologne; I knew he'd put it on with specific intentions in mind. When my mouth reached his chest, I immediately sucked on a perky nipple.

I spread his legs open further with my hands so I could press my body closer, using my lips and my tongue to coax him into arousal. However, I had one rule—I wouldn't kiss someone I didn't have feelings for. I kissed when I wanted to share true pleasure; casual hookups were to release my pent-up frustrations, anger, sadness, and expectations.

I undid the clasp of my pants and pulled my boxers down enough to release my hard cock. With my other hand, I reached for a packet of condoms I'd hidden between the back seats. Several of our clients were into men, and I often brought them back here for a fuck.

I squeezed Justin's ass hard before stripping him of his pants and underwear, and without wasting any more time, I lifted his legs and slung them over my shoulders. I squeezed a dollop of lube from a bottle and spread it around his asshole. Then, I pressed the head of my cock against the pucker and forced my way in.

"That hurts!" Justin cried out. "Aren't you going to help stretch me first? Ouch!"

I threw my head back, closing my eyes and biting my bottom lip. However, his cry of pain and the way his body writhed in agony made me look at him again. I didn't know why, but I suddenly saw Pete's face instead of Justin's.

"Vegas... It hurts!"

I heard Pete's cry in my head and saw how he looked at me. Pete had said he was in pain, but his eyes hadn't looked like he was. I'd been wondering about that for a while. It was strange; I knew that Justin meant it right now when he said he was in pain, and he clearly didn't like that I was hurting him. But with Pete...it didn't seem like he hated the pain. He'd only looked confused.

I knew I was the only man to ever fuck him, and I'd probably hurt his feelings as well as his body. However...sometimes, when he cursed, *"Vegas, you son of a bitch! I hope you rot in hell!"* as I ravished him, he seemed more...*satisfied* than angry.

"Ow... That's enough!"

I ignored Justin and kept pushing until I was balls deep. Just thinking about Pete made me even harder. My pulse skyrocketed as blood rushed through my body, making me damp with sweat.

Pete was astonishing. When I slapped his face or punched him, he would give me a defiant look. It was like he was daring me to keep hurting him until he died. He didn't seem like the type of guy who would do that just to insult me—when I looked into his eyes, my gut told me he meant it.

Most of the time, when I had aggressive sex with Pete, it looked like he was forcing himself to stay angry. He would look like he was in agony, but then his body would relax like he was enjoying what I did to him. I was certain he had no idea he made such a pleading expression when we fucked; he even begged for more with his eyes. Then, when we were done, he would act indifferent, like having sex with me meant nothing. He wouldn't be emotional or distressed. It was like he was testing me somehow.

"*Ah*... Ow... It hurts, I can't—!" Justin's cries reverberated through the car. I swore. I couldn't focus on him at all. Although I kept fucking him vigorously, all I could think about was how different he was from Pete.

Justin looked like he was about to collapse. If he were the one I constantly forced my frustrations on like I did with Pete, he'd be traumatized by now. He would be terrified, curled up with his knees drawn to his chest, eyes gazing blankly into the distance, refusing to eat. Pete, on the other hand, was tough as nails. He looked perfectly fine after I did all of that to him. All he thought about most of the time was food.

"*Let me go! Damn it, Vegas!*"

Pete spat endless profanities, but it only sounded like dirty talk to me. It aroused both of us further. Pete was always holding back, acting like he couldn't let himself enjoy the sex. I knew it must be embarrassing for him, but I was sure he didn't hate it—he was only confused.

One thing I noticed after all of it was that Pete loved the pain. Whenever I reprimanded him or treated him violently, I saw the satisfaction in his eyes.

"Fuck, Pete...cry louder!" I cried, Pete's name slipping from my lips unbidden. I didn't think Justin heard it—he was in so much pain that he couldn't focus on anything else.

I thought about the time I'd hit Pete in the face, the first day he was captured. He'd glared daggers at me, his eyes filled with defiance. It seemed like he was begging to be killed, and I hadn't expected that.

In the beginning, I thought it was only his pride. However, I saw something whenever he looked back at me. He tried hard to hide it, but it kept showing through.

Ugh... Why did the way Pete looked at me make my body surge with lust? I loved that he always fought back. I knew I was a sadist, and I loved inflicting pain on Pete, but I was surprised it didn't traumatize him. He even looked undisturbed.

Shit! Why do I miss Pete so much? I can't hold back...

I came inside Justin without even giving him a second thought. *This is bad. You're gonna be the death of me, Pete.* I didn't just feel content when I was with Pete, I also felt connected with him sexually. It made me begin to fear...fear that I'd lose him...

I drove Justin to his hotel. He complained about the pain the entire time, but I believed it wouldn't affect the business. I knew how to deal with guys like him, so I apologized and tried to comfort him before I let him go.

I pulled Justin into an embrace and petted his hair gently. "I'm so sorry," I said. "If you're not okay, you have to tell me, all right?"

"It hurts," Justin said, his face buried in my chest. I didn't like people who pretended to be fragile like this; it was annoying. I preferred people who were unintentionally endearing. The reason

I changed lovers so often was because I kept ending up with whiny nuisances like Justin.

"I'll be gentler next time," I said sweetly. "You're so cute that I just couldn't control myself."

He looked up at me with a smile. "Make love to me more tenderly next time," he said, leaning closer to kiss my cheek.

"All right." I gently pushed him away and waved goodbye.

I drove away from the hotel as fast as I could. I sighed, feeling fed up with guys who acted too affectionately. Wasn't he a *man*? Why did he want tenderness and protection from another man? Kinn used to like this exact type of wimpy guy, and it drove me crazy! I would lure Kinn's boy toys back to my place to have sex, and it always took so long to cajole them into leaving my house. I wanted to punch all of them in the faces!

Anyway...what's Pete up to now?

I pressed on the gas to get home as soon as possible. If I had to guess, Pete was probably pacing around the room right about now, looking for something to remove his chain.

It wasn't like I didn't know about the bizarre things he did in my bedroom. I found it hilarious, really. I couldn't believe a Major Clan's bodyguard would be so...cute. *Damn it! Why do I find you so adorable, Pete?*

When I opened the glass door to my bedroom, Pete was bending his head up and down to look under the bed. I wasn't surprised that he was acting bizarrely again.

"Pete! What are you doing?"

Pete practically jumped out of his skin. Then, placing a hand over his chest, he sighed.

"Why did you sneak up on me?" he whined. "What if you gave me a heart attack?" He walked to the bookshelf, dodging my question.

"Eat anything yet?" I asked, unbuttoning my shirt. I wanted to shower and rest. Somehow, seeing Pete's face and smelling his familiar scent filled my heart with peace. I'd never felt so relaxed in another person's presence.

"I did," he replied.

"Southern food?" I asked, stepping out of my pants. I was the only one looking at him, while he ignored me.

Pete pretended to be reading a book he'd taken from the shelf. He seemed so carefree, sitting on the sofa with his feet propped up on the coffee table. "Yeah..."

Resigned, I stood with my hands on my hips, staring at him. Was he ever worried about anything? A couple of days ago, I'd yelled and hit him because he'd tried to ask my friends for help. Today, he was acting like nothing had even happened. He wasn't being chatty, pesky, or annoying. It felt as if I liked everything about him.

However, Pete was an intimidating person. He was determined and strong; he never gave up, he adapted easily to any situation, and he was so optimistic.

If I finally fell in love with him and set him free, I was sure he'd decide to go. He would leave me without hesitation. He probably wouldn't even care about me. So I prayed for him to stay like this with me a while longer.

Although I felt I might be falling in love, I was still afraid to open up to him. I hated saying goodbye, so I was trying hard not to make him the center of my universe. However, that was easier said than done...

I could no longer control my feelings. Pete's smiles were my guiding light. He made me feel alive again. He never expected anything from me, never gave me a pressing glare, never set a bar for me to reach. I was just Vegas to him. He understood what I felt, and he knew how to deal with me...

Does someone like this really exist? Someone who understands me...?

Now, stripped to my underwear, I declared, "Pete! Let's shower together!"

"Are you nuts?" Pete yelled, trying not to look at me.

"I want you to scrub my back," I teased, watching him feign disinterest.

"You're a grown-ass man. Can't you shower by yourself?"

It didn't seem like he would be joining me, so I started counting. "Pete! One..."

I tried to hold back my laughter as he suddenly grew anxious. "Two..."

Pete sprang up from the couch. He quickly stepped into his slippers and approached me with a frown.

"Go wait for me in the bathroom!" I said with a grin.

He acted precisely as I'd expected. I didn't even know what I was going to do after I reached three—I just loved seeing him get nervous. I'd only started counting to coax him into doing what I wanted. I loved to be in control, and Pete was good at following directions. He yielded to me every time I counted to two. I bet he loved the challenge and excitement I gave him; otherwise, he'd just ignore my threats. I knew that I had influence over him.

"I'll *only* scrub your back," Pete muttered as he walked past me.

Would he realize that the longer he stayed with me, the less he could hide the fact that he loved being dominated? He wanted someone in charge who could excite and satisfy him—he'd become addicted to pain.

KINN PORSCHE

36

Parting

PORSCHE

"Are you sleepy yet?" Kinn asked, toweling his hair as he came out of the bathroom in nothing but a pair of pants. He looked up at me as I rolled around on the bed.

"Yeah. I'm exhausted," I said.

Four days had passed since my birthday, and it was the end of the semester. Kinn was working me to the bone, making me take documents to the courier, then making me fetch more files from his father's room, then he wanted a snack, then this, then that. Most importantly, he was constantly annoying the shit out of me. Every time I went anywhere near him, he'd find an excuse to grope me, the pervert. The moment he put his hands on me, he'd break into an evil grin. I was so fed up with it all that I wanted to kick his smug ass—once, maybe twice for good measure.

"Are you that tired? Did I work you too hard?" Kinn asked. He fell onto the bed and crawled toward me, reaching out to grab my waist and pulling me into a loose hug.

"Yes!" I said without thinking. It was even worse now than when I was a bodyguard! Things hadn't changed much in this house, despite my change in status. I was still subject to Kinn's every whim.

Kinn began to gently knead my hip. "I'll give you a massage."

I lifted my foot to nudge him off. "Nice try," I chided, sounding a little irritated. I actually didn't mind that much—at this point, I was used to him trying to get handsy with me all the time.

Kinn chuckled. "Fine, fine. I know you're tired, so I'll take charge tonight. Yesterday, you went on quite a *ride*, so of course you're tired—*ow!*"

I swatted at his head without waiting for him to finish that sentence. He rubbed at his head gingerly.

"What the hell are you talking about?!" I snapped, pulling up the covers. *Are you kidding me? Where does he get his stamina?* Kinn's sex drive was ridiculous. If I could find a way to bottle it up and sell it, I'd make bank. I really didn't know how he could want to fuck every damn day.

"What?! If not you, then who am I supposed to talk about this stuff with, huh? Or do you want me to talk with someone else…? How about N'Phe—*oof!*"

I swung and hit Kinn square in the face with a pillow and smothered him with it until he fell back onto the bed.

"You really want to piss me off, don't you? Are you crazy?!" I grumbled, pressing down on the pillow.

Kinn pushed me off and grabbed both my wrists, reeling me in. "But you're cute like this," he said, wrapping his arms and legs around me to keep me in his embrace.

"Cute, my ass. You're a pervert." I lifted my head from his chest to scold him properly, but as soon as I looked up, Kinn bent down to pepper my face with kisses.

I turned my face away as much as I could, pushing at his chest. "Enough already!"

"You're cute when you're jealous," Kinn said as he gently pressed another kiss to my lips.

"*Mmph*...no!" I pushed him off. I was utterly exhausted tonight. I hadn't had a break since my birthday, what with work and... *Forget it!*

Every time I left the room, Khun would tease me, saying that I looked dead on my feet, then badger me into going to the hospital with him. I said I wasn't sick, but he kept insisting I was—fucking hell! I didn't know what the fuck his deal was lately, but he was angling to take people to the hospital every day. He was driving us nuts!

"Heh... Come on, let's get some sleep," Kinn said. I kept squirming, so he scooted up to lie down properly with his head on his pillow, stretching out his left arm across the bed in an invitation for me to rest my head on it.

I pulled my own pillow over instead. "No! I'm not falling for that!"

"I'm not going to do anything... We have to go check on the company tomorrow, so I don't want to wear you out," Kinn said. He pulled me back to nestle against his arm before closing his eyes and going still. I looked at him warily and settled in.

Kinn had been working himself to the bone these past few days, so he must've been just as exhausted as I was. Ever since he finished his midterm exams, he'd been helping his father run the family business without a single moment's rest. The documents on his desk piled higher each day—there was no space left on it for anything but papers and files.

It seemed like Kinn carried every possible responsibility on his shoulders. Some days, he had to go meet clients; other days, he had his face buried in documents needing his signature. Although I complained to myself that he worked me too hard, even if he didn't explicitly ask me to do so, I was fully prepared to help him.

Everything he did was his duty as his father's son; in the future, he would have to take over for Mr. Korn.

Sometimes, I had to question why the middle son was stuck with all the worries and family responsibilities. Look at his older brother! He had karaoke music echoing through his walls every day—with not a care in the world!

I rested my head on Kinn's arm, staring at his blissful expression. "Aren't *you* tired?"

"Yeah, I'm tired," Kinn answered with a sigh.

"You don't have to do so much," I told him. "Look at your older brother. He just lazes around all day doing fuck all."

"I just have to do it. It'll be ours in the future anyway," Kinn said as he rolled over to face me, reaching for my waist to pull me into another hug.

"When you put it like that..." I raised an eyebrow at Kinn, even though his eyes were closed. "Does that mean Father is going to leave everything to you in his will?"

"We'll share. Father has three sons, and each of us gets an equal share."

I frowned. "But you work harder than your brothers."

I didn't know what the future was going to be like, if there really could be an "us" like Kinn said. Right now, I was the one standing at his side, and even I could see that he was at a disadvantage. I wasn't being selfish or greedy—well, maybe a little—but Kinn liked to say that he wanted to slowly show me the ropes, so I'd know what to do when I fully stepped in to help him run things. This business wasn't exactly small, so whenever Kinn said that, it filled me with a strange, new sense of purpose.

Kinn cracked open one eye to look at me. "Khun works. And Kim is...still young."

"What does Khun even do? And Kim's not a kid anymore! He's the same age as me." It was partly my new sense of purpose that made me feel sorry for Kinn. I could still remember what he'd said when we were lost in the forest together. He was already his family's only hope; I didn't want him to put so much pressure on himself.

"Khun's got his chocolate factory," he said.

"What the hell does he even do there? He just takes pictures for their Facebook page. I could do that shit in my sleep."

Kinn smiled. "What, are you afraid our family is losing out?"

"Yes! You're the only one working this hard! I'm not hoping for anything—I don't know how long we'll be together—but I don't want to see you being the only one working his ass off," I said seriously. *I might be a greedy son of a bitch, but if Kinn has to work without rest, it's not exactly fair.*

"We'll be together forever," he said. "But it's good that you're thinking of the family business. I want you to learn everything you can, Porsche. It'll only get busier for us in the future." He leaned over to kiss the tip of my nose.

"I don't want you to shoulder everything on your own, Kinn. Delegate some things to your older brother sometimes. It was one a.m. by the time you were done with those documents, and tomorrow morning, you've still got to go to the company building."

"Come now... It's the family business. It's all the same no matter who does the work."

"It's not fair to you. Kim can work too. I haven't even dealt with him yet for fooling around with my brother."

"I don't know anything about that," Kinn said hurriedly, rolling onto his back.

I huffed. "You don't *look* like you don't know anything, but, well... Apparently, my brother forced himself on your brother, so

I do understand Kim. He's probably feeling a bit lost, like I was at the beginning... Ah, what can be done about that? Of course, my brother will have to take responsibility for his actions." I frowned. The information I'd gotten from Nont was that Chay had gone after Kim. *Ugh, Chay, I've had it with you.* I still hadn't had the chance to speak to him properly about it yet or ask him how it happened.

"Huh?" Kinn's head jerked up. He looked bewildered.

"What? Is there a problem?"

"No." Kinn furrowed his brows, seeming confused about what I'd just said. *What, my brother ended up topping your brother—what's confusing about that?* Sure, my brother was cute, but...if you looked closely, Kim was a cute type of guy too, in a mischievous sort of way. If they were walking next to each other, you really couldn't tell who'd top and who'd bottom.

Unfortunately, I happened to know! *Damn it, Chay!*

"Oh! I've always wanted to ask..." Kinn acted like he'd suddenly thought of something, but his expression made me suspicious. It felt like he was trying to change the subject.

"What?"

"Why are you named Porsche, and your brother Porchay? Doesn't it mean the same thing?" Kinn asked.

"Why do you want to know all of a sudden?"

Kinn pushed himself up, propping his chin on his hands. He looked at me with such fondness that it gave me goosebumps. "It's the same word, just pronounced differently," he said. "Porsche, Porchay."

"Mm-hmm. Well, my parents were in the luxury car business, so they called me Porsche. When my brother was born, they named him Porchay, and my dad said it was because we were both his children. Whether it was Porsche or Porchay, my dad said he and Mom loved us both equally, and he wanted us to stick together no matter what. Our names are written the same and mean the same thing, but they're pronounced differently to avoid confusion," I explained, remembering my parents' faces. Every time I thought of them, it always brought back beautiful memories.

"That's kind of cool," said Kinn.

I smiled at that faint memory, then turned to Kinn. "Yeah, my dad was the coolest. What about your father? Why'd he name you Anakinn?"

"Me? Take a guess," Kinn said with a playful expression.

"Hmmm... 'A-' is 'without.' So...'Nakinn,' like Mother Naki?[5] Meaning 'snake.' When we put it together, you're 'not a snake!'" I smiled and teased him back, jabbing a finger at his face.

Kinn giggled. "I'm not a snake, I'm a *dragon*." He ground his crotch against my leg for emphasis.

I slapped his arm. "Pervert."

"What? You know it's true. Ha ha ha!"

"Be serious!"

"Well, my older brother is Tankhun, which means 'grateful.'"

"And right now, your brother is so fucking *un*grateful," I said, looking at Kinn in disbelief. He smiled widely and gently flicked my forehead.

"When I was born, Father wanted a name that matched Khun's, but also something grand. A name that conveyed authority and power. At first, I was going to be Anachak,[6] but that didn't really match, so he went with Anakinn instead."

---

5   "Nakinn" is a variant of "Nak" or "Naki," the Thai word for "Naga": a race of semidivine serpents from Buddhist mythology.
6   Meaning "kingdom."

"That's it? That doesn't make any sense," I said.

"To tell you the truth, he just based everything on Khun's name without any real significance behind it. As for Kim, Kimhant[7] because he happened to be born in the summer."

"Your father's so unfair. He must really love Khun."

"Well, he's his firstborn son. Actually, Father used to say he wanted everyone who heard our names to think, 'Hey, that man must be handsome because even his name is handsome.'" Kinn chuckled. "Whatever name sounds handsome to Father, he'll go for that one."

"Kinn sounds handsome? Kinn sounds stupi—*mmph*."

Kinn pressed his lips to mine and kept kissing and kissing me.

"That's enough," he said, pulling away. "Go to sleep. We have an early morning tomorrow." He slid his arm under my neck again, pulling me into his embrace. His other arm reached over to turn off the lights.

"'That's enough'? You started it!" I grumbled.

"It's just normal pillow talk."

"Fuck off!"

In the morning, Kinn dragged my sleepy ass out of bed. By the time both of us had washed up, got dressed, and finally made it downstairs for breakfast, it was almost ten a.m. It was fine for us to go in at eleven, apparently—we just needed to check the new shipment—so I was a little bit annoyed that Kinn had made me wake up early. If I'd known, I wouldn't have rushed myself; I could have snoozed for another ten minutes.

---

7   *An archaic word for summer.*

I walked down to the dining room—I'd upgraded from eating in some hidden corner of the kitchen to eating in the bougie dining room. *Must be my merits and virtues.*

At first, I'd felt a little nervous about joining the main table, but I was used to it now. Plus, there were no more dirty looks from Big because he was... Anyway, the most important thing was that *that* entire gang had been removed.

The traitors being gone also meant that Kinn had no bodyguard currently assigned to him. He couldn't borrow Tankhun's men because Khun didn't have anyone with him at the moment either. As for Nont, he was already running around like a headless chicken, running errands for Kim and Khun. I felt bad for Nont, so I'd volunteered to help assist Kinn while we recruited more bodyguards. For the time being, I continued to slave away for Kinn. He couldn't use anyone else, so he ended up using me.

"Good moooorning, everyone!" Tankhun's voice arrived before he did. As I watched him strut into the dining room, I could almost hear the trumpets announcing his presence.

"What ghost possessed you to come down to eat breakfast?" Kinn scoffed at his brother as he added food to my plate. On the days I woke up early, it was usually just the two of us eating breakfast. Father took his breakfast much earlier, and as for Kim and Chay, they normally figured it out on their own—Chay still had school, so he ate there, and Kim simply vanished. It was almost as if he could teleport.

"Any ghost possessing me is none of your business. I'm just so happy today! I'm thinking of celebrating at Madam Yok's place tonight! Please, please, please, please, Porsche!" Khun begged, plopping down next to me and shaking my arm just as I was about to take a sip of my soup. *Shit, I spilled it! Damn it, I won't get to eat anything at this rate.*

"Celebrate what?" I asked, peeling his hand off my arm and turning back to my food. His father might have announced to everyone that I was like one of his own sons, but that didn't give me any more reason to respect Tankhun. He didn't act in a way that commanded any respect. But he didn't seem to have a problem with it—whenever I scolded him or told him off, he'd just huff and puff like usual.

"Today! Today! Today!" Khun excitedly shouted and shook my arm again—right when I was in the middle of picking up some fried pork, so I ended up dropping it on the table. *Argh! I've had enough!*

"Asshole! You made me drop my food!" I glowered at Khun, who was still grinning from ear to ear without a care in the world. "Just say what you want to say!"

"Do you know how long I've waited for this day? I practiced singing every day, just for tonight! You can call Madam Yok right now—I want a Luk Thung theme like last time. I'll buy out the entire bar! Tee hee!" Khun got up from the table with a dreamy expression. I really wanted to crack open his brain to see if there was any space for actual thoughts in that thick head of his.

Kinn helped me pick up the fried pork from the table. "What are you celebrating?"

"Today...heh...today..."

Kinn and I looked at Khun with our brows furrowed.

"Ah..." He bent down and pointed at us cheerfully. "*Sorry to third wheel between you and him, malingkingkong malongkongkang manongmanang palongpongpang!*"[8] He broke into song and started twerking. *Ugh. If he does that at a concert, he's getting the crap kicked out of him.*

"So. Your point?" Kinn asked Tankhun while nudging my arm to tell me to continue eating. Khun was really wasting our time. Plus,

---

8   *Malong Kongkaeng* by Poj Sai Indy; the lyrics Khun is singing are nonsense.

I had that stupid song stuck in my head now—I'd been hearing it blaring from Khun's room for days.

"I practiced my dancing too... Do you wanna know? Do you wanna know why?" Khun stepped between us and threw his arms around our shoulders.

"No," I answered curtly and went back to eating.

"No! You *have* to wanna know," Khun whined, spoiled as ever.

"Don't disturb us. I'm hungry. Annoy me again, and I'll hit you with this ladle." I waved it at him.

"Shit, Porsche, you—" Khun pulled his arm back, stomping his feet. "I'm your husband's older brother!"

"Shut up." I cut him off. Khun huffed for a bit before letting out a sigh.

"Fine, I'll tell you why," he said. "Today, I want to celebrate because..." Without finishing his sentence, Khun ran for the door. Kinn and I looked at him in surrender.

"Ta-daaaa! You guys can come out now!" Khun waved his hands to present the people emerging as they walked in.

"Fucking hell. Took him long enough to give us the signal," Pol and Arm complained while smiling awkwardly at Tankhun. Then, they turned to me and their smiles widened as they rushed over to hug me. I immediately shot up from my chair to hug them back.

"We're back!" Arm declared. They turned to give Kinn a wai, and he nodded at them in acknowledgment.

"You guys left me all alone in this house for too long!" I said. At long last, my friends were back. I finally had some allies in this house!

I'd been so fucking lonely. Usually when I came back to this house, it was these guys who kept me entertained—but they'd been gone for over a week. Yeah, I had Kinn by my side, but I still needed my friends.

"Hey, you... What am I supposed to call you now?" Pol whispered, teasing me. "How about So?[9] I heard you got a promotion. Heh."

I glared at him. *Running his mouth as soon as he arrives! What a dick.*

"It's good you guys are back," Kinn said. He turned to his brother. "Khun, I need to borrow Arm."

Khun was staring at his bodyguards with stars in his eyes. I craned my neck to look behind them, trying to find the other man who should've come in with them.

"Of course. But not tonight!" Khun said brightly. Of course he was happy—his karaoke victims were back, so he was more spirited than usual.

"Where's Pete?" I blurted out at last, my eyes scanning left and right. The whole room went silent, with confused faces all around.

"Pete? Isn't he here?" Arm said, frowning.

Nobody said anything. We stared anxiously at each other. I had a bad feeling about this.

Kinn put down his spoon, suddenly serious. "Pete didn't go back home with you guys?"

"But...Pete was working a job for you, right, Mr. Kinn?" Pol asked, bewildered.

Kinn got up and rounded on Khun. "You said he went home."

"I meant Pol, Arm, and Jess." Khun was starting to panic. He pointed at Kinn. "Isn't Pete with you?"

"No! I asked you that day—you said he went home!" Kinn raised his voice. I looked between the two brothers.

"But you borrowed Pete! I thought you had him investigating something secret," Khun said. Both he and Kinn went pale. Pol and Arm looked stricken.

---

9   *"So" is a teochew term of address for the wife of one's older brother.*

"What is all this?" I snapped. I could tell it couldn't be anything good.

"I didn't *borrow* him. I thought he went home already," Kinn said, squaring off with Khun. He looked extremely distressed.

"I thought you sent him to tail Vegas! That's why I haven't seen him around. I knocked on his door, but he didn't answer, so I thought you had him watching Vegas around the clock. Kinn, what is wrong with you?!"

"Why would you assume that? If Pete didn't inform you he was taking his leave, why didn't you come and tell me?"

"Because you asked to borrow him, and I didn't want to overstep! I wanted him to work without distractions. I thought he was working for you!"

Both brothers kept raising their voices, their shouts booming louder and louder.

"Shit! Don't tell me that Pete..." Arm trailed off, his face the picture of shock.

"What the fuck is this, Kinn?! Answer me!" I turned to tug at Kinn, who rubbed at his face in frustration.

"That means...when I had him go to Vegas's house, he disappeared?" Kinn said pensively.

"What? You ordered him to infiltrate Vegas's house?" I asked just to be sure. My heart plummeted to my stomach. My mind went numb. *What do I do?*

"Yes!" Kinn rubbed his temples. "I ordered him to sneak into Vegas's house to get evidence of Vegas defrauding the company."

I took a deep breath to steel myself and tried to make sense of what had happened. "When?"

"Two weeks ago..."

"Fucking hell! Pete's an entire human being! How could you *lose* him? Why didn't you tell me? Who did he go with?!" I shoved Kinn's shoulder as hard as I could. "Don't tell me you had him go alone!"

"I misunderstood. I thought he was back already. It's all my fault," Kinn groaned.

"Kinn, you son of a bitch! He's probably rotting in the woods somewhere near the Minor Clan's house!" I snarled, furious. This was all Kinn's fault. I could admit that I was losing it, but even more affected than me was...

"Rot...rot...*rotting*? P-Pete!" Tankhun cried hysterically. He ran out of the dining room and headed straight for the front door.

Arm and Pol chased after him. "Young Master!"

"Bastard! How could you think he went home? You fucked up! That's my friend you abandoned!" I jabbed an accusing finger at Kinn, who sank down into his chair. The veins in his temples bulged in distress.

"I'm sorry. I shouldn't have assumed he went home. Fuck! If something happened to him, why didn't he call me?"

"If he got caught by the Minor Clan's men, do you think they'd let him use his phone out of the goodness of their hearts? What were you thinking, letting him go alone?" I raged. I'd have punched him right in the face, but I didn't want to hurt him.

The Minor Clan was just as ruthless as the Major Clan. If they caught a traitor, they'd probably have that person "taken care of." And I knew Vegas and his father weren't exactly normal.

Thinking back to what had happened at the abandoned warehouse...I had no idea what Vegas was truly capable of.

"Mr. Kinn! Help!" Arm shouted from the front of the house. Kinn and I ran toward the sound.

"Let me go! I'm going to Pete! Pete!" Khun yelled. He kept trying to make for the front gate, only to be held back by Pol and Arm.

"Sir, please get a hold of yourself," said Pol. "Calm down. Pete might've really gone home. And if he did get caught, he might still be unharmed."

"Khun, stop! Khun!" Kinn went to help, grabbing his brother's arm. I tried to tamp down my fury, telling myself that Pete might still be okay, even if the chances were slim.

"I'm going to Vegas's house!" I snapped, marching toward the garage.

"Shit! Porsche!" Kinn let go of Khun and turned to grab me instead, but I hadn't totally lost my shit just yet—not as much as Tankhun, anyway. I went with the force of his grip, whirling around to face off against him.

"I'm going!" I insisted. "Pete might still be alive!"

"Pete! Don't rot yet, Pete!" Tankhun's voice cut through our argument.

"Calm down first. Let's try to contact him one more time. Why don't we check with his grandmother before we do anything else?"

"Porsche is right... Young Master, calm down... Let's call his house just to make sure," Arm said with difficulty. "This might all be a big misunderstanding."

"Haven't we misunderstood enough?!" I said to Arm, then spun back to berate Kinn. "You *forgot* him! You kept passing him back and forth, and in the end, Pete paid the price!"

"Porsche... Please, calm down. I'll take care of this." Kinn reached out to touch my forearm, but I shoved him away.

"Take care of it, Kinn? If anything happens to my friend, I swear I won't respect any of you again—I don't care who you think you are!"

"I'm going kill him. I'm going to kill Vegas! Pete..." Khun kept wailing, his eyes red and overflowing with tears.

Rrrrr. Rrrrr. Arm's phone vibrated.

"Give me a second—Pol, hold him for me. P'Chan is calling," Arm said, stepping away to pick up the call. I tried to keep calm, but my mind was running wild with possibilities.

"What?!" Arm shouted at the top of his lungs, making us stop in our tracks, including Khun. We turned to look at Arm.

"They found a body...burned... Th-there was a Major Clan crest in his pocket?" Arm stuttered out, his eyes darting toward us. We were speechless, our faces going pale. Kinn looked at me with obvious worry.

"Of course... At the hospital? I'll be there straight away." Arm's expression was grim as he walked toward us. We stood there, frozen in shock, especially Tankhun, who went stiff as a statue.

"P'Chan wants me to go check the hospital. They found a burnt body this morning in a warehouse on the outskirts of the city, along with the Major Clan's crest. They don't know who it is..." Arm bit his lip, his voice beginning to shake. No one seemed to know what to do. The most worrying was Tankhun, who looked like his spirit had left his body.

"Let's go, sir... Young Master!" Pol rushed to hold Khun up as his knees gave out and he dropped to the ground.

"Pete... It can't be..." Khun whispered in disbelief. Tears slid down his cheeks and his mouth trembled.

"Take Khun to rest in his room first. Arm, you're with me." Kinn went over to help Pol hold Khun up, but Khun shook his head.

"I'm going. I'm going to see Pete!" Khun bawled, his body going limp.

"We don't know if it's Pete yet. You go rest—I'll take care of this." Kinn reached out to wipe the tears from his brother's face.

"No! I'm going!" Khun sobbed so hard, he shook with the force of it. Kinn froze for a second. Then he ordered Arm and Pol to carry Tankhun into a car to go to the hospital.

"Let's go, Porsche." Kinn reached out like he was going to touch my arm, but I held up a hand to stop him. I didn't want him to touch me right now; I couldn't even bear to look at his face. I'd gone numb the second I'd heard the word "body."

I didn't know what I should feel: grief, anger, a desire for vengeance, or something else. This was all thanks to Kinn's negligence, and if that body really was Pete, I was going to wipe out the entire Minor Clan to avenge the death of my friend. *Just you wait.*

Pol drove the van. Each and every one of us was silent during the trip to the hospital; the only sound in the van was Khun's sobbing. A lump formed in my throat as images of the day I lost my mom and dad came rushing back. I hated parting without being able to say goodbye.

My feelings were all jumbled up. I didn't know how I was going to face this sudden loss. And I knew that Kinn felt guilty, so I didn't want to bring it up and make things worse, but I couldn't help feeling angry. Deep down, I blamed Kinn for this. It was his heedlessness that got us here.

We arrived at the hospital and headed straight to the morgue. Pol and Arm had to hold Khun up by his arms; his legs were so weak that he could barely stand.

When we got inside, we were met by a police officer and the forensic doctor.

"Hello, Uncle..." Kinn raised his hands in a wai as soon as he saw the police officer, greeting him with familiarity. He must have been one of the cops on the family payroll.

"Oh, hello, Mr. Kinn. Why so many of you? Really, it's not anything important. Probably just someone 'taken care of,' like usual." The cop sounded so casual, like this was a completely normal occurrence.

"Pete... Is it Pete?" Khun asked, still bawling.

The officer furrowed his brows. "Pete... Pete? What?! You're joking, Khun. How could it be Pete...?" The officer went still for a moment, lost in thought, before looking between Khun and Kinn. "Did something happen?"

This cop talked like he knew Pete, but I wasn't surprised; Pete had been with the Major Clan for some time now.

Khun sobbed, "Pete went missing, Uncle."

The officer paled, turning behind him to look at the doctor. The doctor was standing next to the body, holding various documents.

"Is there any evidence to identify the body?" Kinn asked. He worriedly glanced in the direction of the body, which was covered with an opaque plastic sheet.

"The body was burned posthumously, and there are various fissures in the skin. The neck has signs of strangulation, and there were rope fragments found nearby," the doctor said. "DNA testing to identify the body will take some time, but from an external examination, I can tell you that the body is male, approximately twenty to thirty years old, about five foot nine, and wearing a stainless-steel ring on the middle finger of his left hand. But the rest..."

"...N-no, it's not true!" Tankhun shook his head from side to side.

I considered the physical description against what Pete usually wore, and I nearly collapsed on the floor with Tankhun. Pete wore a silver ring. On his left or right hand, I wasn't sure, but he definitely wore a silver ring…

"Pete!" Arm and Pol couldn't hold it in anymore. Although they looked like they didn't want to believe it, in the end, they walked up to the autopsy table and bowed their heads, motionless save for their shaking shoulders.

"I'm sorry… That day, I was preoccupied with Big," Arm sobbed. "I thought you came back to report to Mr. Kinn already."

"Pete… It's not true, is it?" Pol hugged Arm's neck and cried into his shoulder.

"Oh, Pete…" Khun went to cling to the table as well. He sank to his knees as he wept, his entire body trembling. I'd never seen Khun cry before—his expression was so despondent that there was no trace of his usually cheerful self.

I braced one hand against the wall, my limbs so weak that I could barely keep myself upright. Kinn stood there, staring blankly into the distance, looking lost in thought.

Uncle Cop squatted down next to Khun and stroked his back to comfort him. "Khun, it might not be Pete," he said.

"It has to be Pete. He wore a stainless-steel ring on his left hand," Khun said through sniffles, tears and snot running down his face. He lifted his head to ask the doctor, "Doctor…Pete has a tattoo on the left side of his chest… Is there one on the body?"

"There's extensive burn damage to the skin… If there is one, we won't be able to identify it."

"Pete has a tattoo?" Kinn asked calmly, a slight tremor marring his voice.

Tankhun sobbed. "I was the one who told him to get it… I designed it myself. When Porsche first came to live with us, I thought his tattoo was cool, so I told everyone to get one. Pete was the only one who did... I had him tattoo 'No legacy as rich as honesty' because I wanted him to stay with me forever!" Tankhun's head dropped down to the edge of the table again.

"Young Master...calm down," Arm said, clearly struggling with his words.

"Mr. Tankhun, we'll be using the teeth and bones to test the DNA, and the results will take some time," the doctor explained calmly. "There's still a possibility that this person is not your bodyguard."

Khun sniffed. "But if it is him...I don't want him to stay here alone. While we wait for the DNA results, can I take his body to the temple?" he asked through his sobs. "If it's really you, Pete, I want you to rest in peace. You don't have to suffer anymore... I love you like one of my own little brothers!"

Khun gently stroked the plastic sheet. The image sent an arrow straight through my heart. I couldn't breathe. It was pure agony, the same feeling as when I'd lost my parents. I'd always been afraid of losing another person close to me, and today, that wound had ripped back open. The fear I'd kept buried deep in my most fragile of hearts had fully reawakened.

"Fuck the Minor Clan! Fuck them all!" I cursed, punching the wall. I didn't register any pain as my knuckles hit the plaster. I lunged at Arm to grab the car keys from his pocket and stormed out of the room.

"Porsche... Porsche! Where are you going?" Kinn moved to grab me, but my rage burned brighter than every other emotion; I could no longer control myself.

I stormed out to the van and hurried to unlock it. My fear had entirely dissipated, replaced by the need for revenge. All I wanted was to charge up to the Minor Clan's house and bludgeon those motherfuckers until they joined my friend in death.

I lost myself to the fire blazing in my heart, ready to burn everything to ashes. I didn't even notice Kinn running up behind me until I felt his strong arms wrap around me, stopping me from taking another step forward. Kinn kept shouting, trying to bring me back to my senses, but I thrashed against his hold and tried to shake him off, not caring about anything else.

"Porsche! Get a hold of yourself! The fuck are you doing?! Porsche!" Kinn strained against me as I struggled, holding me tightly from behind.

"Let me go! I'm going to kill those bastards! I'll kill them all!" I raved like a madman. Although I'd only known Pete for a little while, I loved him as a true friend—I admired his sincerity, his caring heart, how he always had my back. If it had been Tem or Jom who'd died, or even Pol or Arm, I would still want the same vengeance. I hated anyone who dared to take away a good friend from me.

Pete, it shouldn't have ended this way. You were too good for all of this. You were a good friend and a good bodyguard. You went beyond the call of duty.

Please, I don't want to lose anyone else.

"Porsche! Calm down! You need to come to your senses!" Kinn succeeded in pulling me back. He grabbed my shoulder and shoved me against the van door, keeping me pinned.

"*Calm down?!* Didn't you see what those bastards did to my friend?!" I roared, not caring that we were fighting in a public parking lot. At least we were in the VIP section, so there wasn't anyone walking by.

"Please calm down first. I'm just as angry as you are, but you need to listen to me! If we charge in there now, the only thing that awaits us is more losses. It's no use." Kinn used all his weight to pin me down. I kept struggling, but I started to lose my strength—maybe my grief was cutting through the anger. My body went limp against the van.

"I've already lost one friend. What more do you want me to lose?!" I demanded, my whole body starting to tremble. The lump in my throat grew until it reached all the way to the bottom of my chest. My heart's old wounds throbbed; images of my parents filled my head, overlapping with Pete's body in that plastic bag. No matter how long it had been, I couldn't let go and make peace with losing the people I loved.

"Porsche! I promise I'll sort everything out. I'll do everything in my power to exact our revenge on the Minor Clan, but you need to listen to me: It's too risky. If you go in now, nothing good can come of it." Kinn softened his voice to soothe me, but I didn't feel comforted at all.

"I'm serious—how could you let Pete go in there on his own?!" I yelled, panting with rage.

"I'm sorry. I can't change the past. Pete was a loyal bodyguard. I saw him as a younger brother..." Kinn's face looked ashen, and his eyes were stricken with guilt. I knew he must be beating himself up, that deep down, he probably felt the same as I did. He was just better at suppressing it.

"Tell me, why were you always so suspicious of Vegas? You've never given me a clear answer." I stopped struggling and finally asked what was on my mind. "Even after Big's death, you barely gave me an explanation, just that he stole confidential documents and sold them. You never told me what you were doing with the Minor Clan or what beef you had with them. Why did you send Pete? What the fuck is really going on here?!"

Kinn had never told me what caused the rift between the Major Clan and the Minor Clan. Even after all that shit went down with

Big, Kinn only gave me short, curt answers. I didn't want to pry, but with everything that was going on now, I felt like I was owed an explanation. The timeline of events was starting to match up, and I could tell there was some secret Kinn was keeping from me. In the end, this was where we'd ended up—with Pete dead.

Now that Pete's gone, don't I have the right to know what the hell is going on? If not, then I don't want to get close to anyone ever again. I'm afraid death will take them away from me...

"It's not like I didn't want to tell you," he said. "I just thought it wasn't the right time. But you have to calm down first."

"What the fuck are you waiting for? Who's next, huh? Pol, Arm, even my little brother? Chay and I live in your goddamn house! Do we have the right to know *anything*?" I demanded, staring at Kinn's face.

"Porsche, calm down... I'll take care of everything. I'm just asking for you to be careful and take things one step at a time." Kinn looked at me imploringly. "Please?"

I took a deep breath and closed my eyes. "Then tell me. Give me one reason not to wipe out the Minor Clan right now!"

"Everything has to be done with caution," he told me. "The Minor Clan is entangled in many of our businesses. I need to find their conspirators, as well as anyone else involved, to be as thorough as possible. At home, we got rid of Big, but at the company...it's more complicated. There are many shareholders, and I need to find additional evidence they can't refute. And Father and I have agreed that we don't want outsiders or other rival families to know we have internal problems. There are people ready to stab us in the back at a moment's notice if we show weakness. If we act too hastily, the company will be in trouble—people on the outside will know how rotten things are within the family.

"I want to take care of things slowly. We have to be quiet and utterly meticulous so no one else can take advantage of the situation. Father and I know that if others realize the Major Clan and Minor Clan are on the outs, then Khun, Kim, Father, even you—none of us will be safe. Our rivals will use the opportunity to take our businesses down and kill us all."

I began to settle down, little by little, silent sorrow replacing my simmering rage.

"Porsche, I promise I'll explain everything to you," said Kinn. "But can it be after we get through this? The Minor Clan is desperate for power over the Major Clan, so they've done so many careless, terrible things... But, please, don't be reckless."

Kinn's hand came up to gently cup my face. I lowered my head, the tightness in my chest unraveling into sobs.

"But Pete...Pete's dead!" I burrowed my face into Kinn's shoulder and cried, unable to hold back. My tears soaked into Kinn's shirt, and my whole body shook. Although the DNA results weren't back yet, all evidence pointed to the body being Pete's; the description was too perfect. There was no use in denying it.

"I promise I'll...'take care' of the Minor Clan," Kinn said, holding me tighter. The warmth of my lover's embrace couldn't fill the emptiness in my heart. I didn't want to accept the truth that Pete really was dead. I wanted to believe that everything that had happened today was just a terrible dream.

The drive back was somber. Pete's body was still at the morgue. We were going to pick him up tomorrow for the funerary rites. There were no words to be said in the car; we sat there lost and confused as silence enveloped everything, even our hearts.

When we got home, Kim was leaning against the door. Nont stood behind him, crying.

Chay was hugging his knees on the front steps. He ran up to us the moment he saw me.

"Hia! It's not P'Pete, is it?" he asked, his eyes full of hope. He must've heard the news, or at least part of it. Arm had probably called to inform everyone else at home.

I could only stand there, unmoving, unable to answer my brother's question.

"Khun. Are you okay?" Kim asked his older brother. But Khun brushed past everyone wordlessly. Keeping his composure, he walked up the stairs and immediately disappeared into his room.

"P'Pete..." Chay called out Pete's name again. I didn't say anything—that was enough of an answer for him.

The bodyguards at the house looked back at us with mournful expressions as we returned from the hospital with red, tearful eyes. Gloom silently wound its way through the whole house.

I went back to my room with Kinn. Neither of us said a word. I hated this suffocating atmosphere more than anything. Although I'd calmed down somewhat, grief still filled my chest.

What Kinn had said to me...his words had enough weight to give me pause. I didn't want to make things more complicated than they already were. Despite how much I wanted to destroy those Minor Clan bastards, I had to hold back.

I couldn't help but blame Kinn, though—he'd had a hand in this. No matter how skilled or experienced Pete was, Kinn shouldn't have let him go in alone. It was utterly careless. I couldn't believe Kinn had been naive enough to assume Pete had already gone home too.

I wanted Kinn to receive his fair share of the bad karma.

"Porsche, where are you going?" Kinn asked as I picked up my wallet and the keys to the BMW. I needed to go somewhere

where I could breathe, where I could process everything that had happened. Right now, I wanted to be alone. My mind was completely numb.

"I'm going out," I said evenly, no emotion coloring my voice. "I promise I won't go to the Minor Clan." I wasn't planning on running away, exactly, but I needed to take a step back and give myself some time.

"No...I can't let you go," Kinn said, pulling me into a loose hug. "I know you don't want to even look at me right now, but I...I need you to stay close. The situation is dangerous. I'm afraid something might happen to you. Besides, at a time like this? I need you, Porsche." Kinn hugged me tighter and dropped his head onto my shoulder. I couldn't help but feel sorry for him, despite my anger. I knew he'd never intended for Pete to die—but it was still his error in judgment that got us here.

"Then I won't go...but I want to be alone." I pried Kinn's hands off and put my things away.

"As long as you're still in this house. That'll be enough."

"Then get out of this room... I need time. Let me be alone for a while."

Kinn nodded, agreeing easily. He gave me one last regretful look before stepping out of the room.

I collapsed onto the couch, letting my mind wander. I'd only just gotten to know Pete, but he was one of the few good people in my life.

I can only hope your good spirit will lead you to a better place, Pete. From this moment on, wherever you are, whomever you meet, I hope the merit you've made will free you from these people.

Don't come near anything like all this in your next life. I want you to be free, to find happiness without needing to serve anyone or having to face such terrible things. Your smile and your sincerity will always be remembered.

I'll think of you as my good friend, always.

I let my emotions flow until I was too tired to hold my eyes open any longer.

Evening came, and Arm knocked on my door to tell me of tomorrow's plans.

"At six in the morning, Mr. Tankhun will go to pick up Pete and take his body to the temple. Are you coming with us, or will you follow later?"

"I'm going," I said.

"Right. We'll meet at six in front of the house..."

"Have you told Pete's grandma yet?" I asked.

"Mr. Kinn will do that himself," Arm explained. "But he doesn't want to do it over the phone, in case Pete's grandparents can't handle it."

"So..."

"He's already sent people to Chumphon to bring them to Bangkok by plane. Then Mr. Kinn will tell them in person."

"Mm," I hummed in acknowledgment.

"Um...I saw Mr. Kinn pacing in the foyer," Arm added. "Can you let him back in to your room, at least to sleep? I think he feels guilty enough already."

"No..."

"He went to Mr. Tankhun's room, but he got chased out. He won't go to Mr. Kim's room, out of concern for Chay. That boy is completely listless—he won't speak a word to anybody."

I knew well how everyone felt. Chay was probably just as badly affected as I was. When I was busy, I'd often entrusted him to Pete—and Chay, like me, also carried the memories of losing our parents. He was probably still in shock.

"Just leave him like that." I did feel a sliver of empathy for Kinn, but what could be done when he was at least partially responsible for this?

Arm nodded and let me go back into the bedroom. I washed up, changed, then collapsed onto the wide, empty bed.

I tossed and turned, unable to sleep. I wasn't tired, wasn't hungry, wasn't feeling anything at all; there was only emptiness. I could only hope that time would heal my heart.

Dad, Mom... Why does the memory of that day keep coming back to haunt me?

The bitter past kept returning. I missed my parents from the bottom of my heart. Losing them without having the chance to say goodbye was more painful than anything. I could never really accept that hard fact of life—that meetings would always be followed by partings. When it was Big or anyone else, I had felt sad for a moment, but I wasn't anywhere as close with Big as I was with Pete. At this point, I just couldn't accept that he was gone.

After waking up in the middle of the night, I couldn't go back to sleep. When morning came, I changed into a black shirt and formal-looking slacks to meet everyone like we'd agreed.

Kinn himself came to knock on the bedroom door, just before dawn, to get washed up and changed. The cooks already had breakfast waiting; Pol called me over to eat, but at a time like this, I couldn't stomach it. Neither could anyone else.

Khun, Kim, and Chay came down to gather in front of the house, and we piled into the van to go to the hospital together.

Khun was despondent, his eyes red and swollen. It looked like he'd been crying all night. Arm and Pol had to prop him up to get him from one place to the next because he was still in such a daze.

When we got to the morgue, the cop from yesterday handed a plastic bag with the gathered evidence to Khun, an uneasy expression on his face.

"This was the ring worn by the deceased," he said with difficulty, "and this is the Major Clan's crest... And most significantly, we found a partially burned business card. It's still legible, bearing the name Pongsakorn Saengtham...which is Pete's legal name."

Khun began to cry even harder.

There might've been a shred of hope that the cop was mistaken and that we should wait for the DNA results, but finding Pete's name made it real.

Khun insisted we take his body to the temple and perform the religious rites so Pete could rest. Although the cop said he was only about 70 percent certain about the evidence, he really couldn't argue against Khun.

We brought Pete to the temple and arranged for a grand funeral. All the evidence had been gathered, so we had permission to cremate him. At first, Khun had wanted a hundred-day vigil, but a lot of the senior bodyguards objected to the idea since Pete had died of unnatural causes; the proper rites needed to be completed to ensure his spirit could rest peacefully. These may have been their personal beliefs, but Khun listened to them. He only wanted to do right by Pete, so he agreed; the funeral was shortened to a more appropriate seven days.

We were all busy at the temple sala for the entire day.[10] Even though he still needed Pol and Arm to help prop him up, Khun

---

10   A *sala* is large, shaded pavilion used as a public gathering place.

took charge of every step of the funeral arrangements, from picking the coffin to finding the florists and arranging the photo memorial outside. Kinn, Kim, Chay, and I helped coordinate with the temple and took care of the tables and seating, recruiting the other bodyguards to help carry things around.

Kinn came over to speak to me. "I've sent someone to investigate the Minor Clan's house, and there's nothing out of the ordinary, but the car Pete drove has gone missing," he said gravely. "When we checked the Highway Department's cameras, there was no trace of his car—they only had images of him driving out of the Major Clan's house. The surveillance footage from after he arrived at the Minor Clan's house is missing."

"And you can't do anything else?" I asked. Everyone else may have accepted that this was Pete, but in my heart, I couldn't help but hope that it was all just a big misunderstanding.

"The Minor Clan's side has police on the take too. It's no surprise that it's been difficult to gather evidence, but I'll try my hardest."

"Just do whatever you can. It might be hopeless, but until the DNA results are here, I don't want to believe that it's Pete." I *did* believe it...but even so, I wanted to do everything I could for Pete.

"Pete's grandparents are here," Nont told Kinn, who took a deep breath and walked out of the sala. I followed after him.

As soon as Pete's grandma and grandpa got out of the car and saw their grandson's name on the sign outside, both of them nearly collapsed. Khun and Kinn ran up to help support them. I couldn't bear to look, so I turned away, biting my lip to keep myself steady.

"Hia..." Chay must have seen that I wasn't looking too great, so he came over and looped his arm around mine, squeezing my hand.

Khun, Kim, and Kinn helped Pete's grandparents into the sala. Both of them were crying their eyes out; it was heartbreaking to watch. It seemed that the Major Clan didn't see Pete as just another employee, but as part of their family. They were clearly close to Pete's grandparents, because Khun kept hugging Pete's grandma and crying along with her.

Kinn crawled up to Pete's grandparents on his knees and prostrated himself at their laps, then briefly conversed with them. Pete's grandpa and grandma seemed to adore those three brothers, so I let them talk and excused myself to help the others with preparing Pete's funeral.

The first night of chanting continued.[11] Mr. Korn and P'Chan arrived around early evening as various guests crowded the sala. Most of them were probably the Major Clan's business partners.

We didn't speak much. Tankhun was a bit more responsive, but still very depressed. We made sure everything went smoothly, and the Major Clan acted as host for the whole seven days.

Tonight, Pol and Nont would stay behind to sleep at the sala and keep Pete company, while everyone else returned home to rest. We'd come back to start again tomorrow.

I sat in the BMW as Kinn drove. I looked away from him, giving one-word answers every time he tried to talk to me. I was even more furious with him now that I'd seen Pete's grieving grandparents.

Kinn told me that the Major Clan owned an edible bird's nest company on the southern island where Pete lived. When they were young, his father would often take his three sons with him on business trips, and Pete's grandma absolutely adored them. Their families grew apart as they got older because Mr. Korn had many subsidiary businesses to see to, and Kinn and his brothers didn't get to go as often; it was P'Chan who took care of things, right up until Pete came to work at the Major Clan's house. That was why the

---

11 At Thai Buddhist funerals, monks are invited to chant the Abhidharma.

family was closer to Pete than the other bodyguards—and why his loss was all the more devastating.

I finally allowed Kinn to come back and sleep in our room because I knew he must be exhausted. I'd hardly eaten, but I wasn't hungry at all.

It'd been three days already. I was still angry with Kinn, but we'd talked more. Over the past two days, Tem and Jom, along with Kinn's friends Time, Tay, and Mew, had showed up to help out. Kim's friends were here as well. I didn't know them, but Chay certainly did.

The sala ended up packed full of people, who all knew Pete and were shocked by the news of his death.

"Khun, let's go eat." I wanted to have dinner now because, as evening fell, more guests would arrive, and it'd be just as busy as on the other days; we wouldn't have time to eat later.

Tankhun had used his authority as the owner's eldest son to order all the family's subsidiary companies to close. Although Mr. Korn was against it, he didn't have it in his heart to deny Khun.

Khun had sat next to Pete's coffin all day. He'd had his head buried in his knees for a while now, and he didn't answer my call to dinner.

"Khun...let's go eat. The monks will be here soon," I said.

"M'not hungry," Khun grumbled.

"Hello," a new voice said.

I turned, following the sound, and brought my hands up in a wai to greet the newcomer. It was Khun's Dr. Top, or Tap, or something like that. I knew Khun had a giant crush on the guy. He'd fallen so hard and so fast; it'd been a little shocking to suddenly find out he liked men too. *Fuck it, forget about that. Maybe this Dr. Top might be able to help Khun feel better.*

"I'll go pay my respects first," the doctor said. He seemed to be talking to me, but his eyes were focused on Tankhun's back.

I squatted down to nudge Tankhun's arm. "Khun, Dr. Top is here."

Khun looked up at Dr. Top. When he saw the doctor finish paying his respects, Khun gave him a wai before dropping his head onto his knees again.

Dr. Top scooted over to sit next to us. "My condolences," he said.

I gently tugged the hem of Tankhun's shirt. "Khun...go take Dr. Top to a seat."

Dr. Top looked at me worriedly. "It's all right," he insisted.

"He won't eat," I told the doctor. "I'll have to trouble you to talk to him."

He nodded, but he looked unsure. "I'll try."

I was only able to keep Khun company for a few more minutes before Kim summoned me to help greet the other guests. As for Kinn, he sat with Pete's grandparents, who'd been crying almost nonstop.

Dr. Top finally succeeded in getting Khun to move to one of the sofas; it was good to see him looking a little better.

Time passed, and another night of chanting was completed. The crowd was thinner today, compared to the first couple of days. Guests began to file out, though a few stayed behind to talk and to eat the food we'd prepared. I was about to get up and fetch Kinn something to eat, since he didn't get to eat much today, when suddenly...

"Sorry, hia, Vegas and I had some business to take care of, so we're late."

I wasn't familiar with his voice, but I remembered his face well: It was Mr. Kant of the Minor Clan.

"It's fine, it's fine," Mr. Korn said, his voice placid. He didn't seem particularly interested in the Minor Clan's arrival.

"And who is this funeral for?" Mr. Kant asked.

"Pete. Khun's personal bodyguard."

"Did you have to arrange such a big ceremony, hia? Isn't this a bit over-the-top?"

I clenched my fists, trying to keep my emotions under control. I had no idea how the two of them could smile at each other after everything that had happened. And if it really was the Minor Clan who did this to Pete, how could they dare to step into this place? Those shameless motherfuckers!

"Khun really did love him like a brother," Mr. Korn explained.

"Hello, Be." Vegas and Macau followed after Mr. Kant, greeting Mr. Korn with wai gestures.

Vegas looked over to where the coffin was set up and stared at the photo memorial in surprise. He looked taken aback, slowly walking up to the photo with his brows furrowed. He stopped in front of the photo, mouth moving silently like he was reading out the name underneath, then sighed and pursed his lips, holding back laughter.

I glared daggers at Vegas. *You dare laugh at my friend?! What's so fucking funny, huh?!* I couldn't stand to see him smiling so blithely; it was the final straw. I launched myself at him and punched him square in the face, catching him off guard. He swayed and nearly fell before he turned back to look at me steadily.

"Porsche...stop!" Kinn pulled me back as I tried to reacquaint Vegas's face with my foot.

"Porsche," Vegas said evenly.

"Why are you smiling? My friend is dead, and you're *smiling*?!" I shouted, not caring about the commotion around me. Everything happened so fast...

"Vegas!" Khun came out of nowhere with a bowl of fish maw soup, aiming to dump it on Vegas's head, but Vegas backed away in time for it to spill all over his shoulder instead.

"Shit!" someone exclaimed as Vegas's black suit dripped with the sticky liquid. So much for serving that soup to the guests.

"Tankhun! What the hell are you doing?!" Vegas yelled angrily, looking down at the state of his clothes.

"Murderer—! Oof! Lemme go!"

Kim quickly slapped a hand over Khun's mouth from behind and pulled his brother away, struggling. Kinn was still holding on to me as he turned to scold Kim.

"Kim! Why didn't you stop Khun?"

"I didn't have time! He grabbed the bowl and just ran over to dump it on 'Gus!"

"Hia! Are you okay? What did you do to my brother?!" Macau patted his brother with tissues, glaring at Khun.

Khun was still kicking the air, trying to cuss out the Minor Clan even with Kim's hand tightly clasped over his mouth. It was so fucking satisfying to see. I'd only managed to get a single punch in, but it was enough.

"Are you crazy?!" Macau shouted at Khun.

"Shut up, 'Cau!" Kim shouted back.

"He started it! If your rabid dog is contagious, you'd better put a leash on him instead of letting him run around, biting other people!"

When Khun heard this, he thrashed even harder to break free from Kim. It was a good thing Dr. Top came over to help; Kim alone wouldn't have been able to hold Khun back.

Kinn loosened his hold on me once he saw that I'd calmed down. "Enough, that's enough. Do you all have no shame?!" he shouted. Guests were beginning to look our way.

Mr. Korn and Mr. Kant came over.

"What's all this?" asked Mr. Korn.

"Nothing, Father, just a misunderstanding," Kinn immediately answered.

"Vegas!" Mr. Kant hurried over to Vegas and inspected his son. "Hia! What did your son do to mine?!"

"Khun was going to bring Vegas some fish maw soup, Zek," said Kim, quickly making up an excuse, "but he tripped, so it spilled all over him."

Judging from the two patriarchs' reactions, they probably hadn't seen me punch Vegas. There'd been flowers and funeral wreaths blocking their lines of sight; plus, they'd been busy talking to each other. Probably only a few people had seen that punch, but everyone must've noticed Khun throwing soup over Vegas.

"Oh? All right, it's good that there's no trouble here. Just a misunderstanding," Mr. Korn said.

"But, hia, your son..." Mr. Kant started.

"Boys will be boys. They're probably just playing around. Forget it; we shouldn't step in. Will someone find a cloth for Vegas to wipe himself off with?" Mr. Korn pulled Mr. Kant back to the sofas to talk.

Vegas huffed, glancing at Kinn, Khun, and Kim before grabbing the tissues in Macau's hands and throwing them to the floor. He closed his eyes, then turned to stare at Kinn.

"Ah... It's such a shame, Kinn. How did Pete die?" Vegas asked with a smirk.

Fuck! I couldn't believe my eyes. This was a side of Vegas I never imagined I'd see. He was able to switch gears so smoothly that it scared me. His eyes flashed with cruelty, but he was still able to smile. I used to think that smile was so bright and cheerful, but now...it was like I'd never even known the real Vegas.

Kinn made a soft noise, like he was at his limit with Vegas.

"Alas, someone so skilled shouldn't have died so young, don't you agree?" Vegas went on. "Did someone do something to him, or...did he go looking for trouble?"

"Vegas, don't you dare say another word," Kim growled, passing Khun over to Dr. Top. He was getting riled up too. I noticed Macau glare unhappily at the two of them.

"Heh... As usual, the Major Clan is one step behind. Let's go, Macau—we're leaving." Vegas tugged Macau's wrist and pulled him out of the sala.

"What do you mean by that, huh?!" Kim shouted. He made to follow them, but Kinn stopped him.

"Kim, that's enough," he said. "Let him go."

"Damn it, I want to kick his teeth in!"

"Let him be. Vegas is all talk. When the time comes, we'll see just how smug he is."

Our friends and various bodyguards went to talk to the guests and soothe any ruffled feathers. "This was all just a misunderstanding. It's all been sorted out now."

We dispersed to see to our own duties. Friends gathered around, asking how I was. I was fine, although I'd have felt even better if I got in another punch or two.

I was still hung up on Vegas's last sentence, though: *"The Major Clan is always one step behind"*? What did that mean?

I was too busy to pay it any mind. We had to send the guests away, make sure everything was in order, and prepare for tomorrow. We were exhausted.

When we got home, Kinn and I took turns using the bathroom. When we were done, we both collapsed into bed. I let Kinn hold me like before. I saw how tired he was, dealing with guests and family the whole day. The anger in my heart was fading with time.

Pete's funeral progressed to its sixth day. Tomorrow would be his cremation. We were busy as usual, but today held more significance.

When we got back home, Khun looked a bit better. Everyone was beginning to accept and make peace with Pete's loss.

We had a fire going in a metal bin. I stood by the tall metal can as smoke billowed from it. Khun, Chay, Pol, and Arm stood by me while Kinn, Kim, P'Chan, and Mr. Korn looked on awkwardly from a distance.

"Pete, if you want anything...just come tell us in Arm's dreams, and I'll send it to you," Khun said with a shaky voice as he threw joss paper into the fire, one piece at a time.[12]

Arm whipped around to stare at Khun. "Why *my* dreams?!"

Khun hiccupped with sobs. "Here... Is this house big enough? I chose the biggest one for you," he said, throwing in a paper house. Arm, Pol, and I continued to throw in joss paper as Chay stoked the fire with a long stick to keep it burning.

---

12 A Thai-Chinese tradition tracing back to Chinese ancestral worship. Joss paper "money" and other paper crafts are burned for the deceased to use in the afterlife, with modern varieties including credit cards and cars.

"Here, have some servants... Just tell them what you want. I've sent you ten, so you'll be comfortable, Pete. You won't have to do anything for yourself." Khun's sniffling and wailing got louder as he spoke.

"Here...a platinum credit card..." Khun threw more paper into the fire. "There's no spending limit, but don't go overboard. You won't be able to pay off the interest otherwise."

"You do realize that burning joss paper is only done for people over fifty and only for your direct ancestors, right?" Mr. Korn asked loudly.

"Shush, Father, what do you know?!" Khun turned to argue. "Pete would also want a house in the afterlife! How will he have a comfortable afterlife if he doesn't have any money?!"

Kim and Kinn shook their heads, staring like they'd had enough of his antics, but the rest of us concentrated on burning the gold and silver paper.

I didn't really know how this tradition worked; when my parents died, I'd just made merit for them at the temple. I'd never burned anything for them, no matter how Chinese I looked. But I was following Khun's lead on this because at least it was one last thing I could do for Pete. I didn't know if it would reach him, but I had to try.

Khun sniffled. "I'm sorry, Pete. I'm sorry I couldn't help you in time. Be at peace. But if you're not...go haunt Arm or Pol. Tell them what you want... I'll make sure to get it for you..." Khun threw a dozen or so paper cars in, making the smoke thicken and ash blow into the house. Kinn, Kim, Mr. Korn, and P'Chan all began to cough and wheeze from the fumes.

Khun hacked and sniffled. "If you're lonely, I'll send Arm and Pol to keep you company..."

"Wait, wait, Young Master—maybe not that." Pol and Arm looked at Khun.

"I want him to have friends…but it's all right. If Arm and Pol don't want to, I've got Madam Yok's picture… I'll burn Madam Yok for you, since you said you liked her bar. Let her open a club wherever you are… Don't forget to play the music I like," Tankhun wept. "Think of me, Pete. You don't have to visit me… J-just think of me, and I'll know." He threw a life-size cardboard cutout of Madam Yok into the metal can. He really had prepared everything. I felt a little sorry for Madam Yok, suddenly having to go to the afterlife like that.

"That's it. Chay, let's go inside. I've breathed in so much smoke that I'm going to get lung cancer," Kim said, beckoning Chay to follow him.

Kinn came up to me and looped his arm over my shoulder, tugging me inside. "Let's go shower."

Behind us, Khun kept wailing, "Pete! Why did you leave me?! Pete!"

The entire house stank of smoke, and the bodyguards and maids had to bring out electric fans to air out the place, but otherwise, the day's work was done. It seemed like everyone was starting to let go of their grief, and the atmosphere in the house began to lighten. In the end, we tried to encourage each other to keep moving forward.

By late morning the next day, I was extra busy: It was the day of Pete's cremation. I'd gone out to buy a few miscellaneous items and more joss paper. Khun said he wanted to burn more offerings because he was still afraid Pete wouldn't be comfortable, so I'd volunteered. There happened to be a religious goods store in my old neighborhood, so I planned to stop and check on my house while I was out. Chay came with me, wanting to fetch some books from his bedroom that he forgot to bring with him earlier.

I'd wanted to come back to our house at least once a week anyway. I wouldn't sell it, no matter what. *I'll keep this house, since Mr. Korn already returned the deed to me. I'm going to keep this place as a memory; it's all Chay and I have left of our mom and dad...*

When we turned the corner onto our street, Chay pointed through the car window to a local shop. "Oh, hia, the khanom krok shop is open.[13] Let's stop by on the way back."

I was somewhat surprised; my little brother didn't really like desserts. "Didn't you say that place makes them too sweet? And you don't like them, anyway."

"Kim has a sweet tooth, hia. Everything he eats is sickeningly sweet. Even his noodles—he puts so much sugar in there that the broth is basically a syrup."

When I heard him say Kim's name, I narrowed my eyes, glancing between him and the road. We'd never really talked about this properly, had we?

"What's going on between you and Kim?" I asked.

Chay panicked. "Nothing! There's nothing going on," he squeaked, voice rising in pitch as he pretended to admire the scenery outside.

"What do you mean, *nothing*? You two are stuck together like glue!" I slowed the car, taking the long way through the side streets so I'd have more time to interrogate Chay.

"We're just...talking," Chay said.

"Hah! Talking, my ass. How many times have you done *that* to him?" *Damn it!* I never thought my little brother would turn out to be this kind of person! And I never thought I would have to ask my brother this kind of question. *Chay, you little...*

"What?! Me? Did *what* to him?" Chay looked at me like he didn't understand.

---

13   A traditional dessert of tiny pancakes made with rice flour, sugar, and coconut milk.

"Uh...you know you can tell me anything, Chay. I accept both you and Kim."

Chay looked even more confused. Or was it that my little brother was too young for this kind of thing, and that they really were only innocently talking to each other? But Nont had told me that Chay had forced himself on Kim!

"Hia, what are you talking about?"

"I've already accepted you. Still, Kim is the injured party here. You should take responsibility and look out for him. I'm not closed-minded about this kind of thing, but if you're going to get physically involved, you shouldn't hurt his feelings," I said because I had some empathy for, uh...my fellow bottom. No matter how good it felt, deep down, there was still some lingering bitterness when another man dominated you like that.

"Kim's the...injured party? Hia, are you crazy?!" Chay exclaimed in disbelief.

"What? Tell me the truth—are you not serious about Kim? Shit, Chay! Consider his feelings too!"

Chay acted like it was the end of the world, like what I'd just said was so very wrong. "Hia! I can tell you anything, right?"

"Of course," I said.

"Hia, listen to me. *I'm* the injured party. I'm the one whose feelings need considering. And the one you should be protecting is your little brother, hia, instead of taking Kim's side! He's the one hurting *my* feelings!" Chay insisted, scowling.

"What did you say?"

"That I'm the injured party?" Chay repeated.

"Nont told me you basically forced yourself on Kim," I explained.

"Well, yeah, I kinda did. He's cute! I like him, but I didn't think he would flip the script on me!"

I slammed the brakes, making us both lurch forward. *Fuck! What the fuck did you just say?!*

"The fuck did you just say?!" I shouted.

Chay rubbed his head. "Owww, that hurt!"

"What did you just say?" I insisted.

"Kim... He's...he's the top, when we..."

I quickly held up my hand to stop him from saying the rest. *How many more earth-shattering revelations am I gonna get this week?*

"Have you ever asked me for permission to date? I raised you, Chay! Didn't you think about how I'd feel about this?" I finally knew how the parents of rebellious teens felt, seeing their kids run off after dubious men and getting into all kinds of trouble.

Chay smiled, trying not to laugh. "Oh, I understand. I really understand you."

"Not funny," I scolded him. *Is there a stick around here? I'll beat both their asses, and I won't hold back!*

"What? When you ended up with P'Kinn, I didn't say anything! Did you ask *me* for permission? Can't you understand how I felt, having my older brother as this cool, macho idol, and then one day finding out the truth? I was in shock too!" Chay joked, before swinging the car door open and taking off.

"Chay! You ungrateful little shit... Why, you—!"

I didn't want to believe it. I couldn't accept it. It wasn't true. *Damn it! Why does trouble keep finding me? How strong does the universe think I am?*

Kim! As soon as Pete's funeral is over, you're dead!

I opened my door and got out of the car, lost in thought.

Suddenly, Chay let out a loud shriek: "Hia!"

I immediately sprinted toward our house.

"What?!"

Chay sounded worried. "Someone broke into our house."

The doorknob was busted. I could sense that something was very wrong, so I went to grab a big stick to use as a weapon before slowly opening the door. I carefully stepped inside, and when I saw the state of our house, I knew for certain that someone must be there. It was a mess—our things were scattered all over the place. I raised the stick, readjusting my grip as I surveyed the house.

"Chay. Go wait in the car," I told him.

"Nope. We're going in together," Chay said, gripping the hem of my shirt.

I swung the door open wider in case we were attacked; that way, I'd be able to push Chay out in time.

Thump, thump, thump came the sound of footsteps walking around upstairs. I was nervous, afraid the thief—or whoever it was—had better weapons than the stick in my hand. However, as I stepped onto the stairs, about to go up, a figure appeared and walked down toward us.

"Oh... How's it going, nephew?"

"Uncle Thee..."

KINN
PORSCHE

Vegas × Pete 8

PETE

[THE DAY THE MAJOR CLAN FOUND THE BODY]

ACHOO!
Ah—ah—ACHOO!
"Fuuuck!"

I'd been sneezing ever since I woke up. My nose was constantly itchy; I'd rubbed it until the skin felt raw. I was starting to feel a bit dizzy too.

"Did you catch a cold?" asked Vegas, lying on his bed and playing on his computer. Meanwhile, I was on my stomach on the sofa, with my head on the armrest. Today's weather was weird—it was making my head spin.

"I don't know. It's probably my seasonal allergies. Looks like it's gonna rain." I gave Vegas a half-assed answer, scanning the shelf for some books to read. Usually, changes in the weather didn't do a thing to me; my body never reacted to the merest sign of rain. I was indestructible! Mr. Tankhun, on the other hand, was very sensitive. When the weather changed even slightly, he would sneeze, cough, and develop a mild fever.

I leaned my head on the armrest and wearily picked a book from the shelf. That bastard Vegas had finished his exams and stopped leaving the house ever since. He kept walking between his bedroom and office, and it stressed me out. I couldn't spend my time daydreaming like usual or trying to pick the lock around my wrist. Simply put, I couldn't try to escape his capture like I did every day! *Yeesh, doesn't he have other business to attend to?*

I was drowning in my thoughts for so long that I didn't notice Vegas walking over to me.

He nudged my side with his knee. "Hey!"

"Hm?" I sat up on the sofa and turned to him, confused.

"Take this." He held out a glass of water in one hand and a yellow pill in the other.

"What's that?" I asked, but I took it anyway.

"For allergies. Your face is red. Are you sick?" He sat down next to me and reached his hand out to lightly feel my forehead. I immediately averted my eyes.

I didn't know why, but I hadn't been able to look him in the eye ever since he shaved my face and...*kissed* me yesterday! I couldn't face him directly. There was a strange feeling inside me; it wasn't fear, nor was it disgust, but it definitely wasn't good. It was just some weird feeling I couldn't place.

My body froze up. "It's all right, I'm fine," I told him. I was sticking to my plan of no resistance, no stubbornness, just following orders...but I still liked to subtly deny him.

"Take it," Vegas said flatly.

I took the water from him, sipped it, then swallowed the pill. After Vegas saw that I'd complied with his order, he turned off the AC and headed to his balcony, where he drew back the curtain and slid open the glass door.

"I guess you've been staying in an air-conditioned room for too long," he said. "Let's switch to a fan." And he left his bedroom.

I looked after him in confusion. What was wrong with him? He was being exceptionally kind lately—it was like some kind of saint had possessed his body. He didn't get mad at me or shout at me at all. It was fucking weird!

Vegas returned with a black standing fan. He plugged it in and set it to oscillate with a remote. Then, he sat on the bed, rested his back against the headboard, put his laptop on his stomach, and beckoned me over.

Did I really have a choice? I didn't want to be anywhere near him. I wanted to fling my foot at him, like Porsche loved to do to Mr. Kinn, and yell, "In your fucking dreams! Like hell I'm going over there!"

But obviously, I couldn't do that, so, frowning, I went over to him. I flopped on the bed, crossed my legs, and glared at him.

Vegas grabbed my arm, pulling me toward him. "Sleep here."

"Sleep? I just woke up!" I protested, trying to resist him.

He insisted on pulling me closer, though. "That allergy pill will make you drowsy. You'll need to sleep eventually."

"I can sleep on my side of the bed. Why did you bother pulling me over here?" Although I mentally reminded myself to obey him, my body tensed up every time he touched me. Damn it, I felt like some naive fourteen-year-old girl trying to keep her virtue intact.

"Don't be so stubborn!" Vegas barked. "Do as I say!"

I went from feeling mild unease to abject horror. I was terrified that my plan had been ruined. *Never forget, Pete! Make him get bored of you. Just listen to whatever he says!*

"I'm sick," I reminded him, in case it might save me from his wrath. I knew full well, though, that I wasn't ill; I'd just sneezed too many times. Was someone talking about me behind my back?[14]

---

14 A common superstition in Thai and some other Asian cultures is that people talking about you behind your back, or just mentioning you in your absence, will make you sneeze.

"Come here!" Vegas yanked at me again, this time so hard that my face smashed into his chest. He immediately slipped his arms around my body, pillowing me against his torso. *Fucking gross.*

"What do you want to watch?" he asked, using his free hand to click on a folder on his laptop. It looked like he had a variety of films saved.

"Wait!" I perked up and leaned closer to the screen. My eyes sparkled as if these video files were precious gems. "You're going to play a movie for me?" I asked, so excited, I almost forgot how uncomfortable it was lying down on his body.

"Yeah...I downloaded some. And the laptop is offline—don't get any ideas."

"Yeah, I can see that," I said without looking at his face. I shoved his hand away from the laptop and scrolled through the list of movies in the folder.

Which one should I pick? Holy shit, finally a taste of civilization! Considering the state that I was in, access to entertainment absolutely counted as a taste of civilization to me.

I was so excited about picking a movie to watch that I unconsciously propped my chin up on Vegas's stomach. I even forgot to tell him off when he slipped his hand into my hair. Right now, all I wanted to do was stare at the screen.

"I've seen this one already, this one, too... This one was too sad... Can we watch this?" I turned my head around to ask for Vegas's opinion. I thought I saw him smile for a second, but it completely vanished once I fully faced him, as if it was never even there.

"Yeah, sure," he replied.

"Okay, just don't call me a man-child," I mumbled. "I just really want to watch a cartoon."

After I put the movie on full screen and adjusted the volume, Vegas pulled me back to lie on his chest and wrapped his arms around me. He'd never done anything like this with me before. I could hear his heart beating and feel the warmth emanating from his body.

We'd spent a lot of time together in this room by now, but I'd never felt this energy from him. I felt strange and conflicted—what had happened to Vegas, and why had he suddenly changed into a completely different person?

I let him hold me as he pleased while we focused on the screen. I'd chosen a Disney cartoon about a Mexican boy whose love of music led him to travel into the land of the dead. I'd seen it before with Mr. Tankhun. The story was lighthearted, and you didn't need to think about it too much to watch it. My life was already stressful enough. I just wanted to watch something that could cheer me up.

We burst out laughing simultaneously; we had become so engrossed in the story that we clearly had forgotten about the outside world. Vegas shifted his posture occasionally, putting one arm behind his head, but his other arm remained firmly around my waist. I tried to rest my head on his stomach, but he kept guiding it back to his chest. Maybe I was blocking his view, but it was a dick move.

"Have you seen this before?" I asked, looking up at him. He shifted his attention from the screen to me and shook his head.

"Can you guess who owns the guitar?" I kept asking him. I blamed Mr. Tankhun for this bad habit. He loved to pause movies to ask for people's opinions. Plus, I wanted to know if Vegas was clever enough to figure it out.

"It's not that hard to guess," Vegas said.

I squinted at him skeptically. "Tell me, then." He could be bluffing. If his guess turned out to be wrong, I'd laugh my ass off.

"Just keep watching."

"No...you have to tell me who the owner is first." I tilted closer to his face, demanding an answer. I wanted him to be a fool! I couldn't wait to witness his downfall!

"Well...I want to keep watching." Vegas pressed my head back down.

I resisted his force and tried to lift my head up again. "No! If you don't know, just say you don't know. Who do you guess?" A cunning smile spread across my face. I was certain Vegas wouldn't know. *Ha! Dumbass! This is a kid's movie. You like to act all tough and in charge, but you can't even figure out this stupid cartoon?* Maybe he was afraid of looking stupid in front of me.

"Well, let me tell you," I said. "The guitar belongs to..."

"Hey! I don't like spoilers," Vegas threatened, pointing his finger at me.

Aha! Just as I expected. "The guitar belongs to—" Vegas immediately covered my mouth with his hand. I pulled his hand away. "The guitar belongs to...*oof!*"

This time, it wasn't Vegas's hand against my mouth that shut me up—it was his lips. My eyes widened in shock as he kept kissing me; the feelings from yesterday came back in an overwhelming wave. For a moment, my heart felt empty.

Before I could get lost in my thoughts, Vegas pushed the laptop away and pressed me flat against the bed. It happened so suddenly, I was caught entirely off guard.

Vegas straddled me and kissed me hard. He started nibbling at my bottom lip, coaxing it open so he could explore my mouth with his hot tongue. The new sensation made me dizzy.

Vegas had never done anything like this since he'd locked me up in here. All he ever did was give me pain. He was never gentle with me, never made me feel good.

He caught me by surprise, probing his tongue against mine before sweeping it through my mouth. I began to feel the heat of lust surge through my body at the sensation of his warm breath mingling with mine. His kiss was gentle yet laced with passion.

"*Mmph!* Mmm..." I protested with a groan and pushed at his chest, hoping he'd get off of me.

Vegas finally let go, smiling at me and stroking my hair. The way he looked at me had changed—his gaze, instead of burning with anger and frustration, was filled with another emotion that I couldn't quite place.

"The guitar is Hector's," he said with a sly smile. "I've seen this movie before."

I frowned. *You fucking liar!*

Before I could even open my mouth to scold him, he pressed his face into the crook of my neck and inhaled. I tensed, a shiver running down my spine.

"Vegas...don't," I said.

I wasn't sure if I should be surprised by his new attitude or try to stop him. In the end, I couldn't do anything. I needed to listen to my brain telling me to follow his orders. I needed Vegas to get bored of me.

However, it still felt difficult to accept my fate. I was conflicted about staying passive; I wanted to resist him in every way. But I needed to just lie there and let him do whatever he wanted to me. Hopefully, he'd begin to realize that I wasn't resisting him, and he'd let me go.

I was scared. I was so scared of what Vegas was going to do next because I knew how much it would hurt.

"Vegas...don't," I whimpered again while he sucked and bit at my neck. His saliva dripped from my neck to my collarbone, making me shudder. I felt his touch more intensely this time, which put me in a challenging position.

My heartbeat skyrocketed. I tried pushing Vegas away, but he stopped me. I startled when his hot tongue licked across my chest; then, he closed his lips around my nipple and sucked.

"I'm scared, Vegas..." I gasped, trying to keep my emotions under control. My mind spun with a whirlwind of thoughts, but my body went limp.

Vegas left my chest to press his lips to mine for another kiss, slipping his tongue in quickly. He was good at this—like he was taking his time to savor me. My awareness was starting to fray at the edges. Although I'd had girlfriends before, none of their kisses had ever felt this intense.

As Vegas swirled his tongue in my mouth, I let my guard down for a moment. I could no longer hold back my arousal at his touch. I breathed evenly, trying to calm my nerves.

My body spasmed when Vegas fondled my crotch through my pants. *No. No!* I'd never felt this way with a man before, but I was being turned on by the tiniest of his touches. Maybe it was because I hadn't had any sexual release for weeks. When Vegas had assaulted me, I'd been too terrified to experience any sort of arousal; I hadn't reached orgasm even once. My body's frustration was making itself known.

Vegas broke the kiss, putting a slight distance between our faces. "Pete are you scared of me?" he asked, nuzzling his nose against my cheek.

"Mm," I whined, both hands tightly clutching the sheets. My body and mind battled against each other. Though I was physically responding to him, my mind was still full of dread. Vegas had inflicted torturous pain on me before; if I resisted him now, it would only hurt more. But how could I just give in? I didn't want him to defile me again!

Vegas ran his hand over my erection, eliciting a flood of horrific memories.

"If you're a good boy, I won't hurt you. I promise," he cooed, pressing his nose against my cheek and giving it a big kiss. I closed my eyes as his thick palm slid into my underwear and gently wrapped around my cock. My breath hitched; an uncomfortable feeling was building up inside of me.

"Umm...Vegas?" I asked, panting. "If I tell you no...if I resist...will you beat me up?"

My mind erupted into chaos as Vegas's firm hand caressed my dick. I couldn't fight him—not out of a lack of strength but out of practicality. I was still chained up, and if I managed to break free from him, the farthest I could run was the sofa. I'd end up getting the shit kicked out of me no matter what I did.

"Oh... I don't have the heart to be rough with you anymore, Pete," Vegas said. "But...I don't want to stop. It won't hurt, I promise. I'll make you come."

I squinted at him in suspicion. I'd never heard him sound like this; he was practically pleading with me. His eyes were full of an unfamiliar gentleness. I was still scared enough to shiver slightly.

I reached down and grabbed a pillow to cover my face. *Fuck!* I should have known that this would happen again, but I couldn't believe that my body was responding to it!

Vegas's mouth moved down to my chest again as his hands stripped away my pants. I bit my lip, knowing what would come next. His tongue dragged down to my belly; he nipped at it gently, not violently like before.

Vegas's hand wrapped around me again and stroked. It was disgusting. Obscene. But another feeling emerged alongside my revulsion—pleasure.

I'd told Vegas I wouldn't let him violate me like this again. But since I was still stuck here, I supposed I had to swallow my pride and get through this with as little pain as possible.

When Vegas rubbed a circle around the leaking tip of my dick, I bit my lip as hard as I could, trying to hold my voice back. It was uncomfortable. I wouldn't dare finish off in Vegas's room.

"Ugh...uhhh."

It made sense that my shaft was so responsive to the stimulation. My heart thumped against my chest as Vegas's hand worked and his lips glided down my thighs.

"Ughhh... Vegas," I groaned.

My body began to writhe as Vegas skillfully stroked my cock. He lifted my legs and spread them apart. At this point, my mind became a blur. He picked up the pace with his wrist, his other hand brushing over my asshole. It made my body tingle from head to toe.

"Ughh...ugh." I dug my nails into the pillow and held it tightly.

I flinched and gasped as I felt a sudden smear of cold liquid on my hole. I stiffened in fear, droplets of sweat forming all over my body, yet somehow, I craved his touch even more. It was so fucking confusing.

"Pete...I'll be gentle," Vegas told me, but I didn't care what he said anymore. His hand moved diligently, making my dick ache with need. When he slipped a finger inside my ass, though, I immediately tensed up.

"Ow! That hurts!" I yelped.

Vegas pulled his finger out. "Pete...relax."

He pulled away the pillow I was hiding my face with and pressed a soft kiss to my lips. At the same time, his hand kept stroking my dick. He showered my face with kisses before breaking away and squeezing out more lubricant onto his finger. He applied it to my asshole before slipping his finger back in.

"Ughh... Ngh..." I felt my ass getting fuller and my dick approaching an orgasm. I didn't know when Vegas added another finger, but he soon hit a spot inside me that made my whole body squirm.

The pain slowly dissipated, leaving only the feeling of fullness, and...I started to...feel something so thrilling that I couldn't hold back my voice any longer.

"*Ahhh...*" It felt different, so different that I couldn't believe that this kind of sex—which I'd only experienced before as vile, disgusting torture—could feel this good.

Vegas's hands picked up the pace until I couldn't take it anymore. My mind went blank as my body spasmed and I came, spurts of white liquid painting my lower belly. I took in a big gulp of air, my heart pumping hard.

Vegas didn't lose out on his own pleasure. He slid in between my legs and lifted them up, raising my hips above the bed. Wasting no time, he grabbed his dick—already sheathed in a condom—and slowly pushed the tip against my hole.

"Sss... *Ahhh...*" Vegas hissed and groaned as he shallowly thrust into me, sending another shiver through my body.

"Nngh... It hurts," I said, my eyes tightly shut. Yes, it did hurt, and I felt full, but this wasn't like the other times. It wasn't the usual body-ravaging agony; what I was feeling now was so different that I couldn't really describe it.

The fullness inside me felt hotter and hotter as Vegas pushed all the way in. I tried to control my breathing so I didn't have to focus on what was happening down there. Without knowing why,

I narrowed my eyes and watched Vegas. He wiped the sweat off his brow and bit his lip hard, as if he was holding back his movements.

Vegas looked down at me and gave a tiny smile before lowering his head to give me a light kiss on the temple.

"Good boy... Do as I say, and it won't hurt."

He stayed still inside of me, kissing me from my forehead down to my lips. He then straightened himself up, supported my hips with his hands, and slowly started to thrust.

"Nghhhhh..." I immediately reached out for something to hold on to; I found a pillow and dug my nails into it. As Vegas moved his hips back and forth, he tilted his head and moaned.

"Ahhhh... Ummmm." I shut my eyes again when he changed his rhythm, the movements shifting between hard and soft. My heart hammered like it was going to explode. The feeling of fullness dissipated, and when Vegas hit my prostate again and again, it sent my body spasming for a moment. He softened his thrusts in response, but he still hit that same spot repeatedly.

"Ugh...you pervert." I grabbed the pillow and threw it at him. When he saw that my dick was responding to him again, Vegas cracked a devilish smile. The way he looked at me was different now—it wasn't threatening like before. Instead, it made butterflies flutter in my stomach.

Vegas proceeded to quicken his pace. One of his hands grabbed my hardening cock and stroked it along with his thrusts.

"*Ahhhhh*... Mmmm."

We moaned together in harmony as my body rocked to Vegas's rhythm. He was starting to lose control of his strength, his thrusts getting faster and more forceful, making my body feel hot all over. It was so exhausting, like I'd been running on a treadmill for miles, yet the pleasure poured over me nonstop. Every time I felt him move, I couldn't control my reactions.

I bit my lip hard. "Mmm...Vegas," I moaned, my voice trembling.

"Ssss... I l-love it when you call my name... I'm so close—*ahh*..."

I couldn't make out a single fucking word out of Vegas's mouth. He let out a deep groan. As he approached his climax, he leaned over, bracing himself on the bed and thrusting his hips even faster. His body was covered in sweat from the exertion.

My mind went blank, and my cock ached; then, I reached orgasm once again. But this time, I just wanted to pass out. I was so exhausted, and the allergy pill that Vegas gave me had doubled my drowsiness.

Vegas thrust a couple more times before he found his own release, then he pulled out and collapsed next to me.

We lay there panting, our hurried breaths heaving in concert.

"Are you all right?" Vegas pulled me into a loose hug.

"Define 'all right,'" I panted, both my legs still trembling.

"Heh..." Vegas chuckled. "How did your innocent little cartoon turn into a porno?"

I gathered all my strength, rolled off the bed, and hurried toward the bathroom. *You animal! You fucking jerk!*

As I cleaned up and finally came back to my senses, I wanted to bang my head against the wall until I put myself out of my own misery. The fuck did I just do? *Pete, you dumbass! You only agreed to do this absurd shit because your judgment was clouded by horniness!* Baser urges were dangerous things. *Ugh, Vegas, you shithead! I gotta scrub this stain off of me!*

"Hurry up, Pete. I want to wash up too. If you take too long, I'll join you in there."

I gave the bathroom door the middle finger, but I did hurry up like he said to. I grabbed a towel off the floor and wrapped it around myself before I opened the door.

"Heh," Vegas chuckled as he walked past me, entirely naked. He didn't forget to look me in the eye and crack a shamelessly evil grin before he disappeared into the bathroom.

I quickly climbed into my pants, then jumped into the bed and buried myself under the blankets. *What the fuck, Pete?! Fuck! What have you done, you freak?! Huh?!* I mentally scolded myself. And what was wrong with Vegas, anyway? He was acting so damn weird! Too weird! It was getting suspicious!

I kept cursing at myself until the allergy pill and the exhaustion dragged me into a deep slumber. I didn't even notice when Vegas left the bathroom.

The next time I opened my eyes, I saw him pacing back and forth between the bedroom and his office with piles of documents in his hands. I couldn't bear to face him. *What do I do? Fuck!*

Vegas came back to the bedroom, this time with a tablet in his hand. I quickly lay back down and proceeded to throw the blanket back over my head.

"Pete! Stop pretending to be asleep," he said casually. "It's eight in the evening already. Time for dinner." He reached out to pull the blanket off of me, but I held on to it tightly.

"No! I'm not hungry!"

"C'mon, hurry up. And I don't have any instant noodles left, so don't hold out on that hope if you get hungry later." He laughed. What was so fucking funny?

"I'm not eating," I said.

"Pete! Don't make me count! One...two..."

"Aahhhh!"

I didn't know why I was so scared of him counting, but as soon as he started, I instantly jumped out of the bed. I made a face at him and went over to sit down on the sofa, stomping heavily with each step.

On the coffee table was some of the Southern food Vegas had bought me. Even better, there were two plates of plain rice, steaming hot. Yeah, well, I *was* hungry…but I still couldn't bear to face Vegas.

"Nop brought it over earlier in the evening, but you refused to wake up, so I had him reheat it." Vegas sat down next to me and pulled one of the plates of rice toward himself.

I played with the rice on my plate, wondering if Vegas was going to eat with me.

"Which dish tastes the best?" Vegas asked, placing his arm on the headrest behind me. I could see him staring at me out of the corner of my eye, but I was too scared to face him directly. I couldn't muster the courage to answer his question either.

"Pete?" Vegas called my name, but not harshly. I sighed and scooped one of the side dishes onto my plate.

"You haven't eaten?" I asked him faintly as I grabbed the spoon and scooped food into my mouth.

"Not yet—I was waiting to join you."

Why the fuck did he want to join me? These side dishes weren't enough for the both of us. If I ran out of food, was he going to buy more for me? *What a nosy, imposing little fucker.*

But that was just a thought. A thought that would stay in my head because I didn't dare utter it out loud.

"Let's see… Which dish tastes good?"

Which dish tastes good? All of them. *Fine, you wanna eat with me, huh? Ha ha! Take this!*

I proceeded to pour sour yellow curry onto his plate. I even gave him a piece of shrimp—how generous of me.

He lifted his plate up to smell it, then slowly picked up a spoon. "It looks spicy."

I pretended not to care and carried on eating with a smirk. *Hee hee.*

Vegas looked at it hesitantly for a while.

"Try it," I told him, without looking up from my food.

"Fine." Vegas slowly scooped up a small amount of rice and curry and prepared to put it in his mouth. I watched him out of the corner of my eye, feeling annoyed.

"Ugh! A small bite like that won't give you any flavor. Give it to me!" I put my plate down and took his. I scooped up a spoonful of rice and curry, then held it up to his mouth. "Eat up," I said.

Vegas's lips tugged into a little smile, and he opened his mouth.

As soon as he chewed on it, the Southern chili paste started to work its magic. He choked and coughed, grabbing a glass of water to drink right away. *Hah!*

I put his plate down and continued eating mine. *Serves you right, motherfucker! That's the South for you, jackass! Don't mess with us!*

Vegas put the glass down and turned to scold me. "That was spicy as hell!"

"Well, you asked me which one tastes the best, and that one does," I replied innocently and continued to eat.

Vegas resorted to eating the omelet instead. "Damn! Keep eating that shit, and I'll laugh if you end up with a stomachache," he muttered.

I'd eaten spicy food my whole life; I was used to it, shithead! *What a sad little critter, actin' all foolish. Just a bite of good ol' Southern curry, and he starts cryin' like a baby! Quit yer bellyaching. Don't make me laugh!*

Vegas huffed petulantly. "It did taste great, though," he conceded. "Now I get why they say the South is hot—both its cuisine and its people. Heh." Vegas leaned forward, his face so close that I had to move to the side to dodge him. *Bastard.*

I shot him an annoyed look. "The fuck are you saying?!"

Vegas leaned back, looking at his plate before cutting his omelet.

"'*I'll never come for a bastard like you!*'" Vegas mocked me, parodying my voice. I put my plate down and quicky drank my glass of water. *Son of a bitch! Don't you dare mention that disgraceful moment! I can't take it!*

"'*I'd rather let the maggots...*'" Vegas mimicked me again.

I shot up from the sofa. "Hey, Vegas! What the fuck are you saying, huh?!" *You little shit!*

"Aww... Are you done eating?"

"I'm done!" I snarled before grabbing my towel and disappearing into the bathroom. *Ugh! I'll never let it happen again!* I wouldn't give in to Vegas's advances. Maybe I'd let my hands slip and kill him by accident! *If you dare to touch me again, I'll kick your ass, you bastard! Go to hell!*

After I showered, Vegas gave me more allergy medicine. He said that I'd be sleeping under the air conditioning, so I should take it just in case. Good—I wanted it to knock me out as soon as possible. I was tired of talking with this dickhead!

Once I got into bed, Vegas went to take a shower. As I was dozing off, I could sense someone hugging me from behind. I was so sleepy that I didn't have the energy to resist him. How did I know it was Vegas? His unique scent hit me right in the nose.

Whatever. I'm just gonna sleep.
I didn't want to acknowledge the ache in my heart.

The next morning, Vegas got Nop to bring breakfast: a simple bowl of congee. He sat on the sofa and ate with me. Once he finished, he got up to start working, but he didn't do it in his office—instead, he carried in piles of documents and spread them all over the bed. *Look at him, scattering his shit everywhere. I bet he's gonna force me to make the bed tonight too.*

What ghost was possessing him, anyway? What was going on in his head? Where had the demon wearing Vegas's face gone today?

He lay on his stomach, working on the files in his binder, wiggling his toes cheerfully as he did so. *This shithead has so many goddamn mood swings, he may as well be bipolar.*

I sprawled out on the sofa with a book on my chest. If Vegas invited me to watch any fucking movies today, I would refuse entirely! I wasn't going anywhere near him, so history wouldn't repeat itself!

I'd really stopped caring about the sex, but what could I do? I was the captive here. Getting depressed over it wouldn't help. But to go, "Whatever, I had sex with a man," just like that? No.

I hadn't gotten over that, but I was trying to see it as a part of life. Most human beings had sex at some point in their lives. I'd just ended up experiencing a different side of the sexual spectrum. *Sigh...*

I needed to put my time into figuring out my great escape plan. When was this motherfucker going to go outside?

I was letting go and accepting the truth, which might be thanks to reading all these books full of Buddha's teachings over and over. It was almost as if I could hear the prayers constantly ringing inside my head. It gave me a weird sense of relief, like I'd been blessed... *Ah, shit, I think I'm hallucinating.* So I put the dharma book down and picked up a pop-psychology book instead: *Your Personality Based on Blood Type*.[15]

I had a lot of time to kill, and with Vegas here in the same room, I didn't have many options. So having a book like this to distract me was at least a halfway decent entertainment.

Let's see if it's accurate. I'm type O.

"*Smart and talented.*" Obviously. "*A little bit lazy, mostly optimistic, likes to be a giver rather than a receiver. Quick-tempered, but cools down fast. Not petty. Tends to be serious under certain circumstances.*"

Was I like that? Hmm. To get a real answer, I needed to ask someone's opinion of me and analyze that, right? People couldn't really be objective about their own personalities. *Should I ask Vegas?*

I needed to know what he was thinking. If he was planning to kill me, I wanted to have time to prepare. I wondered what was on his mind that was making him act so weird lately. I didn't ask him directly, because I feared he would refuse to answer. But using this book could be a good excuse to get into his head.

With that plan in mind, I called out to him, "Vegas?"

"Hm? What is it?" Vegas replied, his eyes fixed on his computer screen.

"What's your blood type?" I asked.

"Me?"

---

15 *Blood Type Personality* is a pseudoscientific belief from Japan that one's blood type can predetermine one's personality and compatibility with others. It is also popular in other Asian countries outside of Japan, including Thailand.

Who else, dipshit? It's only you and me here. Are you brain-dead?

"Yeah."

"AB," Vegas said.

"Damn, that's so cool," I murmured. When I was a kid, I always wanted to be type AB. It was such a rare blood type; type O didn't feel unique at all.

All right, let's see, AB. What's on his mind? I couldn't figure him out at all, but maybe his blood type would illuminate me.

"Read it out loud for me," Vegas said.

I made a face and skipped to the AB section. "*Mysterious, like a secret waiting to be uncovered. Complicated. Lacks self-control*—heh, this book is accurate!" I laughed out loud, unable to stop myself. "*ABs hate illogical people, yet they are the illogical ones themselves.*"

Vegas smiled a bit and shook his head. "Are you making that up to insult me?"

"It's written in the book!" I showed him the page. Vegas looked up from his work to read some of it, then turned back.

"What about you? What's your blood type?" he asked.

"O."

"What does it say?"

"Handsome, kindhearted, and cool," I said with a chuckle.

"Throw that away, it's all bullshit," Vegas said. His smile made mine fall.

"Fuck you," I mouthed, then proceeded to read more.

"*Who you really are deep inside.*" Hmm... *What's in your head these days, Vegas?! I have to know!*

"Vegas," I called out to him again.

"What now?" he asked plainly, not bothering to look up from his work. He picked up documents, riffled through them, and typed on his laptop.

"*One day, you are camping with your friends, and you find a very beautiful rock. You stop to admire it for a little while, and once you look up, you find that all your friends are gone. What would you do in this situation?*

a. Proceed to go straight.
b. Leave the pathway to find a river.
c. Toss the stone and ask it to show you the way.
d. Cry for help." I read the scenario from the book. "Which one would you choose?"

"Hmmm... I don't like camping," Vegas replied.

"It's a what-if scenario."

"Uhh...but I wouldn't stop to look at a rock in the first place," he insisted.

"Ugh! What *if* you did?"

"I would stand still."

"That's not one of the choices."

"Fine! I'd cry for help!" he said, not looking up or paying attention to me at all.

"Do you really mean it?" I asked him, annoyed.

"Yeah. I'd cry for help."

"Okay, okay, second question: *Now you see an abandoned house. What do you do?*

a. Knock at the front door.
b. Knock at the back door.
c. Go inside through the window.
d. Just wait outside."

"Aren't I supposed to be crying for help right now?" Vegas asked, laughing.

"Well, apparently, you found an abandoned house."

"If I'm crying for help, how did I manage to see it?"

"I guess you were turning around when you cried for help and just saw it?" I pushed myself up from the sofa and made a spinning gesture with my hand.

Vegas raised an eyebrow at me. "What? How big is this house? How did it appear out of the blue?"

"You didn't see it at first!" *Stop being such a stubborn little shit!*

"Fine, fine, I choose to wait outside the house," Vegas said, shaking his head again.

"There. That wasn't so hard," I grumbled, then read the next part: "*You decide to go inside the house.*"

He whipped his head toward me. "What?!"

"Listen to it first! *You decide to go inside and explore the living room. What do you see?*

a. A big mirror.

b. A cute little wolf cub.

c. A recently deceased body.

d. A skeleton."

"I said I would stand outside the house. How would I see any of this?" Vegas laughed in my face.

"Because you thought, 'Aww, let's go inside to explore.' What *if* you entered the house?"

"What if? Again? But I don't wanna go inside."

I sighed and rolled my eyes. "Fuck it, I'm done!" I closed the book and threw it on the table.

"All right, all right... Fine, I found that teeny, little wolf cub."

"I'm *done*!" I repeated. I got up from the sofa, aimlessly walking around the room.

"Come here," Vegas said, beckoning me over with his hand.

I immediately shook my head: *No. That's enough from you, motherfucker.* I made a face and dropped down onto the floor to start exercising. This was my life, an endless loop of the same old shit. I lay down on the rug and started to do sit-ups.

"Pete, are you lonely?" Vegas asked.

"I am. Are you gonna let me go?" I shot back, giving Vegas a sidelong glance. He seemed to be deep in thought.

"Nah, I wanna keep you all to myself," he muttered, though I couldn't really hear him clearly. "I won't be here tomorrow."

"Why are you telling me that?" I asked. What happened yesterday made me doubt his words.

"I have to stay the night at the casino with my father. I'll be back the day after tomorrow." Vegas started to pack up his laptop and documents from the bed, taking them to his office.

Hmph! Good! Without you around, I'll be able to plan my escape! And I wouldn't have to keep constantly watching my back...

Vegas came back with his guitar and put it on the sofa. "Pack me a bag, will you?"

I sighed hard at him ordering me around, but I had no choice. I stopped doing sit-ups, got up from the floor, and walked straight to his wardrobe.

"Which one are you taking?" I asked him, unimpressed, as I pulled out his fancy-ass designer luggage from the drawer.

"Any bag works. I need one business outfit for a meeting with the client, two casual outfits, and one pair of pajamas."

Should I sabotage his wardrobe? I could pack only shirts with no pants... No underwear either! He'd be hoodwinked with no clothes to wear! He'd taste the feeling of utter humiliation!

But I could only fantasize about it. I picked out some shirts—I sort of knew his favorites. Nop always took Vegas's laundry basket down to the maid, and once the clothes were dry, I was the one hanging them back up. That's how I knew what he liked to wear.

Damn it! How come no one else in his house has realized that I'm in here?!

"Just don't fight with your dad when you're away, okay?" I said. If he came back grumpy, I didn't want to be his emotional punching bag.

"Can't promise that," Vegas said as he started strumming his guitar.

"Does your dad know I'm locked up in here?" I asked.

"Huh?! Are you crazy? If my father knew, you'd be dead," Vegas said with a smirk.

"Then why are you keeping me alive?"

"Because I like it..."

"Psycho," I muttered quietly. *You get off on torturing people, huh? Sadistic pig.*

"The only people here who know are Nop and some of my men."

"So...what's next?" I asked reluctantly.

Vegas paused for a moment. "What do you mean?" he asked, raising an eyebrow.

"What's next for the Minor Clan and the Major Clan...? Mr. Korn isn't a bad person, I think—"

"I don't know when I'm gonna be taken out. We're all hiding behind masks and smiles for now, but I'm pretty sure they're plotting to get rid of us. It's all thanks to you for feeding them the evidence, right?"

I was stunned. I shouldn't have brought it up. Well, I had been completely cut off from the outside world; I had no idea what the Major Clan was planning to do. I was worried for them, but I believed the evidence I sent them was enough to bring down the culprits.

But...when I looked at Vegas's face, my heart always fluttered for a moment. When Vegas was sane, he wasn't so bad. He was just a troubled boy.

What he had done to me was unforgivable, though.

"Well, if that happens, I wouldn't mind. If my clan has nothing left, if the Major Clan gets fucking serious and takes everything away from us—I wanna see how Father's new wife copes with *that*. But I'm worried about Macau. I don't know what his life would be like. I'm guessing Kinn won't spare me. I mean, look at what I did to his precious wifey. He's definitely holding a grudge." Vegas sighed, staring out into nothing.

"I don't think it's too late, if you stop everything now," I said. "Just stop messing with Porsche and stop embezzling from your cousins' businesses. It's not too late."

"I haven't messed with Porsche in a long time... And I've been laying low and letting Father take care of everything for a while."

"Take care of? You mean having Big destroy the evidence every time?" I said. I couldn't keep the emotion out of my voice. The Minor Clan had been traitors all along.

"Big is missing," Vegas said. "I think someone might have got to him already."

I frowned. If what Vegas said was true, the Major Clan must have been taking it seriously this time around.

"And..."

"Forget it, Pete!" Vegas snapped. "I'll just let my dad decide this shit. I'm too tired to deal with it. If they want to wipe out our clan, then so be it—as long as they spare Macau! I don't want to compete with Kinn anymore either. No matter how hard I try to be good, no one notices. I'm just waiting to see my father's downfall. I want to know if his wife and their kid will stick around after this."

All I could do was stand there and stay quiet.

"Vegas... If you can let it go, let it go," I said at last. "Just stay in your lane and don't mess with the Major Clan. Things aren't that bad—it's not too late to back out. Mr. Korn loves you and Macau. Regardless of the clan rivalry, you're still his nephews. You can learn from your mistakes and better yourself. You know what you're doing is bad, right?" It was an attempt at levity, but I wasn't sure if it made things better or worse. Vegas just glanced at me calmly, which made me shudder. *Ah, shit! I need to stop running my mouth. It's getting me into trouble again.*

"If I die, become a monk for me, will you? Sounds like you're approaching nirvana," Vegas said, cracking a faint smile. *Phew! I almost had a heart attack!*

"Um…so you like the guitar?" I awkwardly changed the subject, fearing for my life. *Enough of this serious talk. Don't want Vegas to turn into a monster.*

"Yup."

"Why guitar? You don't like the drums or bass?" Great, now I sounded like a nosy grandma invested in his hobbies. What a nice way to change the topic without looking suspicious. *Smooth, Pete. Very smooth.*

"It's cool, I guess? A senior classmate told me that playing the guitar makes it easier to flirt with girls. But I like boys, so I used it to flirt with the boy I like."

"Oh? Did it work?" *Ugh!* I wanted to slap my fucking mouth! I didn't know what else to talk about, and I sure as hell didn't want an awkward silence! We'd just been discussing a serious topic. *Argh! Now I'm panicking!*

"Not sure… After the most recent attempt, he just threw a pillow at me," he said, smiling. "Not sure if it was from embarrassment or hatred."

I froze. That sounded familiar. I hoped it wasn't what I thought he was implying.

"Hatred, I guess...?" I mumbled, quickly shifting my focus to packing his luggage.

Vegas strummed his guitar. He gazed at me and started bellowing out a song; meanwhile, I was trying to concentrate on packing the handful of outfits he needed. I repeatedly folded and unfolded them. Once I folded them all, I unfolded them again. *Ah, fuck.* Well, it was awkward that he kept staring at me like that—anyone would agree with me.

"I keep the memory of us forever etched in my heart,
Those bright blue skies and beautiful smiles.
Love filled our lives with joy;
When you smiled, it brightened the whole world.
I'm thankful for every happy day I shared with you..." [16]

I kept my head low so I wouldn't have to look him in the eye. He was still staring at me, and it was freaking me out.

"...So, do you think I succeeded?" Vegas asked.

"Which boxers do you prefer? These or these?" I held up underwear in two different prints, but he just smiled and ignored my question completely.

"Guess it's this one, then?" I continued. "All right. Done. I'm gonna head to the bathroom now..."

I put his luggage in front of the wardrobe and paced back and forth a little before walking straight into the bathroom. As soon as the door was shut, I leaned against the wall and grabbed the left side of my chest.

"Fuck! He's going to give me a heart attack!" I cursed, glancing occasionally at the bathroom door.

The fuck was he saying? What was this "most recent attempt" bullshit? I wasn't stupid—I just didn't want to accept the truth! It couldn't be true, right?! But what he'd described earlier was

---

[16] Lyrics from Kae Lub Ta (Just Close My Eyes) by the Thai rock band Bodyslam.

literally me! *Argh! What do I do? Was he for real or just fucking with me? Ah, shit!*

I spent a long time in the bathroom calming myself down, chewing my nails down to nubs. *Aaahh! He's giving me a fucking stroke!*

Eventually, I cracked the door open—and sighed in relief when I saw Vegas had left for his office. He was talking to a few of his men with a serious expression. I half walked, half ran over to the bed and sat down. Since I had no idea what to do next, the book beside me became my first option. I wouldn't be able to focus properly, but it was better than nothing.

In the afternoon, Vegas ordered Nop to bring me a sandwich. It wasn't my favorite, but I couldn't do much about that. When night came, Vegas joined me for dinner, just like last time, but unlike lunchtime, we had Southern food. I stuck to the same old rice and curry. But after only a few bites, I put my spoon down.

"Why'd you eat so little?" Vegas asked.

"I don't know. Feels like I'm full..." I gulped some water down, staring blankly at the plate. Why did I feel so full lately? It weirdly felt like when I went to the temple to make merit... *Hey! Is someone out there making merit for me?!*

"Weird, you always wolf your food down like a beggar. If you get hungry later tonight, tell me."

I nodded without caring much. Fuck, this whole situation was so gross. *Vegas, dude, you have to change your mind. A guy like me? A guy who looks like me? Seriously? Disgusting.*

That night, Vegas held me from behind while we slept. My eyes stayed wide open almost the whole night; I couldn't fall asleep, but I had to pretend I had. I had to admit, though, that his warmth helped me get through another night under the cold air conditioning.

He held me close to his chest the whole night. We were under the same blanket, his arms and legs intertwining with my body as he softly snored.

Damn it, I had no idea what I'd done to make Vegas interested in me. I was nothing like Porsche at all! That guy was cool, handsome, and his skin was as perfect as a prince's. Meanwhile, I looked like a bog creature. Well, I could admit I had a handsome face, but my overall appearance was mediocre! I was pretty muscular and scary-looking—I couldn't believe it!

Vegas, what's your type, exactly? What's your kind of guy? How would Porsche react if he knew about this? Is he gonna cry? Fuck!

I must've fallen asleep at some point. The moment I next became conscious, I felt someone nuzzling at my cheek. I tried to brush them off because it was annoying. When I cracked my eyes open, I jumped back in shock.

Vegas pressed his nose against my cheek and gave me a big kiss. "I gotta go now. I'll be back soon. Behave yourself while I'm away, all right?"

I was still confused and sleepy, so Vegas's sudden affection caught me by surprise. After he finished saying goodbye, he grabbed his luggage and left the room.

I sat up on the bed and sighed. I was going to go insane before I ever got the chance to escape this place, huh?

I showered and did some morning exercises, which was all the routine I had. When I ran out of things to do, I sprawled myself out on the couch.

My brain couldn't stop mulling over Vegas and my great escape plan. I hung my head back off the armrest, looking at the bedroom upside down; maybe the different angle would be more entertaining. Maybe it would give me a new perspective.

"Nop... Please, you have to let me goooo." I dragged out my voice, still lying in the same position. "Let me go, come onnn." Though I knew it was useless, I still wanted to beg to him over and over, just in case I was lucky enough to manifest my freedom. *Who knows? I'm feeling the power of merit lately.*

"The fuck are you lying down like that for?" Nop replied, arranging my food on the table. "Aren't you gonna come eat?"

"Nop... What do I dooo?" I whined until Nop looked at me in pity.

"You won't die. Don't worry," he said.

"Really?"

"But he won't let you go, that's for sure. What did you do to him?" he asked, and I frowned. "I'll say this," he added, "keep doing what you're doing, and he might thaw out and unchain you one day. But that doesn't mean he'll let you run away. You get what I mean?"

I lifted my head up, looked at Nop, then rolled over on my belly to fiddle with the books on the nearby table.

"What do you mean?"

"You haven't realized?" Nop said. "That he's...?"

I raised my hand to cut him off because I knew with all my heart what he was implying. *Ughhhh! I'm so stressed out!* I didn't want him to feel that way for me. It gave me the creeps!

I picked up a book and skimmed through it. I glanced at the personality-analysis book I read yesterday and remembered something: AB blood types hated illogical people.

I opened the book. "What kind of person do you think he'd hate?" I asked Nop.

"Why? What are you gonna do?"

"Just asking. Spill it."

"The type of guy Mr. Kinn is, I think? He says he hates him pretty often."

The type of guy Mr. Kinn was...? A perfect one. He was the most logical of the three brothers, if a little self-centered and silly sometimes. Maybe it was from being dominated by Porsche. But even so, he was a calm and stately sort of man. It wouldn't surprise me if Vegas hated that kind of guy. But Mr. Kinn was his rival! What did I have to do to become a guy like that?

All right, next question! "How do I annoy or bore him enough so he'll let me go?" I revealed to Nop the plan I had been trying to put in place. All this time, I'd been trying to spoil Vegas's mood, to wear him out, to make him bored. How had it turned out like this? Maybe what I'd been doing wasn't effective. Maybe I needed a new plan.

"Oh, heh, well...it's too late for that, Pete."

"No. I don't think it's too late. What type of guy do you think would bore him?"

Nop rolled his eyes, fed up. "He's not going to get bored of you."

"Not true! What type of guy?!" I sat up and started reading the AB blood-type personality description.

Nop sighed.

"Answer me," I insisted.

"A guy like Tankhun, I guess? That would annoy him, I think. What the hell kind of nonsense are you up to, anyway? I'm leaving now. Bye."

Oh, right! Why didn't I think of that? It was literally straight from the book—ABs hated illogical and self-centered people! That was Tankhun to a T. "Logic" wasn't a word in his vocabulary. When things didn't go his way, he'd throw a tantrum. If he wanted something, he had to have it. He was obnoxiously loud and constantly moody.

Huh. Why hadn't I thought of that in the first place? *Keep following Vegas's orders? That shit isn't working at all!* So what did I need to do? I needed to tap into my brain to come up with another plan to make him bored of me.

Whenever we went out, Mr. Tankhun loved to harass us with annoying phone calls. *Hah! Great! Let's do it.*

"*NOP!*" I shouted for Nop, who had just left. I threw a tissue box at the glass door because the chain wouldn't let me reach it myself.

The door slid open. Nop walked in, looking annoyed. "What?"

"Call that fucker Vegas."

Nop frowned, looking like he was wondering if he misheard me.

"Hurry," I urged him.

"Why do you want to call him?"

"Come on, please, please, please. Call him for me," I begged, giving him a pleading look.

"Okay, okay. You're acting weird, though. Don't give me that look—it makes me cringe." Nop fished his phone out of his pocket. "Good thing he told me that if you wanted to call him, I had to let him know right away," he muttered. "It's like he could see the future."

My eyes sparkled with excitement. I hadn't expected a chance to carry out the next stage of my plan so soon!

Nop tapped Vegas's name on his Contacts list and hit the call button. He handed me the phone, and I eagerly accepted it. *Heh.*

"Yes, Nop?" came Vegas's voice.

As soon as Vegas picked up, my heart pumped faster with excitement. *Here we go!*

"Where are you?!" I made myself sound snappy, copying the exact words I'd heard so many times from Tankhun.

"Hmm...? Pete? How are things? Is Nop there with you?" Vegas lowered his voice, speaking to me in a cheerful tone. *Gotcha!*

"I said, *where are you*?!" *Heh, this is fun!*
"Um...on a toll road, stuck in a traffic jam. What's the matter?"
Ah, shit. What should I say next? "When will you be back?!" I screeched, trying to keep my voice harsh.
"Tomorrow. I already told you that."
"*No!* You gotta come back *now*!" I exclaimed, then bit my lip, holding back my laughter.

Nop widened his eyes at me. "You want him back?" he mouthed.

"Trust me," I mouthed back.

"Are you all right?" Vegas sounded surprised.

"It doesn't matter! Come back *now*!" I yelled.

"What's wrong with you, Pete? I'm on a business trip with Father; I can't just rush back."

"Dunno. I don't have a reason. You just have to come back. *Bye!*" With that, I disconnected the call and broke into a shit-eating grin.

Nop took his phone back and eyed me in disbelief. "Why did you say that?! What if he really comes back?! I don't wanna see him."

"He won't. Heh." That was satisfying. Life was so fun when I got to irritate Vegas! *Wait... What if he beats me up when he gets back? Fuck! I completely forgot about that.*

I decided to space out the calls. Mr. Tankhun would keep spamming you with calls over and over until you couldn't concentrate for shit...but, well, that was Mr. Tankhun. Everyone let him get away with it. Vegas wouldn't—I could guarantee it.

So, I had to rearrange the plan in my head. I could still do the prank calls, but I had to keep some distance. Enough to keep him annoyed, but not enough to make him mad.

I went back to my food and let my thoughts run wild. I'd been thinking about it all day—pacing the room, doing random stuff as usual. It seemed like the more time I had to myself, the more my mind went, *"What do I do? I'm so fucking bored. I wanna get out of here!"*

I stayed in bed, rolling around onto my back, then my stomach, then my side, letting time pass until it was eight in the evening. I planned that around ten p.m., I'd ask Nop to call Vegas. I estimated that he'd be sleeping by that time, and it would piss him off to get woken up by my call.

I thought through every possible outcome. If he got so angry that he wanted to beat me up, he wouldn't be able to come back and do it: He'd already be at the casino by then. *Hee hee.*

It was possible Vegas would make me pay later when he came home, but it was such a long drive that by the time he got here, his anger would've cooled down. I had it down to a science!

The door slid open with a *creak*. I looked up to see who it was—Nop, on the phone with someone. He spoke a few words before shoving the phone into my hand.

"It's Mr. Vegas," he said and went to sit down on the sofa.

I gulped in fear. Was this just to scold me for the call earlier this morning?

I pressed the phone against my ear and spoke timidly: "Hey." I hadn't had the chance to make the second prank call, and he fucking beat me to it. *Man! There goes my plan.*

"Are you in bed yet?" Vegas asked in a normal tone of voice, with not a trace of a foul mood. That was a relief.

"No."

"Have you had dinner yet?"

I pulled the phone away and looked at it, confused. *Vegas, can you stop giving me more anxiety than I already have?! Huh?*

"Yup," I grumbled.

"No need to be harsh. Are you mad at me or something? I can't leave now, all right? My dad'll kill me. I'll be back by tomorrow, okay? Do you need a snack or something?"

I rubbed my face and sighed heavily. What next?

"Where are you?" I asked.

"At the hotel, about to sleep. Gotta be up early tomorrow."

"Come back...right...now!" I said hesitantly. I felt kind of nervous and awkward.

"Why? Miss me so bad that you can't sleep?" Vegas laughed.

Fuck no.

"Come on... I'll be back tomorrow," Vegas said.

"Mm. What time?" I asked.

"Evening, I guess. Don't know the exact time."

I took a deep breath. "*What time?!*" I barked back.

"Fine, fine! Before six. I'll have dinner with you. Okay?"

"Hmph. Buy me some rad na,[17] then, I wanna eat some." I tried to keep my voice harsh, but I ended up getting distracted by the prospect of tomorrow's meal. *What else can I get?*

"Got it, Pete. All right, I'm turning in early so I can finish things quickly tomorrow and get back faster."

"Okay. Get me some dessert too," I demanded. "Anything sweet."

"Okay... Tell me good night," Vegas instructed.

I made a face. No fucking way was I saying that. "Just get back fast. That's all."

I cut the call as soon as I heard Vegas's laughter ring out on the other end of the line. Damn it! I was trying to drive him crazy! Piss him off! Why wasn't he mad at all? *Ugh!* What should I do, insult his dad instead? That'd get my ass kicked for sure.

---

17   Rad na is a Thai-Chinese dish of stir-fried noodles in a thick gravy, with boiled vegetables, mushrooms, and pork or chicken.

Nop came over to get his phone back. He shook his head at me as I freaked out.

I tossed and turned on the bed. Sleeping in the same bed as Vegas was a challenge, but why was it harder *without* him here? What was wrong with me? Maybe it was because of all the bullshit daydreaming I did today.

By the time I finally started to doze off, it was almost dawn.

I woke up just before noon. The food that Nop had brought in at fuck-knows-when was already cold. I looked at the clock in anticipation. *Yikes! What am I doing?!* Was I really *that* eager for the rad na tonight? *Damn my gluttony!*

"Nop!" I yelled, throwing the tissue box at the glass door again. It was time to harass Vegas with another prank call. Maybe he was in a bad mood today, and I could rile him up.

Nop walked into the room at just the right moment; he happened to be on the phone already.

"It's Mr. Vegas... Man, are you guys psychic or something?" He lowered his voice and gave me the phone. Vegas had happened to call me at the same time? Shit!

"Yeah?" I said into the phone.

"Pete, I might be back late," Vegas said.

"Why?!" I exclaimed, making a face despite myself. That made Nop laugh—from his expression, it looked like there was something going on that I didn't know about.

"If you're hungry, just eat without me. I'll bring you some rad na later tonight."

"*Why?!*" I repeated myself, frustrated. My heart felt achy all of a sudden.

"I have to go to a funeral."

"Who died?" I asked, my voice somewhat grating. Did I really have to be this grumpy over a lack of rad na?

"I don't know. Father's secretary just brought me some black clothes. I heard the Major Clan is closing down their offices for a couple weeks."

When I heard his words, the blood drained from my face and tingles went down my spine. "What?! What does it have to do with the Major Clan?"

"Well, they're holding the funeral," Vegas replied.

"Who died?!" I asked in a panic. Various scenarios whirled through my head. Were Mr. Khun, Mr. Kinn, and Mr. Kim all right?

"I don't know. I'm not at the temple yet. I'll tell you as soon as I know…"

"*Vegas, who are you talking to?*" I heard Mr. Kant's voice cut in.

"It's not Khun, Kinn, or Kim, I'm sure of that—otherwise it would be on the news by now," he said hastily. "See you." With that, he hung up.

As the phone went silent, I couldn't shake off what Vegas had told me. If the Major Clan had closed their offices, it meant whoever had died was important! But to be honest, it would hit me hard no matter who had died in the Major Clan.

Shit! I wanted to run back to the main house right now! *Damn it! This is horrible!*

KINN
PORSCHE

Vegas × Pete 9

PETE

I PACED IN CIRCLES around the room. I'd asked Nop what was going on with the Major Clan, but he said he didn't know anything. He told me he wasn't Vegas's personal bodyguard, who followed him around, just a guard stationed at the house, so he didn't have any insider gossip. In fact, his main job right now was looking after me.

I panicked, my thoughts running wild. P'Chan? Couldn't be; he was still young and fit. There was no way he'd die so soon. Auntie Prik, Mr. Tankhun's favorite cook, who made the best Southern food this side of Bangkok? No, she was still healthy, so it couldn't be her…or could it? *Argh, I can't think of anyone!* But it certainly couldn't be Mr. Korn or any of his sons; that would spell disaster for both the Major and Minor Clans.

Oh! Could it be P'Jess? Shit! That's possible! That guy was pushing sixty and still got shoved around by the young master, so he'd probably died of resentment. *Or shock, I guess… Ah, what a shame.*

Regardless of whose funeral it was, I was sad about it. If it was someone I knew, what was I supposed to do? I wanted to go pay my respects at least once, but I was chained up in this fucking place!

Argh! And Vegas wasn't back yet—didn't he know I was waiting for news?!

As I waited anxiously for Vegas to get home, I knelt on the bed, clasped my hands, and began to recite the Mettā mantra. I went all out, chanting every other mantra that I could remember, from the Sarapanya to the Chinnabanchon, and thought of every venerated monk I knew of. It was a good thing Grandma took me to the temple a lot as a kid. Although I couldn't attend the funeral—I didn't even know whose it was—I could still dedicate some merit to them. I hoped it'd reach them because everyone at the Major Clan was important to me.

Ah… Life is short; forgive me for any past offenses. I continued to pray and meditate, taking refuge in the Triple Gem. *Let merit send them to a better place. Be at peace. Don't concern yourself with worldly things; be on your way… If there's an opportunity, I'll make merit for you. Sathu.*

I opened my eyes from my meditation, saluting the Buddha, the Dharma, and the Sangha, but as I bowed down, the smell of food tickled my nose. Maybe it was rad na or fish maw soup… *Ah, I'm getting hungry. Vegas must be back with my food.*

"Ve— What's this?" I turned toward the door, about to call his name, but I stopped short in surprise.

Vegas looked at me, equally surprised. "What are you doing?"

My hands were still clasped together, and my back was bent; I was just getting up from my prostration. I didn't answer Vegas's question, but I got up from the bed and walked over to take a look at him.

Sticky liquid dripped from Vegas's clothes. I snorted and tried to hold back my laughter, quickly covering my mouth. "I asked for rad na," I said, "but why did you pour it over yourself? Ha ha!"[18] I really couldn't help it. What had Vegas done this time?

"Fuck, it was Tankhun!" Vegas scowled. "What the hell was he trying to pull? He poured fish maw soup all over me! Look."

I stopped short and came back to my senses. Hearing the young master's name, I was reminded of the funeral. "Who was it?" I asked urgently. "Who died?"

Vegas made a thoughtful face and looked me over from head to toe. He stilled for a moment—then it was his turn to purse his lips and stave off a laugh. "Hah!"

"What are you laughing at?" I furrowed my brow, scolding Vegas in my head. *I'm being serious here!*

"Fuck! Such a fancy fucking funeral, I thought Chan died. Turns out... Ugh, whose corpse have they got in that coffin?" he muttered, scratching his head.

"P'Chan? It's P'Chan? Speak clearly!" When I caught P'Chan's name, my heart dropped to my stomach. P'Chan taught me everything: how to shoot a gun, how to handle a knife, how the business was run—I learned it all from him. *Such a shame...*

"It's not Chan," Vegas sighed. He took off his shirt, jacket, and slacks, leaving only his boxers.

"Then who was it?!"

Vegas threw a towel over his shoulder and stared at me steadily. "It's my lover!"

Vegas wasn't making any sense. I frowned even further. *His lover?* I felt a strange prickle, almost like my heart had skipped a beat. Damn it, what did he mean by that?

Before I could figure out what Vegas meant, he spun around and slammed the bathroom door in my face.

---

18 The name "rad na" means "to pour over."

Bang, bang! I pounded on the bathroom door, wanting Vegas to come out and explain himself. "What are you saying, huh?! Who's dead?! Who's dead, Vegas?!"

I heard Vegas turn on the shower. Why couldn't this fucker just tell me who died?! I kept banging on the door, completely forgetting he could yank it open at any moment and shut me up with his fist.

The door creaking open made me jump. Vegas was completely soaked and entirely nude, but he clearly didn't care that I was standing there. He left the door open like that, then walked back into the shower to continue washing up. I panicked, hurriedly looking away. *Shameless bastard! Who the hell showers with other people watching?*

"Just say what you want to say." Vegas scrubbed himself with soap, unfazed. Even worse, he acted like this was perfectly normal. *This freak!*

"Y-you finish showering first," I said, lowering my voice and turning to the side. I blindly reached for the doorknob to close the bathroom door.

"Wait," Vegas said.

I stopped short, swallowing thickly. I chanced a glance at him, and he crooked his finger at me. "Come here."

"No!" I snapped back without thinking, ready to close the door again.

"Wait!" he barked, raising his voice.

I froze. "What?"

"Come in here!"

"Why? I'll get wet."

Vegas raised an eyebrow, the corner of his mouth lifting. "Don't you want to know who died?"

"Then say it. Why do I have to go in there?" I looked left and right, anywhere but at him. I felt self-conscious, even though I'd been through the Territorial Defense program and showered with the other cadets. But that had never felt like this. It was definitely because of Vegas. He wasn't exactly normal—his head was probably full of evil thoughts. I didn't trust him at all.

"If you don't, I won't tell you," he said.

I grunted and let out a long sigh. I wanted to know, but I didn't want to go in. It was too risky.

"It's fine if you don't want to know," Vegas said, turning back to grab his shampoo and lather up his hair.

"Fine, I'll come in." I crossed my arms and stepped into the bathroom.

"Closer." Vegas deepened his voice and turned to fully face me, his hands resting loosely on his hips.

"Fine." I inched forward the tiniest bit.

"Closer!" Vegas shouted.

"Argh! I can hear you just fine from here! I'm not deaf," I snapped, getting more annoyed by the second.

"Come into the shower with me. If you don't want to get wet, then take off your pants."

I could sense the danger, so I pulled a sardonic smile and turned back around. "I'd be an idiot if I did that," I muttered to myself.

"Pete! One..."

I stopped in my tracks and rolled my eyes.

"Two... I promise you, if I count to three, you'll regret it," Vegas threatened, but when I turned to look, he was smiling gleefully. *Damn it!*

In the end, I had to do as he said. I stomped over to him, trying not to look down. Instead, I stared into the distance.

"Motherfucker!" I hissed.

"You're whining like a girl," said Vegas.

I clicked my tongue in frustration. Stray droplets from the shower hit me, making my skin wet.

"Who died? Just tell me, and quickly… Shit!"

Vegas grabbed my wrist and pulled me toward him. I squeezed my eyes shut against the spray of warm water.

"I missed you so fucking much," he said. Without waiting for me to get my bearings, he held me tightly and pushed me back against the wall. Then he pressed his nose to my face, alternating between my left and right cheeks.

"Vegas! Let me go!" I pushed at his chest, but he just stared at me hungrily. I opened my eyes with difficulty. My hair, my face, even my pajama pants were soaked through. "Let me go!"

"Don't you want to know who died?" he asked slyly, his sharp eyes staring deeply into mine. The tip of my nose brushed against his, our breaths mingling together.

"You can tell me like a normal fucking person, you know." I struggled against him, but Vegas had me cornered. He plastered his naked body against mine, keeping me pinned with his weight.

"Do you want to know?" he asked.

"W-well, yes, but you don't have to tell me. It's fine." I turned my face away from him, but Vegas followed the motion.

"It's someone important," he said, singsong. "You really don't want to know…?" He trailed off teasingly, making me pull a face at him again.

"Just spit it out!" I wanted to know, but I was also wary—Vegas had started rubbing up against my leg.

He broke into an evil grin. "If you want me to tell you, you have to kiss me first."

I backed up further still, practically fusing with the wall. "Like hell! Get off!" I said, pushing his face away.

Vegas pulled back and looked at me with a haughty expression. "It's fine if you don't want to kiss me. But your young master wept so hard today that his eyes were all swollen," he said.

He moved back under the shower spray, but when I thought about how Mr. Tankhun must have known this person well, I couldn't help it; I needed to know.

My body acted before my brain could stop it. I tugged at Vegas's wrist for him to turn around, put my hands on either side of his face, took a deep breath to gather my courage, and pulled him down into a kiss. I closed my eyes, thinking I'd just quickly get it over with, but inside, my heart was hammering wildly.

I didn't know what kind of expression Vegas was making; I didn't dare open my eyes to look. My whole body shivered, and all other thoughts melted away. There was only the warmth of his breath and the touch of his lips.

Abruptly, I came back to my senses and pulled away. Vegas stared at me, not even blinking.

I avoided looking at him and gingerly pushed him away. "Can you tell me now?"

Vegas grabbed my wrists and drew me in toward him. "What was that?" he asked, furrowing his brow, but still smiling at me.

"Just tell me, don't play any tricks," I said, even though I knew that I didn't have any room to argue. I didn't know how to act. My face felt hotter than normal.

"Why? You haven't done what I asked you to," he said.

"I already did! Don't you dare—"

"That was just a peck, it doesn't count... *This* is a kiss."

Before I could react, Vegas grabbed my face and gently pressed his lips to mine. He nipped at my lower lip and sucked until I instinctively opened my mouth, allowing his hot tongue to lick inside. My body went weak; Vegas pulled my arms around his waist, and I had to hold on to him to stop myself from sliding to the floor. His hands moved down to hold on to my hips before he reached down further and gave my ass a firm squeeze.

"*Mmph!*" I inadvertently responded to Vegas sucking on my tongue. He surged forward until there was barely any space left for me to retreat.

I knew I was at a disadvantage, letting Vegas take control like this, but somehow, the fighting spirit inside me made me want to retaliate against his every touch. Our tongues tangled together, each of us trying to overpower the other, but I wouldn't give up that easily! We pressed closer, and while the kiss had started with Vegas in full control, we now took turns trying to take charge.

"Mmm..."

At first, I was a little lost in the moment, but when his hand slid into my pants, my awareness came back. *Wait... Fuck! What am I doing?!*

"Mmph!" My eyes flew open, and I jerked away. Vegas frowned as I shrank back as far as I could. "Vegas, get your hands off me!"

I peeled his hands from my ass and pushed him away. Vegas giggled and licked his lips.

"Pervert. Asshole. So, are you going to tell me or not?!" *What a waste of effort, fuck! What the hell are you doing, Pete?!*

"Hmm... Should I tell you?"

"Fuck it, I don't want to know! You're a liar. You can't be trusted."

"Fine, fine, I won't tease you anymore. This time, I promise I'll tell you." He glanced at me, his sharp eyes piercing me like I was his prey.

"What now?! I've done what you asked," I muttered under my breath, but I knew he heard me. He smiled and leaned in close, but I twisted away.

"I'll tell you, but you have to...sleep with me," he said slowly, emphasizing every word.

I lost it. *Motherfucker! Selfish piece of shit! Give him an inch, and he'll take a mile! You think someone like me will let you get away with this? Fuck no!*

"Forget it!" I struggled out of his grip and stomped off, thinking that if I stayed there, I'd just be a target for him to wind up.

When I got to the bathroom door, Vegas called after me, "Fine, fine, I'll tell you."

I turned back to give Vegas a nasty glare. "I don't want to know," I said, even though I desperately did. *If I have to suffer, I should at least get something back.*

He sighed. "I won't tease you anymore." He turned the shower back on to rinse himself off, so I stood there, waiting for him. His cheerful expression turned serious.

I turned to the door, not wanting to look him in the eye. "What?"

"I'm just wondering whether it's a good idea to tell you or not," he said somberly.

"Is it that bad?" I adjusted my tone. Judging from Vegas's reaction, it was weighing on him.

"In a way...I think you're just better off not knowing some things," he murmured, almost like he was talking to himself.

I frowned at him. "What are you saying?" I asked, confused.

Vegas looked even more uncomfortable. "I'm not sure how you'd feel..."

"Of course I'll be upset. I know everyone who works for the Major Clan." Why did he have to act so serious? This couldn't be good.

"You don't..."

"What?! Didn't you just say—?"

"I mean...*I* don't know him. The guy who died," Vegas said evenly. He grabbed a towel and wrapped it around his waist.

"What are you talking about?! Didn't you say Mr. Tankhun was crying his eyes out?" I had the courage to glare at him directly now that he wasn't naked.

"It's...one of his men, maybe," he said.

"What about a name? You said the funeral was big—how could there not be a name?" This guy was crazy. How could he go to a funeral and not see the name or a photo of the deceased?

"It was...Pong...Pong-something." Vegas came over to the sink and started brushing his teeth. He acted so casually, like he wasn't interested in the subject at all. He must really not have known whoever it was.

Pong, huh? People in the Major Clan named Pong... Aside from my legal name, Pongsakorn Saengtham, who else was named Pong? I scratched my head, thinking hard.

"Pong... Uncle Pong!" My eyes widened. "Are you serious?!"

"Maybe?" Vegas squeezed out his face wash and carefully scrubbed his face, occasionally sneaking glances at me.

"Uncle Pong...the security guard at the young master's chocolate factory! Shit... I can't believe he died so young."

Vegas lifted his eyebrow and looked at me through the mirror. I stood at the bathroom door and rambled on, thinking about Uncle Pong. "I heard that he was sick here and there, but he was still going strong. I wasn't that close to him, but he used to share his moonshine with Arm and me when the young master visited his factory."

Although I wasn't that close to him, Uncle Pong was still someone I knew, so I couldn't help but feel sad. At the same time, as I let my mind wander, something suddenly occurred to me—*the young master cried until his eyes were swollen? And put on a big funeral? He went that far? Mr. Tankhun didn't know him that well.*

Mr. Tankhun usually only did the bare minimum when he visited his factory and left as soon as he was done—he barely remembered his employees' names. Really? He cried? The young master did have a sensitive side, but this was odd. What was going on?

"The young master cried? And put on a big funeral?" I asked in disbelief. Whenever an employee died, the Major Clan family usually only took the responsibility of the funeral host. They didn't get personally involved; at most, they'd send a bodyguard as their representative. It was rare for even P'Chan to attend a funeral himself.

"It's…the Major Clan. You know how they love to be over-the-top." Vegas rinsed his face and patted it dry with another towel.

I was baffled. Was Vegas lying to me? *Is he crazy, saying the young master was crying?! Maybe Mr. Tankhun is just obsessed with some new soap opera… Anyway, I'll just offer my condolences for Uncle Pong.*

I sighed. "Rest in peace, Uncle Pong. All meetings end in parting; that's a fact of life," I said, then gloomily walked out of the bathroom.

I saw the corner of Vegas's mouth twitch upward, but I had no time to argue with him. I quickly wrapped my towel around myself and changed into a fresh pair of pajama pants before Vegas could come out.

I didn't want Uncle Pong to have died—or anyone, for that matter—but I'd confess I was relieved it wasn't anyone I was close to. I really wouldn't have been able to handle it. It was still tragic, but

I didn't have much of a connection with Uncle Pong. I just felt sorry for his wife and kids.

Vegas came out and rifled through his closet for pajamas. "Still thinking about it?" he asked.

"Well... Hmm... I'm just worried about his wife and kids. Think about it—if you lost someone you loved, what would you do? It's fucking depressing, you know?" I went to sit on the sofa, still thinking of Uncle Pong. "But as the saying goes, meetings are followed by parting. How can you stay together forever? I just think parting when you're both still alive hurts less than parting through one's death."

Maybe Uncle Pong's death was getting to me, so I was being more talkative than normal. But I didn't have anyone else to open up to—it was just me and him in this room.

Vegas's silence made me suddenly aware of his unusually somber mood.

"Vegas...Vegas, what's wrong?" I turned to ask him.

Vegas sat in a daze at the foot of the bed. I wasn't sure how, but lately I'd been able to notice even the slightest change in his mood; as soon as I started talking about death, his discomfort became clear.

"I...don't like parting," he said.

I wanted to pull my hair out. *Argh! Why did I ramble on about death to him?!* I completely forgot that his mother was dead and his beloved nanny had gone missing. And he was always talking about how alone in the world he felt! *Damn it, I did it again!*

"Doesn't matter if it's parting while alive or dead—I don't like it," he said. "My mother died, my nanny disappeared... No matter how much I miss them, I can never meet them again."

I was right; that was Vegas. There was so much pain hidden inside him. Even if he could smile and laugh, his eyes held so many more unfathomable emotions.

"In the end, you've got to accept what's happened," I said. "If you're still stuck in the past, you'll never be able to move forward. I'm not trying to lecture you, but if you accept reality, you'll be happier. I'm serious." I wasn't sure why I felt the need to comfort him, but maybe I was afraid he'd get angry and take it out on me.

"You know, today," he said suddenly, "it was kind of funny…but then, I imagined if it were real. I probably wouldn't be able to accept it either." I couldn't make heads or tails of this.

"What? I don't get what you're saying."

Vegas fixed his gaze on me. His eyes cleared, and he slowly smiled. "I'm happy that it's not real. I came back home and saw you sitting on that bed, doing your thing… Do you know how damn relieved I was right then? Even when I knew nothing had happened to you." I was even more confused now. Was this asshole drunk or something? He wasn't making any sense!

"How could anything happen to me?" I laughed. "You've got me chained up in here. If anything's going to happen to me, it'll be that I've died of boredom."

Vegas shook his head and walked toward me. He stood over me and used his hands to carefully bring my face toward his stomach, gently holding me.

"Can you stay with me forever?" he murmured.

My heart skipped a beat before I was interrupted by another thought: *Shit! I forgot to act unreasonable!*

Vegas was especially besotted with me these days, and that was no good. I couldn't act like I understood life, that I saw the truth that all things were impermanent—I couldn't have the dharma in my heart! I had to fuck with him first! I had to cause chaos and annoy the shit out of him so he'd get fed up with me! *How could I forget?!*

I pushed Vegas away from me and looked up at him obstinately. "Where's my rad na?"

"Hmm?" He looked bewildered for a moment, but then his eyes widened in sudden clarity. "Oh, right."

"Don't tell me you forgot!" I snapped when I saw his guilty look. *Oh...I'm mad, all right. You can forget whatever you want to forget, but you can't forget my food!*

"Tankhun splashed fish maw soup all over me!" he protested. "I came straight home. I completely forgot."

"Bastard! How could you forget?! I'm starving!" I hadn't eaten anything since noon; I'd been too busy worrying about what had happened with the Major Clan to eat.

"What?! I told you to eat first."

"But you promised to bring me rad na!" I got up from the sofa and stared him down.

"Tomorrow, then," he said with a straight face.

Oh, now I was even more pissed off. My hunger took over, and I forgot to calm myself down, forgot that Vegas could just punch me. Right now, his face was completely blank. He just kept staring at me.

"What do you mean, tomorrow? I'm hungry right now," I said, pretending to kick the sofa in anger. In truth, my heart was beating hard, especially when I saw Vegas frown and let out a sigh. I started to waver, wondering if I should keep going or quit while I was ahead. *What should I do?*

"Then why didn't you eat? And now you're angry with me?"

"You said you'd come back to eat with me!" I blurted, but I softened my voice a bit at the end. If I hadn't done that, I'd have been eating a kick to the face right now instead of dinner. Maybe it was time to abort the mission and just go to sleep so I could forget how hungry I was.

I figured Vegas was about to explode, rage simmering under the surface. Judging from his mood, he'd put up with enough from me. I stomped toward the bed and climbed in, pulling the blanket over my head so if he wanted to kick me, he'd have a harder time aiming. *Phew!*

Secretly, I was scared.

"Pete..."

Under the blanket, I couldn't see what sort of expression he was making; I could only concentrate on my breathing. *Breathe in, breathe out, breathe in, breathe out.*

"Fine, fine, I'll order delivery," Vegas said, sounding tired.

He wasn't angry anymore, but he should at least have been annoyed with me—or was it just because he'd been through a lot today? I decided to push him a little more. If he was tired, at least that meant he'd be too sleepy to kick me.

I threw the blanket back and glared at him. "No! You said you were going to get it for me!"

"Isn't this the same thing? I'm ordering it now," he said.

"...It's not the same."

"Argh... So I have to go out and buy it?" He pulled at his hair in frustration. I nodded slowly. He heaved a long sigh and got up to grab his robe and car keys, marching out in a huff.

I sighed in relief that he hadn't laid a hand on me. *Fuck, I nearly had a heart attack there.* I stared at Vegas's back, waiting until he'd left the room before I burst out laughing.

"Ha ha! That was fun. Whoo!" I cheered, getting up from the bed. I was on a roll! "Heh, bet you're thinking twice now. See how annoying it is for me to stay with you? I'm a perfect copy of Mr. Tankhun! Ha ha!" I ambled over to the sofa and sat down, propping my feet up on the coffee table as I waited. Who knew that getting whatever I wanted would be so much fun? *Now I know why the young master does it! Hah!*

Vegas disappeared for almost an hour. He came back with a bowl, and I happily sorted out our rad na. He'd bought three servings, and he ate with me, although he only managed to eat half of his portion. As for me, I polished off two servings. He sat and stared at me as he waited for me to finish. *You must be wondering whether or not to let me go, huh, bastard? I'm so excited!*

I felt satisfied as the night drew to a close. The only snag was when Vegas pulled me into an embrace as we slept, wrapping his arms and legs around me like he did every other night. *Damn it! You can still hug me? You'll think twice tomorrow. When will you stop being so smitten with me?*

At the start of a new day, I broke out into song:

"What should I do? Just one glance
An' I'm scared to get close.
It's love from my heart, I'd like ya t'know.
When I see ya, I get nervous,
I take one look and run.
Dunno when I can let ya know,
There's somebody who thinks yer the one.
But ma looks ain't yer type,
Just a country boy raisin' cows in this life.

Don't have any papers, but I got my scythe. Mahalai Wua Chon!"[19]

I wanted to mess with Vegas from the moment he got up—this would annoy him for sure! I'd confuse him for the whole day. Singing in the Southern dialect was a great way to start. *Have you ever even heard it before? Heh.*

Vegas emerged from the bathroom. I saw him smile as he went about his routine, doing this and that. Why was he so happy? *You can't be happy—you have to be annoyed! Your ears have to hurt! It's supposed to be annoying!* This wasn't good. I had to sing louder.

"*I get up early an' take the cows down the ol' country road.*

Lady, ya don't even know ya make this country boy quake

Each time ya look at—what are you laughing at?!" I scowled at Vegas when he burst out laughing. *It's mortifying when someone laughs at your singing. And rude!*

"If you're happy, I'm happy," Vegas said cheerfully as he buttoned up his shirt. *What?! Aren't his ears bleeding yet?* When Mr. Tankhun sang in the mornings, I always got so fucking annoyed.

"Where are you going?" I frowned, staring at Vegas as he got dressed and drenched himself in cologne.

"Meeting clients with Father," he said.

"Didn't you say the company was closed?"

"The Minor Clan's side of things isn't…" He came over and bent down to kiss my temple. "I'll get you something once I'm done."

I didn't say anything.

"My country boy can keep singing while he waits… Just be careful not to strain your vocal cords," Vegas chuckled.

---

19 Mahalai Wua Chon (Bullfight University) by Phattalung Band.

Once he'd left, I flipped him the bird. *Asshole.*

I walked in circles, thinking hard again. *What now?* I had maybe two hours before Vegas returned. *Heh! What other annoying shit does the young master like to do?* I'd do all of it.

Whenever I went home on leave, Mr. Tankhun loved to call and pester me with stupid questions, and I'd have to pretend the signal was bad every time. I'd be swimming with my friends, and Mr. Tankhun would ring me every ten minutes. That was why I'd started turning my phone off altogether when I went home. *Fuck it, let's do that!*

I sat on the sofa and flipped through magazines, my eyes barely skimming them. Then, I came across an astrology page. *What's his zodiac sign? Hee hee!*

Two hours had passed—now was the time. "Nop!" I shouted, flinging the tissue box for emphasis.

The door slid open.

"You want to call him?" Nop asked, frowning at me. He knew exactly what he was supposed to do: He pulled out his phone to dial Vegas's number before handing it over to me.

"Thank you! Heh, how's this?"

"I can't believe it. Keep this up. When he finally snaps and kills you, I'm going to laugh," Nop muttered, sinking down onto the couch next to me. I held the phone to my ear. I could barely contain my excitement as I listened to the dial tone.

Vegas picked up the call with a snarl: "What?!"

"Vegaaas," I cooed, my eyes scanning the magazine.

"Pete? What is it?" His voice was much softer and quieter this time, almost like he was whispering.

"What's your star sign?" I asked.

"Huh?"

I strained to hold in my laughter. He was still working—I could hear people talking in the background. It sounded serious. "What's your star sign? I'll read you your monthly horoscope."

"What?! I'm with a client right now."

"Your star sign!" I raised my voice, trying to get an answer out of him.

"This isn't funny, stop pestering me! This isn't the time." In the background of the call, I heard his father call his name sharply. *Oh, fuck! I completely forgot about his father. Shit, now I feel bad. Is his father going to scream at him again? Did I go too far?*

"Pete...Pete?"

"Mm. Sorry. Bye," I mumbled, chagrined. I forgot how rude it was to call and disturb him like this. I was having fun, but I'd forgotten to consider that he might get in trouble with his father.

"Capricorn. December 25. I'll listen to you read it when I get back. See you later." With that, Vegas hung up.

Now I was paranoid. *Shit, what have I done? Is Vegas gonna fight with his dad again?*

Nop snatched his phone back and shook his head. "Huh. Were you calling to annoy him, or did you miss him?"

"You can leave," I said, waving Nop away. My guilty conscience took over. The Minor Clan wasn't like the Major Clan; if Mr. Kant got angry, Vegas would get a beating. *Argh! Why am I worrying so much? This is good, Pete! It's good! He'll see me as a troublemaker now!*

I did my own thing for the rest of the day, but my heart felt restless. My eyes kept going back to the clock.

It was early evening when I heard the bedroom door open. I scrambled to get up from the bed—I'd been rolling around on it for a long while now.

Vegas entered with a sigh, tossing his bag down and wrenching off his watch. He looked exhausted. Seeing him like that, I didn't dare say anything. I could only watch him in silence.

He looked at me and came over to sit down beside me. "Hey, Pete... Your call got me in trouble."

"...Did your father do anything to you?" I asked hesitantly.

Vegas reached out to cradle my face in his hands and pulled me into a hug. "Just a little... Forget about it. So, what's my monthly horoscope?" Vegas asked, kissing the top of my head and sighing again. He seemed more at ease than he had earlier.

"Are you sure?" I pulled away to ask, looking at him with worry.

Vegas gently stroked my hair. "It's nothing..."

Even if he said it was fine, I still felt guilty. I was the one causing difficulty for him in the first place.

"Don't think about it. What about you, calling and calling—did you really miss me that much?" He smiled wickedly.

"That's not it!" I pushed him away. *What do you know? My goal is much more complex. You wouldn't understand.*

"I'm here! I'm back! What should I do so you'll stop missing me?" Vegas grabbed my wrists and pushed me down onto the bed, climbing on top of me.

"What are you doing?!" I yelled and thrashed against him, my heart pounding.

"Calling me so often... I'll make sure you won't miss me anymore!" he said with a smile, bending down to plant a big kiss on my cheek.

"Let me go!" *Asshole!*

But no matter how much I struggled, when Vegas pressed his lips to mine and pushed his tongue into my mouth, my mind blurred, and my body went limp. *What's wrong with you, Pete?!*

"You can call my name as much as you want... I missed you too, heh."

"Let me go!" I shook my head from side to side, trying to muster the strength to throw Vegas off. He nuzzled into my neck, then moved down to my chest. *Don't you dare! Not when my body has been so strange lately. One little flicker and everything is ready to ignite. I hate this traitorous body.*

[FIVE MINUTES LATER...]

"Ngh... Vegas...no," I begged.

Vegas slid his hand into my pants and took hold of my cock. My heart skipped a beat, and a shiver ran through my body. *Not like this! You misunderstood me! I wasn't missing you!*

[TEN MINUTES LATER...]

"Mmph... V-Vegas...slower... Bastard, that hurts!" I cursed for the millionth time, even if it was more...*tingly* than painful. *Fuck!* I was ashamed of myself.

The second Vegas took his clothes off, and I felt the cold lube, I knew it was over!

[FIFTEEN MINUTES LATER...]

After that, the only noise in the room was our moaning and groaning. I yielded to Vegas, silently berating myself. What had made him think I missed him? I was acting like a little shit to drive him crazy! Was I not bratty enough? I'd acted exactly like the young master—the guy who gave me headaches every day. Damn it!

Mr. Tankhun's antics made me want to run away or punch his lights out. How could Vegas get it so wrong?

You completely missed the point, Vegas! Argh!

It was almost noon by the time I woke up the next day, all because of that asshole Vegas. *Motherfucker!* By the time he let me sleep last night, it was a few hours past midnight. Where did he get all that energy?

When we'd finished on the bed, I ran into the bathroom, but that fucker followed me and went for round two! It felt like I was being split open, and all the while, he kept saying...

"Did you know? You're getting cuter every day."

Cute? Yeah, right! Open your eyes and look at me! I've done everything exactly the same as Mr. Tankhun. If you hate the young master so much, you should hate me too!

Was I really *cute*? Did I have to act violent and wild like Porsche? Shit, though, he was into Porsche... No, no, that would be way too risky.

Vegas walked in and out of his room, working on his documents. I lay on the sofa, hanging my head off the side like before. There were so many thoughts swirling around in my head that I didn't know where to start. *Does a crazy bastard like Vegas need someone to act even crazier?*

"Are you hungry yet?" Vegas asked.

"Naw, I ain't peckish. How 'bout you, ya eat yet, dickhead?" I played up my Southern accent as much as I could, holding back from laughing at my own stupid joke.

"What did you say?" Vegas asked, picking up a file.

I smiled as if nothing had happened. "I'm not hungry yet. Have you eaten?"

Vegas squinted at me in suspicion. "No, I was waiting for you. What the hell was that?"

"This how the homefolk speak. Idjit like you... Porch lights are on, but ain't nobody home." Being able to mess with him like this made me so happy. It was like I'd found a release. *Whoo!*

"Did you just call me an idiot?" he asked.

"No, I didn't call you an idiot. Really."

"Heh. I know you're insulting me."

"Dunno yer ass from yer elbow, do ya?" I said. "Yer the boss, how come yer half a brick short of a load?" *Heh, this is fun!*

"Argh! You're giving me a headache!" Vegas shouted and stormed out of the room. I looked up and stared at his back as he left before bursting into another laughing fit. *Ha! He's got a headache again! Not long until he can't put up with me anymore!*

Vegas must've been stressed about his work today. Or maybe it was all the Southern dialect I kept spewing at him. Who could say?

We usually ate together, but Vegas looked particularly hassled by his work today, so he didn't have the time to bother with me. *Heh, let's keep bugging him until he goes insane! Serves him right.*

I was already asleep by the time he came back into the bedroom. The day had passed without much excitement, and I'd just been playing around. I didn't know if Vegas had started thinking about getting rid of me at all, but I'd keep hoping. *Who knows? It might happen sooner rather than later.*

The next day, I planned to torment him like before. If he asked me anything, my answers would only make sense half the time.

But it turned out Vegas was busy. He did manage to come over to kiss the top of my head or hug me a few times, but when evening came, he showered and got all dressed up. Then, he sprayed on so much cologne that the whole street would be able to smell him.

I leaned against the bathroom doorframe with my arms crossed, glaring at him suspiciously. "Where are you going?" I asked.

"I'm going to a junior classmate's birthday party tonight," he replied. "I might come home late. You don't have to wait up for me."

That answer irked me for some reason. "You didn't tell me that."

"I'm telling you now." Vegas looked at himself in the mirror without paying any attention to me. My frown deepened. *Asshole! You had the whole day, and you didn't say a word—now you're telling me when you're about to go out?!*

And why am I so pissed off about this?!

"When will you be back?" I asked.

"When the bar closes," he said nonchalantly. "After midnight."

"Come back at ten!" I insisted. I didn't even know what I was doing.

"Heh." Vegas smirked and looked at me expectantly from in the mirror.

"What are you laughing at?" I grumbled.

"Eleven, then."

"Ten. Ten o'clock *on the dot.*"

Vegas sprayed on even more cologne, making me gag. He pulled away from the mirror to walk toward me and leaned in, smiling. "You've blown away all my expectations."

"What expectations?" I grumbled. "So, will you be back on time?" I followed Vegas as he walked over to put on his watch.

"Hee hee. Yes, honey," he cooed, so I glared at him. He lifted his bottle of cologne again.

"Hey! What are you doing, spraying on so much of that?!"

"Am I handsome yet?" he asked. He gave me another smile, so I glared at him harder.

"Yer as fine as frog's hair," I drawled. "Whatch'er ma and pa eat to make you so handsome? So purty, my skin's a-crawlin'."

Vegas groaned and shook his head before giving my forehead a quick peck, quickly grabbing his car keys, and leaving the room.

Bastard... Where are you really going, dressed for the runway like that? Asshole!

Argh! What is wrong with you, Pete? It's good that he's gone! You won't have to feel so on edge all the time. Plus, it looked like he was getting fed up with my Southern nonsense. Why wasn't I seeing this as a mission accomplished? *Damn you, Vegas!*

Nop came in as I grumpily tried to concentrate on the book in front of me.

"Pete?"

"What?"

"I'm getting off my shift," Nop said. "You want anything?"

"No!" I snapped.

"Er, I'll go, then. Parm will be watching you, but you probably can't borrow his phone—Vegas didn't give him permission."

"Ah? Then what happens if I need to call him?"

"He'll be back soon," said Nop. "Let him be. Don't you like this better? It's awkward when he's around. You need to be careful, Pete. Vegas is messing with your head. Why do you keep calling him all the time? He hurt you! Do you even know what you're doing?"

I spun around to stare at Nop.

"Vegas is cunning!" he said. "Who knows what's real and what's fake? I'm warning you because I mean well, Pete. He's making it so you can't bear to leave him. Be careful!" With that, Nop turned around and left.

"Wait, Nop! What did you mean?!" I shouted after him. *What did you mean, so I 'can't bear to leave him'? No way! I want to get away so bad! It's not that, Nop, you dumbass. I'm trying to find a way to escape!*

I'd been in this room for too long. It had to be too much stress building up. There wasn't much to do, so I kept mulling over the same shit again and again; plus, I was in low spirits, so when I was alone with my own brain, I overthought things more than usual.

My mood kept swinging up and down because I didn't know what to focus on. It was like I was adrift; I couldn't do anything else. When Vegas was here with me, at least it felt like I was playing a game. Finding ways to mess with him helped distract me from my thoughts, but I wasn't planning on staying with him or suddenly becoming enamored with him. Right now, when everything was quiet, and I was the only one in the room, it was eerie. Strangely lonely too...

My eyes stared at the clock. *Why does it feel creepier the later it gets?* I thought back on what the hell I'd been doing and how Vegas was acting around me. He'd been so kind to me lately, a completely different person from before. What bullshit was he trying to pull? *Who exactly is messing with whose head here?*

The sound of the glass door sliding open grabbed my attention. I glanced at the clock; it was ten minutes past ten.

"Not asleep yet?" Vegas asked.

I fell back onto the bed and lay there without answering. As he got closer, the smell of alcohol completely overpowered the cologne he'd basically bathed in earlier.

"Are you sleepy?"

I didn't reply.

"Why aren't you answering me? What happened to that smart mouth from earlier?" Vegas squatted next to the bed, so I turned over to face away from him. "What's wrong?" Vegas touched my shoulder like he was trying to flip me back over to face him. "Oh... I'm ten minutes late."

I didn't say a word in response.

Vegas succeeded in rolling me over to face him. "I did get home exactly at ten o'clock," he told me. "I just stopped to pee downstairs."

"You can't piss in your own bathroom?" I muttered darkly.

I tried to analyze Vegas's actions. Did he actually have feelings for me, or was I thinking too highly of myself? He might just be amusing himself by messing with me.

"I ran out of there as soon as it was half past nine. I had way too much to drink. I needed to pee so bad," he said, half joking.

"That's your problem. I'm sleepy. Scram." I pushed him away and pulled the blanket over my head.

Vegas hugged me tightly before getting up. I heard his footsteps heading for the bathroom. I threw the blanket off of myself and sighed. After what Nop had said, I had to rethink my plans. *If he's playing games with me...am I winning or losing?*

Vegas was a liar. Two-faced. Heartless. He spent every day thinking of ways to one-up the Major Clan. His parents hadn't raised him right. He was a monster.

Vegas had been a menace since we were young. One time when we were kids, he pushed me down from a tree, and I cracked my head open—and he pinned the blame on Kinn! He even stole Kim's boyfriend in preschool. *At least Kim wasn't serious about that boy, heh.*

All the times Mr. Tankhun had cursed Vegas came rushing back to me. In all the years I'd spent with the Major Clan, I'd listened to countless stories about Vegas; of course, none of them were flattering.

As I got lost in thought, my eyes strayed over, and I noticed that Vegas had left his phone unattended on the vanity. My heart sped up in excitement. He must really have been sloshed to be this careless! Vegas almost never made mistakes, but he was probably drunk out of his mind right now. I hurriedly grabbed the phone, my hands shaking uncontrollably. I finally had a way out. I could call someone from the Major Clan.

Ah, fuck, he's got a password lock… I tried different passwords, including the same one as for his computer, from that fateful day, but it still wouldn't unlock. *Should I use the emergency-call option to phone the police? What should I do?*

Suddenly, Vegas's phone vibrated, and a LINE notification popped up:

Yimmy_Yummy: is P'Gus home? ^_^
Yimmy_Yummy: thank u for the present, i love it! but it's so expensive
Yimmy_Yummy: and…thank u for bringing out the cake. i'm happy it was u, P'Gus

"What are you doing?!" Vegas yelled, snatching his phone out of my hands.

I sat frozen for some time, my ears ringing. I hadn't even noticed that Vegas had come out of the bathroom until he'd snatched the phone from me.

"What were you trying to pull?" he pressed, glaring at me.

"...Actually, you didn't have to hurry back," I mumbled, my emotions all jumbled up. *What am I supposed to feel right now?*

Vegas furrowed his brow and looked at the screen before widening his eyes and smirking.

I walked back to the bed and sat down. "Was it someone special's birthday? ...You can tell me the truth."

"Hmmm...in a way, but what can I do? That was all the time you gave me," Vegas said cheerfully as he let himself fall onto the bed.

"The time *I* gave you?" I repeated. "Do I even have the right to order you around?"

Vegas reached out and hooked his hand around my waist, pulling me toward him. "You're so cute when you pout, you know that?" he said, wrapping his arms and legs around me.

"Let go of me, Vegas!"

"If you're jealous, just say so... You don't have to act out." Vegas poked his head over my shoulder to try to kiss my cheek, but I pushed him away.

"Why would I be jealous? Get off me." I kicked rapidly at Vegas with both legs, pushing him to the edge of the bed.

"Ow, Pete! That hurt!"

"I'm going to sleep!" I told him, curling up and yanking the blanket over my head.

Vegas sighed loudly. After a while, he settled back down next to me. Then, he snaked his arm under the blankets for another hug.

I peeled his arm off of me. "Let go! Get off of me!" I snapped.

"You're acting like some chick on her period," Vegas said, backing away from me. "I really can't keep up with your mood swings."

"That's your problem!" I snapped. I should've been happy that Vegas was getting fed up with my behavior...so why did I feel angry?

Vegas sighed. "Fine, fine, sleep. I'm tired. I don't want to argue with you." With that, he turned over, one hand reaching to turn off the lights. He fell asleep just like that, as if nothing had even happened.

I couldn't sleep no matter how hard I tried. I kept thinking about everything that had happened. What was I doing? Why were my feelings all over the place? I hated that I couldn't get a grip. It was like I was losing my mind. It was just a message on his phone—why had my chest tightened at the sight of it? What was wrong with me?

I was probably deluding myself that Vegas was into me. How could he be? What was so special about me? I wasn't his type when it came to looks—not to mention my personality. *Ha! I'm so stupid.*

I'd been overestimating myself when I thought I could make him stop being smitten with me. Someone like him probably never had those feelings for me in the first place. That had to be true because if I was in his shoes...if I liked someone, I wouldn't chain them up.

And when I acted crazy, he probably thought it was funny. He must've been secretly laughing at me, enjoying that I was going insane, proud that he could mess with my head.

I wasn't winning; I was about to lose...

I tossed and turned until the sun came up, then tossed and turned some more.

In the late morning, Vegas and I ate breakfast together. He was pretty badly hungover, complaining about a headache, but I didn't pay attention to him. I must have seemed quieter than normal; I couldn't escape the confusing thoughts swirling around in my head.

Vegas carefully touched my forehead with the back of his hand. "Are you sick?"

"No," I said evenly, twisting away.

"You haven't eaten much." He glanced at the half-eaten congee in my bowl. "I need to head to campus this afternoon. The club needs to borrow my guitar," Vegas told me, eyeing me carefully. He raised his eyebrows. "Oh, what do you want to eat? I'll pick it up on the way home."

"Don't want to eat," I said.

"...What's wrong?"

"Nothing."

"Pete...you can't act like this just because I came home ten minutes late."

Since last night, I kept asking myself if I was still sane: *What's wrong with me? What am I really feeling?* I'd felt irritated ever since he left yesterday, and my foul mood had bled into everything else. I really needed to reflect on myself.

Vegas sat up and turned to face me. "Okay, okay, I'm sorry. How many hours will you let me stay out today? What time do you want me back? Just tell me."

"That's your business," I said. With that, I got up from the sofa and spun around to go into the bathroom. I just didn't want to see his face. Why did he act like he cared about my feelings when I was just a toy for his amusement?

"You're just one of his stupid loyal dogs... And now, you're my chew toy!"

Vegas's words came rushing back to me. Even if he was acting kind enough right now to make me falter, the horrific things he'd done to me could never be erased.

"Vegas is messing with your head. He's making it so you can't bear to leave him."

Nop's words brought me back to my senses. *Yes! What am I doing?! Why was I calling Vegas so often? Did I rely too much on him? No, I only did it to mess with him...but why did it feel so real? Shit!*

What was Vegas planning? He was a liar. What did a monster like him need to care about or pay attention to me for? He acted like he was enamored with me, but I was starting to doubt it. Vegas's personality was so carefully curated that nothing seemed to be real—not even his feelings...

"Pete, I'm going out now. I'll hurry back." Vegas came over to where I sat at the edge of the bed. He reached out to cradle my face and kiss the top of my head like usual, but I got up to escape from him.

"Mm." I hummed my acknowledgment.

Vegas let out a long sigh at my reaction. "Be good while I'm gone," he said.

I didn't reply.

When Vegas walked out, I sat back down and stared at the chain looped around my wrist. That was answer enough, whether the things he did were real or fake... If he really loved me, he wouldn't keep me locked up like this. Nobody wanted to see the person they cared for mistreated, right? So Vegas's affections had to all be an act.

I needed to stop feeling everything I was feeling; stop the confusion, and stop the things I did unwittingly. I'd been isolated for so long that it felt like Vegas was the only person I had to rely on, even when he was the one who'd locked me up in the first place. I couldn't forget that. I had to stop feeling sorry for him. I had to stop being considerate of his tragic past—especially when I didn't know what was real and what was a lie.

While I wallowed in my thoughts, Vegas was gone for quite some time.

In the evening, Nop came in with his phone and held it out to me. I didn't need to guess to know who it was, but even if I didn't want to answer the call, I had to...

"Mm-hmm?"

"Have you eaten?" Vegas asked, sounding completely normal.

"No," I said.

"Good! Can you wait for me? I'll be back around eight. I'll bring you something to eat."

I didn't reply.

"Did you not miss me at all today? Heh. You haven't called all day! I've been waiting."

"If that's all, bye," I muttered.

"Pete..."

"P'Gus, are you done?" Another voice piped up in the background of the call: "I'm waiting... Ugh... P'Gus, it's poking into me. It hurts."

I frowned. *Poke? Hurt? What?* "...Ve—?"

"I've got to go. Bye," Vegas said, then hung up.

That same strange feeling flooded my mind once again. I handed the phone back to Nop, who was waiting on the sofa. I was trying to get things straight in my head. *Shit! I fucking hated feeling like this last night, but right now, everything is worse. It hurts more than ever.*

Nop touched my arm. "Pete...are you okay?"

"Nop...can you let me go?" I bit my lip, pleading with him.

"I don't have the key," he said. "Did he do anything to you?"

"...Why do you think he locked me up, Nop?"

"To...to get revenge on the Major Clan, probably... I really don't know. I feel sorry for you, Pete, I really do. But I'm afraid of death too. I don't know what crazy shit Vegas is pulling, playing house like you're his wife. Actually, I think he's already got someone, that N'Yim or something. The guy whose birthday party he went to last night. I'm confused too—I used to see that boy come around here, morning and night, but he hasn't been here lately. Probably because you're here. But I'm not sure. Hey, I've got to go now."

I went still with shock. I thought back to the video files of Vegas and his various bedmates, more certain about what I feared: In the end, he was only keeping me around to satisfy his urges. It was all just a game to him, some fun to pass the time.

I pulled at my chain again and again. I didn't know where I got the strength, but it was like a fire had been lit under me. I was so furious that I wanted to shatter the chain in my hands.

In the end, Vegas only saw me as another body: worthless. Nameless. Meaningless.

Just being chained up here was bad enough—why did I have to feel this way? I was only human; I had a heart, I still had feelings. I didn't want to feel like this. What was wrong with me?!

I was so wrapped up in trying to pull my wrist out from the chain that old, healed bruises began to reappear. Time became a blur as I felt my heart being wrenched out and stomped on. Vegas was playing with me; he never saw me as a person.

In the end, the only one caught up in this game was me.

I heard the glass door open, but I didn't care. I pulled against the chain like my life depended on it. The fire inside me crackled and burned; I drowned out everything else, focusing solely on breaking free.

"I'm back! I brought all the stuff you like, to say sorry for last night... Pete, what are you doing?!" Vegas came in, set his things down on the vanity, and immediately rushed over.

I sprang up from the edge of the bed. "Let me go!"

Vegas grabbed my wrist to inspect it, alarmed. "Pete, what's wrong with you?!"

As soon as I saw Vegas's face, my patience snapped. "Let me go! I'm not staying here any longer, asshole!"

"Pete! Why are you doing this?"

"Stop pretending, you liar!" I yelled in his face. "Don't try to act all nice with me!"

Vegas looked taken aback, gaping at me in confusion. "Pete, I didn't think you'd be so angry with me."

"I've always been angry with you, Vegas! Cut the bullshit and talk to me straight!"

"Pete! I already said I was sorry about coming home late."

"I'm not concerned with something that petty," I spat.

He and I stood there, glaring at each other.

"Then...don't tell me this is about the LINE message. I didn't think you'd care about that—that's my peer mentee at school," Vegas said seriously, trying to convince me with his eyes that what he said was the truth.

"Did you have fun?!"

"Pete! I don't think of him like that!" Vegas insisted.

"That's none of my business. If you want to *poke* him, that's your own fucking problem!" I was at my limit, so overwhelmed by everything that I wanted to just explode and be done with it all.

"What?! No! I was carrying a drum set, and I asked him to hold it for me. The metal stand was poking him, that's all." Vegas tried to grab my hand, but I twisted away.

"I told you, that's your own damn business! I'm not some dumb water buffalo, so don't treat me like one." I spat each word in his face.

"I've never thought of you like that."

"Then what is this?!" I held my chained-up arm up to his face. "You treat me like I'm less than human, like an animal in a cage waiting for its owner to bring it food and water... You told me I was a dog—is this enough for you?! Is this enough for you?!" I took another step forward, getting up in his face, no longer scared.

"Pete! I never thought of you like that. Can't you see? Everything I've done is in consideration of your feelings!" Vegas took a step back, his arms coming up as if to grab me.

"Hah... If you really cared, you wouldn't treat me like this! Let go of me!"

Vegas hugged me tightly, but I flailed against him, refusing to give up. I smashed my chained wrist into the wall, not caring about the pain.

"Pete... Stop it! Pete!" Vegas struggled to hold on to me and stop me from hitting my arm against the wall. My rage was out of control.

"Let me go! I won't stay here!"

"Pete! That's enough, Pete!" Vegas used all his strength to shove me toward the bed. I lost my footing and fell onto it.

"Let me go right now, Vegas! I won't obey you anymore! Even if I die today, I'm not afraid of you!"

Vegas wiped at his face, looking frustrated. "Pete! You have to calm down."

"Calm down? You want me to *calm down*?! I've put up with enough. You treat me like an animal. I won't put up with living like this anymore!" I stood up, the words spilling out of me. "I've got feelings, I've got a heart, and I've got people I love. Have you ever considered anyone else's feelings in your life, you selfish asshole?!"

"Pete... I didn't want you to feel this way. I only did this because I wanted you all to myself," Vegas said.

"Hah! Easy for you to say. But, of course, you've never been loved—you wouldn't understand what love is. Your father raised you to be selfish!"

When Vegas heard that sentence, he lifted his head to glare at me, his eyes flashing. He pushed me with so much force that I stumbled to the floor.

"What did you just say?" he hissed through gritted teeth.

Once he'd pushed me, my rage only grew stronger. I was so furious, I was close to tears, the lump in my throat tightening like a dam about to burst.

"Vegas!"

He must've seen something in my expression because his face suddenly softened. "Pete, does it hurt? I'm sorry," he said, his eyes full of guilt. He bent down and tried to help me up.

"You've done much worse. Go on! Punch me! Hit me however you like!" I pulled his wrist and used his hand to slap my own cheek, bringing it down hard as if to remind myself of how he'd hurt me.

He tried to pull his hand back. "I'm begging you...don't be like this!"

"Begging me... You're *begging* me? That day I begged you to stop, did you listen to me?!" I shoved him, making him stumble and fall. Warmth pricked around my eyes, and wet tears slid down my cheeks.

"I'm sorry... Pete, I'm truly sorry. Please, stay with me," Vegas begged, his voice shaking.

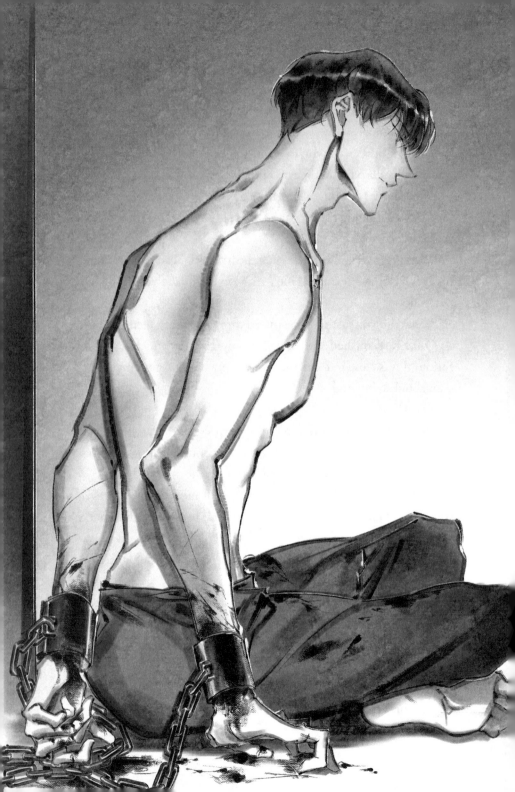

"I won't stay! Let me go!" I bashed my wrist against the floor again and again. No matter how hard Vegas tried to stop me, I flung him away without a care. I couldn't feel the pain at all anymore, even though I could feel the stickiness of the blood smearing all over my wrist and smell the acrid tang of it in the air.

"Stop it! I told you to stop!" Vegas grabbed hold of my wrist until I stopped thrashing. "I yield, Pete. I yield to you," Vegas said, tears streaming down his face. I'd never seen him cry before.

With reddened eyes, Vegas reached into his pocket and pulled out something. I could barely believe my eyes.

"Pete... I'm sorry," Vegas repeated. My heart raced as he brought the key to my wrist and unlocked the chain. In that moment, I was speechless, not sure if I was awake or dreaming.

"Stay with me. Promise me you won't leave me," Vegas sobbed, pulling me into a hug. I was barely holding on to my sanity. I didn't even know what I was supposed to do.

"I promise I won't hurt you again. I'm sorry for making you feel that way. I can't lose you, Pete. You're all I have. You've changed me. You make me want to be a better man. Don't leave me. Stay here with me, Pete. I like the version of myself I am when I'm with you... Stay with me, please!" Vegas's body shook as he held me tighter, as if he was afraid I would vanish into thin air.

I sat there in silence, frozen in place. I hadn't quite adjusted to reality yet. I couldn't even describe how I felt, the joy and sorrow bleeding together.

"Pete..." Vegas finally pulled away and stared at me longingly. He wiped the tears from my face with his finger. "I can't live without you... I love you." He slowly emphasized each word as if trying to convince me that everything he said was true. But I didn't need convincing; I could see it in his eyes.

Painful tears spilled out once again at the strange feeling welling up inside me. I was caught in an impossible situation, especially when confronted with the sincerity in Vegas's declaration of love. I hated the thoughts running through my head; my mind and heart clashed together in a battle of logic against emotion.

"Vegas..." My lips trembled, and the searing pain won out against what I felt inside. "I'm sorry..."

I grabbed the heavy chain on the floor and swung it at Vegas's head as hard as I could. The weight of it knocked him out instantly. He collapsed onto the floor, blood seeping from his head.

"I'm sorry," I sobbed when I saw Vegas crumpled on the floor, completely still. I felt my anguish with stunning clarity; I didn't feel happy at all. I was a wreck over my own actions, but what I wanted more than anything was freedom.

The door swung open, and Nop burst in. "Pete! What are you doing?!"

I stood up from the floor, blood dripping down my wrist. "Nop... please let me go," I pleaded with him, my voice shaking. My tears hadn't even dried yet.

Nop stood there, shocked at what he saw.

"Think of it as feeling sorry for me one last time," I said, biting my lip.

Nop gave me an uneasy look and turned around. "Do what you need to do. Make it quick. I'll give you one minute, but after that, I need to do my duty."

At that, I ran to the wardrobe, grabbing a shirt without looking. It was one of Vegas's white shirts. I threw it on hastily, but I didn't forget to grab Vegas's wallet to shamelessly pull out a thousand-baht note. Then I headed straight for the balcony and threw the door wide open.

"Nop...look after him for me," I said.

I looked left and right before steeling myself and jumping down. I ran toward the back of the house to climb the wall.

When my feet touched the ground outside the property, I scanned my surroundings again. I half walked, half jogged to the main road without a single thought of turning back to look at the house.

I waved down a taxi and jumped in, giving the driver the address to the Major Clan's house. The driver looked at me strangely—after all, I was dressed in a white shirt stained with blood, and I wasn't wearing any shoes. I'd run out of there barefoot, without feeling any pain in my feet.

I leaned back against the seat, using my shirt to dab at the blood on my wrist. I still couldn't deal with my feelings. I finally had the freedom I'd longed for, but right now, the joy of escape was being replaced by worry for Vegas. What would happen to him after this?

I'm sorry, Vegas, but I can't live like that. I had my family waiting for me. He couldn't keep me locked up forever, and I didn't want my feelings to get any deeper. I knew that some fraction of me still felt something for Vegas, but Nop's words had reminded me of the horrible things Vegas had done to me. That was what woke me up and reminded me that I needed to escape...

"This house right here," I said, paying the driver and getting out. I felt so relieved to be standing here again, heading for the house I'd been away from for so long.

As I slowly approached the front gate, I started coughing. I didn't know what they were burning, but a thick blanket of smoke hung in the air. "What the hell is all this smoke?"

I hadn't been outside in so long. My eyes stung, and I rubbed at my face with my bloodied hand. *Shit! I've got blood on my face! I'm so fucking stupid.*

I started coughing again. "Young Master…"

Argh! I can't see anything. Is the house going up in flames? Do I have to call the fire department? I slowly made my way forward, straining to see anything through the smoke. I spotted a faint outline of what looked like Mr. Tankhun in the distance, so in my excitement, I called out for him:

"Young Master…"

37

Topsy-Turvy

PORSCHE

"Peeeeete!" Tankhun wailed, loud enough for the whole house to hear as smoke filled the sky.

After Pete's cremation last night, Tankhun had barely been able to stand. He'd just kept crying and shouting Pete's name in front of the crematorium. I had felt a twinge of sympathy at the sight; Khun and Pete were close—they'd basically lived together for years—so I could understand how he felt. Of course he'd have a hard time accepting that this was goodbye forever, especially when we just saw Pete's grandparents off on their plane back to Chumphon last night. Tankhun had already promised to personally bring Pete's ashes back to their island for the loi angkarn,[20] but we'd have to wait to fly over until after the ceremony was completed tomorrow morning.

"I forgot to send you the house and car keys yesterday. Here."

The metal can was back, set up in front of the house. There was even a second can this time. It was another evening of Khun burning joss-paper offerings for Pete; he was still afraid Pete wouldn't have everything he needed in the afterlife.

---

20 *The morning after cremation, the deceased's ashes are gathered, then taken for loi angkarn, or the ceremonial scattering of the ashes over water, either at sea or a major river.*

"Why are you burning offerings today too?" Mr. Korn said wearily. "He's at peace now—why are you still mourning?"

"Well, if he doesn't have a key, how is he supposed to get inside his house?!" Tankhun snapped back. His father could only shake his head.

By now, only Khun, Arm, and Pol were left standing in front of the fire. Everyone else, including me, was watching from the front door.

Kinn threw his arm over my shoulder. "I've sent people to investigate. I don't believe he's dead."

"Who did you send? You're sending them to their deaths," I half joked. Even though I still had a lot to think about when it came to Kinn, I tried to act as normal as I could.

This afternoon, I'd talked to Uncle Thee, and the things he told me made me doubt everything I thought I knew.

"I had P'Chan pick someone," Kinn said, gently petting my hair. "He's been checking the security cameras along Pete's route to recover their data."

I wasn't *fully* convinced the body was Pete's, not until the DNA results came back, but...

"Your brother's really going overboard. If Pete's really alive, then... I can't imagine it. Heh." I glanced at Tankhun's tearstained face. He was still burning joss paper; worse still, he'd gathered over fifty bodyguards to stand vigil in a row next to the metal cans.

"Here... Southern curry paste. I had Auntie Prik make some this morning. I know you like her cooking. Here!"

Whoosh! The fire grew, and the fumes from the chili, garlic, and other assorted spices stung our eyes and noses. Kinn, Kim, Chay, and I—even Mr. Korn, P'Chan, and the other gathered guards—all hacked and wheezed and had to cover our noses and mouths with our black shirts, bending down to try to escape the smoke. *Bastard! Who the hell burns spices for the dead?! Fucking Tankhun!*

Khun coughed and squeezed his eyes shut, waving the smoke away as he shouted, "Enjoy your Southern curry...! And here's gas for your car..."

"Wait, wait, Khun! You can't burn gasoline!" Mr. Korn immediately protested.

"Whyyy?" Khun asked, still coughing. "Why, Father? How will Pete drive his car, huh?"

And before Mr. Korn could reply, Khun threw the gasoline onto the fire.

Foom! The flames exploded, nearly scorching the house. We all dashed inside to put the front door between us and the smoke, which was much thicker than before. *Damn it, Tankhun, you asshat! Were you planning on cremating* us *with Pete?*

"Somebody remove him from my house!" Mr. Korn snapped in exasperation. Smoke hung thickly in the air; from the look of things, it wouldn't be long until we all choked to death.

"What's that? What else are you trying to do?!" Kim shouted, his hand coming up to cradle Chay's head against his shirt. My little brother was coughing so much that it looked like he was going to puke.

Khun walked up to the other metal can. "Hah! I'll have my revenge," he said, coughing. "The Minor Clan...I'll make them all pay!"

Both Arm and Pol were covered in black soot, tasked with fanning the flames.

"Two pounds of chili peppers...and salt, pour it all in... Are you guys ready?" Tankhun turned to the sneezing and coughing guards. It finally clicked for me when he lit the fire in the other metal can to burn the salt and chili peppers[21]—he'd specifically set the second fire to curse the Minor Clan. *Argh! I can't believe you!*

"Porsche, can we go wait upstairs in our room?" Kinn pulled me toward his chest and tried to use his shirt to cover my face. "There's so much smoke."

Fucking hell! Am I going to die?

"Throw the chilis in. I'll curse the Minor Clan so hard, they won't be able to escape hell to be reborn. More, Arm, more!"

I felt so sorry for Arm and Pol. They had tears streaming down their faces from the fumes, but what could they do? Khun was their boss, and they had to follow orders.

Tankhun glared with a vengeance at the chili peppers being poured into the can. He gritted his teeth and clenched his fists, looking like a soap-opera villain. "All right, all of you—all together now!" *What? What's he doing now?*

Khun turned to the bodyguards behind him, who hesitantly raised their fists and started shouting in unison:

"Curse the Minor Clan! Destroy the Minor Clan!"

The booming chorus left me, Kinn, Kim, and Chay completely speechless. Even Mr. Korn, P'Chan, and the maids were shocked. I had no words.

"Louder! I said louder…! Pol, more salt!" Tankhun encouraged his men between his coughing fits.

"Curse the Minor Clan! Destroy the Minor Clan!"

"I need to lie down," Mr. Korn muttered in disbelief. He rubbed at his temples, then turned around and disappeared inside. P'Chan followed after him expressionlessly but made sure to tell the maids to clean up the ashes and soot.

"Good! Just like that… *Ack*," Tankhun coughed.

---

21 *Burning chili peppers and salt together is a folk method to place a curse on someone.*

"Curse the Minor Clan! Destroy the Minor Clan!"

"Louder, so that their karma catches up to them and the curse can work faster! Louder!"

"Curse the Minor Clan! Destroy the Minor Clan!"

Kinn couldn't take it anymore. "En...enough! Stop!" he raised his voice above the racket and pulled me behind him, gearing up to scold every man looking at him dejectedly.

"Curse—"

"What the hell do you think you're doing?!" Kinn snarled at the bodyguards. "What's this nonsense?! Don't you all have anything better to do?"

One of them spoke up hesitantly: "Th-the young master ordered it, Mr. Kinn."

"And you, Khun, instead of helping sort things out at the company—which, by the way, is in complete chaos—what the fuck have you been doing?"

"I'm helping the family, Kinn!" Khun shouted. "You shut up!"

"Can't you find another way? Are you crazy?" Kinn put his hands on his hips in exasperation. He probably couldn't stand to see his older brother acting so stupid.

"You really have to ask?" I said, still dazed from the smoke.

"Well, if we can't get the Minor Clan with evidence, doing it this way is our only choice!" Khun insisted. "Haven't you heard the saying? 'If you can't get it with cunning, get it with tricks.'"

I just wanted to give Pol and Arm a bath. They looked particularly sooty and scruffy, like they'd just rolled around in the dirt. I couldn't bear to look at them.

"You've been ruminating over him too much. If you're not careful, he's going to come haunt you," said Kim. He used his shirt to dab at

Chay's face, which had begun to drip tears and snot. The smoke and fumes really did sting.

"I already said that if Pete wants to visit, then he can go visit Pol and Arm over there... He'll tell them what he wants, and I'll sort it out for him."

Pol and Arm quickly shook their heads. I was starting to get annoyed too. If Khun wasn't Kinn's brother, I would've punched him right in his stupid face.

A distinctively burnt smell still clung to the house; I had no idea how we were all going to sleep tonight. *And think of the environment! I'm going to call the Ministry of Natural Resources on you for contributing to climate change, bastard!*

"You should be careful," Kim warned his brother. "Ghosts come back to the people who miss them. And the first seven days after death is when they retrace their steps, so he'll return to the places he feels attached to! Especially people who died unnatural deaths—those kinds of ghosts are especially fierce. Maybe Pete doesn't even realize he's dead. He'll go about his daily routine like..." He trailed off, lowering his voice.

As I followed his train of thought, I reached out to grab Kinn's shirt. *Fuck! I'm scared of ghosts! Why does he have to bring that up?!*

"He usually comes and goes by your room, so right now, his ghost might be walking around there... He'll head to the bathroom, then prepare your pajamas... Then around ten p.m., he'll watch a TV series with you..." Kim giggled. "Then, the routine will repeat."

"Enough, Kim! You've been listening to too many spooky podcasts!" Chay elbowed Kim, but his face was starting to go as pale as mine was, and he kept looking around nervously.

However, the person who looked the most frightened was Tankhun. "Is that true...?"

"Of course it's true. You don't have to worry about Pete having enough to eat or drink in the afterlife because, as long as his death is still a mystery, he'll still be wandering our mortal realm. Ha ha ha!" Kim burst out laughing.

I hugged Kinn's waist. The more I thought about it, the more clearly I could picture it. The house had been quiet for the last few days as our grief lingered; everything was shrouded in an eerie silence. With the wispy smoke and the sound of dogs barking in the distance, I was starting to get goosebumps.

"Kim, stop talking." Kinn turned to scold his younger brother. "Look at Porsche, you've scared him enough." But Kim just kept laughing uproariously.

"Fine, fine, we can do this again tomorrow when it's light out," Khun conceded. "Pack it up. Arm, you're sleeping in my room tonight."

Arm, who was putting out the fires in the metal cans, looked uneasy, like he wanted to refuse the order. We helped clear away the smoke and were about to go back inside, when we heard a sniffling voice:

"Young Master…"

"What?" Khun turned to Pol, who was putting away the bag of coals.

"Yes?" Pol asked, perplexed.

The rest of us were confused too. Pol hadn't said anything. *What's wrong with Tankhun? Is he spooked? High on the smoke? Crazy? Well, he's already crazy…*

"You called for me," Khun said.

Kinn stroked my arm. "It's probably nothing…"

"I didn't say anything," Pol said.

"Huh… What did you want, Arm?" Khun switched targets.

Arm quickly shook his head. "Nothing. I'm putting out the fire over here."

"Then, you guys..." Before Khun could finish asking, the other bodyguards all waved their arms as if to say it wasn't them. In that moment, the voice spoke up again:

"Young Master..."

This time, we all went still—everyone had heard the voice. I plastered myself against Kinn's back. My legs went stiff, and my heart skipped a beat. *No, no... I must've misheard.*

"What? Who's calling for me?!" Tankhun yelled. I saw him gulp in fear, but he kept his head high as he looked left and right, searching for the source of the voice.

"Young Master, i-it's...me," came a faint, shaky voice, echoing.

This time, I hugged Kinn tightly. I didn't care if anyone saw. Kinn hugged me back, his eyes darting around. He'd gone pale now too.

"Kiiiim...did you hear that?!" Chay burrowed his head into Kim's shirt, his hands clasped in a fearful wai.

"Who is it?! Who's calling for me?" Tankhun was still acting brave, the crazy motherfucker. He craned his neck. "Who's over there?"

Khun held one hand over his eyes and squinted at the front gate. The bodyguards, including Pol and Arm, retreated into a huddle on the front steps, staring at the gates in fear.

"Young Master...can you see me?" There was a faint shadow there, waving at us. The figure and voice made my breath catch. "Over here."

Kinn, Kim, Chay, and I backed away, ready to run.

"Nont, is that you? What the hell are you doing over there?" Khun said.

I don't know if Khun's worldview is so optimistic that he isn't afraid, or if he's so damn crazy that his brain can't process anything.

"I'm over here!" Nont raised his hand, moving to stand behind Kim.

"Argh, then is that Jess? Oh, you all really love me, huh? What's everyone so afraid of? That's Jess," Khun insisted, hands on his hips as he scolded the bodyguards backing away from him.

"P'Jess has been on sick leave since this afternoon, Young Master," Pol told him, starting to back away as well.

"Young Master..." came the faraway voice.

"Who's there?! Come out!"

"Why did you have to call him over?" Kim held on to Chay, face twisting as he looked around.

"Young Master, help me..."

No matter how scared everyone was, we stared at the scene in front of us, all eyes locking onto the source of the voice. Even if I was so terrified that my legs shook, I still wanted to know who it was.

When the tall, shadowy figure came closer, we were all shaken to the core: *That's definitely Pete!* He slowly inched forward, step by step, blood covering his face and the white shirt he wore. My mind went blank, a chill went down my spine, and...

"Aaaaahh!"

We all scrambled to get inside. I shrieked and jumped onto Kinn, hooking my legs around his waist.

"Wah! Pete! *Sabbe satta, all the creatures of this earth*[22]—HELP!" Tankhun stood, shaking, with his hands clasped, all alone in front of the house as the rest of us ran for our lives. I was still clinging to Kinn.

---

22 An abbreviated Chant of Mettā, a Buddhist chant.

"Get inside!" Kim shouted at Khun, hugging Chay tight.

Tankhun didn't move a muscle, still rambling, "Help...m-me, my legs won't move! Help! *Sabbe sa*— What's the rest of the chant?!" He glanced over at the slowly approaching Pete and shuddered.

"Khun! Porsche, get off of me. I'll go drag him in." Kinn tried to peel my legs off of his body, but I quickly shook my head.

"No! Don't go! What if Pete haunts you to death? What'll I do?" I buried my face into Kinn's shoulder and held on tighter. He carried me on his back and tried to bend down to deposit me on the floor.

"Pete! Go someplace else you like, and I promise I'll make merit for you!" Kim shouted at the gate. Both he and Chay had their hands clasped together.

"But I like it here... Ouch...it hurts!" Pete looked down at his wrist, which had been dripping blood the entire way. "Young Master? Why are you so afraid? What's wrong with everyone?"

"Don't scare me like this! Help! I'm gonna piss my pants!" Khun shouted at the top of his lungs.

"Young Master, I'll take you to the bathroom. Let's go," Pete said, about to reach Khun. The closer he got, the harder Khun trembled.

"He must not know he's dead." Kim turned to Kinn, who'd finally succeeded in peeling my arms and legs off of him.

"Wait here," Kinn told me. "I'll go help Khun first."

I stayed slumped on the floor, my limbs limp and my mind a muddle. The scene in front of me was so terrifying that I thought I might pass out. I'd never thought I'd see a ghost with my own two eyes. I couldn't believe this shit was happening to me!

"Kinn, don't go!" I tried to reach out to Kinn, but he had already run off to help Khun, whose chanting had progressed into loud wails.

"Mr. Kinn, I'm back," Pete said, moving toward Kinn.

Everyone inside started yelling.

"Khun, come on!" Kinn tugged at his brother's wrist to pull him along. Just as Kinn was about to yank his wobbly-legged older brother off the ground, Pete stared at them like he was upset by what he saw.

"Mr. Kinn, Young Master? I'm back now," he said.

"Pete…we'll make merit for you." Kinn was pale as he pulled Khun into his arms. Khun looked like he'd gone completely nuts; he had his hands clasped together, and he was mumbling complete nonsense.

Pete looked confused. "What are you talking about?"

"Tell him, Kinn! He doesn't know!" Kim yelled. I glared at him.

"Why don't *you* tell him?!" I yelled back. *Why the hell are you telling Kinn to do it? If he gets haunted to death, I'm going to kill you, Kim! And don't think I don't see how you've been hugging my little brother and hiding behind Nont!*

"Kinn's luck is better than mine! Tell him, Kinn!"

"Pete," Kinn said, hauling Khun backward toward the house. "You're dead. Be at peace."

"Really? I'm dead?" Pete touched his own face and began to inspect himself.

"Pete, we love you, but you don't have to appear so clearly before us!" Arm shouted, giving Pete a wai.

"Wait! When did I die?" Pete furrowed his brow, muttering something to himself. "Vegas wouldn't have killed me… Or was I already dead, and Vegas wouldn't let me out…? What do I do?" He seemed to be lost in thought.

I saw Kinn pause before he grabbed Khun and ran inside, throwing Khun to a waiting Kim. The bodyguards stuffed a statue of Buddha into Khun's hands as he mumbled incoherent chants.

Kinn walked back outside, and I called after him, "Kinn, where are you going? Kinn!"

"Mr. Kinn, I'm not dead yet... I just escaped...from the Minor Clan," Pete sighed. With every step Kinn took, the men inside the house yelled out.

"Argh! Kinn! I told you to get inside!" I shouted. No matter how much I wanted to get up and run over to grab my lover's hand, I couldn't do it; it was like my body refused to respond.

"Pete! We just cremated you today, and you're saying—" Kinn left a bit of distance between himself and Pete. He put on a brave face, but he was clearly afraid as he cautiously stared at the man in front of him.

"Cremated me? Today?" Pete pointed at himself. Kinn slowly nodded. He still looked like he had questions, but his fearful expression began to calm.

"Really? But I woke up normally today. I wouldn't really call it waking up because I barely slept, but I ate rice soup in the morning and Vegas said he was going out... Am I dead? Then who was Vegas talking to?" Pete still sounded lost. I could barely make sense of what he was saying.

Kinn looked Pete up and down incredulously. "Pete...you're really here?"

"Pretty sure I'm not dead... I just escaped from the Minor Clan's house, Mr. Kinn. Here, you can touch me to see if I'm solid," he said, offering his arm to Kinn.

"Don't do it, Kinn!" Kim shouted. "You're gonna get haunted! The ghost is trying to trick you!"

"*Ithipiso... Namo tassa... Namo,*" Khun's glassy-eyed chanting cut in.

"Pete... Shit!" Before I could yell out a warning to Kinn, he reached out to grab Pete's arm. His expression immediately changed into one of relief.

"Kinn!" I cried out in alarm.

"Are you all right? I'm sorry, I'm sorry, I'm so sorry," Kinn babbled. He grabbed Pete's wrist and dabbed at the blood there with his own shirt.

Pete showed a relieved smile. "Mr. Kinn... I'm fine."

"I thought I would carry that guilt for the rest of my life... Shit! Thank you for coming back." Kinn looked like a great weight had been lifted off his shoulders. A faint smile appeared on his face.

"Kinn, you're getting haunted," Kim insisted.

Kinn turned around to happily shout, "Everyone! Pete's not dead!"

"Pete!"

Pol, Arm, Nont, and the rest swarmed around Pete, overjoyed.

"Dead, dead, we're dead!" Kim groaned. "Everyone's getting haunted."

"Stop trying to stir up trouble, Kim," said Chay. "Are you asking for a kick? You can see that Pete's not a ghost." He broke away from Kim and ran over to Pete.

I finally came to my senses. If Pete really was a ghost, he probably wouldn't be smiling and talking with us and letting us hug him. *Even if he does look like a ghost. He's covered in blood!*

Chay led Pete inside with Kinn following behind them. I couldn't really explain how I felt—I'd gone from being so scared I couldn't lift a finger to being utterly relieved. My heart was finally put at ease, and so was Kinn's.

"Porsche?" Pete said.

I pushed myself upright and threw my arms around him.

"Fuck! Where were you?!" I hugged Pete tightly, my heart racing in excitement. The flicker of hope that had gone out suddenly shone brightly again.

"I missed you so fucking much," Pete said, hugging me back.

"I was so scared, you bastard! Are you okay?" I pulled away to inspect him.

"I..."

"*Namo tassa...*" Khun chanted.

"Before everyone gets all sappy, come take a look at this guy. His spirit's probably left for the next world already. '*Namo*'... what? Is it '*tassa*'?" Kim laughed and sat down next to Khun, pretending to pray with him.

"Go to him. Go," I told Pete, patting him on the shoulder. He walked over to Tankhun and carefully squatted down in front of him.

Tears spilled down Khun's cheeks. "*Namo...*"

"Young Master...I'm not dead." Pete took the Buddha statue from Khun's lap and placed it next to him. Khun froze, then looked up at Pete with watery eyes.

"Pete! Pete!" Khun bawled, throwing himself at him.

"I'm here now, Young Master," Pete said.

Khun kept holding on as Pete let out a long sigh. Pete looked quite relieved to be hugging Khun.

"I was so afraid... I thought I'd never see you again," Khun managed to say through his sobs and sniffles.

"I'm here now," Pete said, stroking Khun's back in soothing motions. Khun's whole body shuddered with the force of his sobs.

"You're really back, right?" Khun wailed. "Don't leave me again... I won't let you!"

"Who's making all this noise?!" Mr. Korn demanded as he strode out of his office. He was momentarily taken aback at the sight of the newcomer, but in the end, he just let out a sigh. "Pete! When did you get here? You almost gave me a heart attack," he said, smiling.

Pete pulled away from Tankhun to greet Mr. Korn with a wai. "Still alive, sir."

"Come, let's have a seat and talk properly. And will someone hurry up and get rid of this burnt smell?" Mr. Korn chased everyone else away. The smoke had cleared up a fair bit, but the odor still lingered in the house.

We all gathered in the foyer—Kinn and me, Khun, Kim, Chay, Mr. Korn, P'Chan, Pol, and Arm. Everyone else split up to do their jobs, some procuring fans and air fresheners, others putting out the fires in the metal cans.

"Here... Your ashes are still warm. We cremated you earlier this evening." Khun smiled and handed the urn to Pete, who received it with a confused expression. "And this is your picture. I picked it out myself..." Khun handed him the memorial photo, complete with Pete's date of death.

Pete set both down on the coffee table. "So, who did you cremate?"

Khun stared at the urn curiously. "You're right... Who is this? We put on such a big funeral; I spared no expense—a hundred grand per day—we sure fed the guests well!"

"Ahh... Don't tell me the funeral you held was for *me* and not Uncle Pong?" Pete asked. His question left everyone confused. He gritted his teeth and muttered under his breath, "Vegas, you tricked me..."

"You knew about the funeral?" Kinn asked from his seat opposite Pete.

Pete was silent for a moment before he answered, "Yes."

Kinn eyed him in surprise.

"Who's Uncle Pong?" Khun asked.

"It's nothing..."

"Can you believe it?" Kim said, smiling. "We had fish maw soup, Buddha Jumps Over the Wall,[23] imported Japanese scallops... The guests were really impressed."

Pete's eyes went wide in surprise. "You did all of that?"

"Yeah, and that's not all," Khun said with a nervous laugh. He scratched his chin awkwardly before his expression turned serious. "We just saw your grandparents off on their flight back."

"Grandpa and Grandma know about this? No, no, no, no! What do we do? Won't they be shocked?" Pete was freaking out like this was the end of the world.

Mr. Korn sighed. "Kinn, deal with his grandparents," he ordered.

Kinn nodded. "I'll sort it out myself, Pete. Though I don't think you should call them right away. I'll slowly broach the subject to them tomorrow morning. If you call them now with no warning, they might not be able to handle it."

Everyone agreed. If Pete called them now, his grandparents might drop dead from the shock!

"Grandpa and Grandma... By now, they'll..."

"I'll take responsibility for everything that has happened," Kinn said quickly, trying to put Pete at ease. "Don't worry."

If I were Pete's grandparents, I'd hop on the next flight to Bangkok, grab the biggest stick I could find, and beat the ever-loving shit out of these Major Clan fuckwits. They literally just finished cremating their grandson, and now you want to call and say, 'Oops, just

---

23 A variety of shark fin soup known for its decadent ingredients. The name comes from the idea that it's so tempting, even the Buddha, a vegetarian, would leap over the wall of a temple to try it.

kidding! Pete's not actually dead!' Hell, I want to beat their stupid asses myself!

"I'll have to leave that to you, Mr. Kinn," Pete said. "So why did everyone think I was dead?" he asked as Pol and Arm helped tend to his injuries. They wiped away all the blood and patched up the wound on his wrist, which looked kind of suspicious. Kinn must have felt the same way because he stared straight at it with wide eyes.

"It's all because of P'Chan... It's P'Chan's fault," Khun said.

P'Chan pointed at himself. "Me?"

"Yes. P'Chan said they found a corpse on the outskirts of the Minor Clan's territory," Khun said, vexed. "The body had the Major Clan's crest in his wallet, a business card with your name on it, and he wore a stainless-steel ring on his middle finger, like you."

"Huh? Really...? Hmm..." Pete glanced at his left hand, currently devoid of any ring. "Was it Thom?"

Pete's statement intrigued us all: "Huh?"

"Thom. He quit last month...said he was going to work for another company. When he quit, I gave him my card so he could call if he had any problems..."

"Thom...Thom... Oh! Thom, who used to be your lackey for a while?" Khun recalled. Pete nodded.

"That's right!" said Arm, seeming to slowly remember. "Thom used to say, 'Pete is so cool, Pete is so handsome.' Pete was his idol, remember? He wore a ring like you."

"Uh-huh," said Pete. "I bought a ring while we were out one day, and he bought one to copy me. I already stopped wearing mine because it was so itchy."

"What...? Why didn't you tell me?! Arm!" Khun pointed an accusing finger at Arm.

"I really didn't think of it until now," Arm said.

"So this is all a big misunderstanding?" Mr. Korn asked, eyebrows raised.

Pete looked down at the urn sadly. "Oh... So this is really Thom?"

"Enough, enough. Don't jump to conclusions yet," Mr. Korn said. "We'll have Chan investigate first to make sure it's not someone else. That way, there won't be any further issues."

"I'll personally check if there's any hidden agenda behind his death," P'Chan said. "If it really is Thom, we need to be certain this was not a targeted attack on the clan."

"I nearly cried myself to death," Khun muttered darkly.

"He was probably taken out by a rival of his new company," Kim suggested. "Don't think about it too much, Pete. It's a good thing that nothing happened to you."

"Think of it this way—you've suffered for your karma, and now you're done with it, P'Pete," Chay said, helping Pol dress Pete's wounds with cotton gauze.

"And the Minor Clan...what did they do to you?" Kinn asked, staring searchingly at Pete. He looked like he still had a multitude of questions—and there seemed to be something he was too afraid to ask. When Pete noticed how intently Kinn was looking at him, he tugged the collar of his shirt shut and avoided his gaze.

I could tell that something was off. Pete had no other marks or signs of a beating except for the wound on his left wrist and the faint marks on his neck and chest. I didn't want to say for certain that they were...

"Vegas," Khun said. "It was Vegas, right? What did he do to you—tell me! I'll *take care* of him personally." He clenched his fists and banged them on the table, his eyes determined and flashing with rage.

"Just let him be," Pete mumbled meekly. "I'm fine."

"What did he do?! Lock you up? Did he starve you?" Tankhun asked. "Actually...you look like you've gotten fatter. You're looking kinda chubby."

I agreed with Tankhun there. On the outside, Pete looked pretty healthy, if neater and cleaner than normal. He didn't even have his typical stubble.

"It's... I..." Pete stammered, looking pretty damn awkward about it all.

"*Hmph!* I'll kidnap Macau! Or Vegas, too, and torture them like he tortured you, how's that? Those monsters!" Khun spat, anger laced in every word, ready to act as Pete's vengeful shadow.

"All right, it's getting late," Mr Korn cut in. "Let Pete get some rest. We can discuss what steps we'll take tomorrow." I had to agree with Mr. Korn. Pete looked miserable; his eyes were gloomy, and he clearly had a lot on his mind.

"Pete, do you want to go to the hospital?" Kinn asked. "I'll take you."

"No, Mr. Kinn. I'm fine, really," Pete insisted.

Khun squeezed himself between Pete and Arm and clung to them both. "Come sleep in my room tonight, yeah? I'm scared I'll wake up and you'll have disappeared again, Pete!"

Pete gently patted Khun's hand. "But I'm back now."

"I don't know why, but I want you with me. Pol and Arm too," Tankhun whined, showing his spoiled side. Everyone else shook their heads at his bratty behavior.

It was Mr. Korn who pulled Khun away from Pete and urged him up to his bedroom. "Khun! Let Pete rest! Stop making trouble," he said. "Go. You're all dismissed."

"As for this urn...I'll have to ask you to deal with this, Arm," Kinn said. "For now, we can put it in the Buddha room."[24]

Kinn grabbed my hand, tugging me away from the foyer. I felt lighter than I'd ever felt before; the painful images that had overlapped with the day I lost my parents now slowly faded. In my heart, a hope that I'd never dared to hope for made itself known. Although I knew there would be no miracles for my parents like there had been with Pete, it was like I'd finally unlocked something in my heart. Things were coming to light that I'd kept hidden in the dark for so long.

I slowly sat down on the bed and carefully dragged my fingers through my hair. After going through so much misery, I needed answers about one more tragedy...the death of my parents.

I pulled out a photo from my wallet. It was the one Uncle Thee had stuffed into my hand this afternoon after all those ambiguous words...

[EARLIER]

"Oh... How's it going, nephew?"

"Uncle Thee..." I froze at the sight of a man I hadn't seen for a long, long time: Uncle Thee, my only remaining relative besides my little brother.

Uncle Thee was skin and bones, dirty and ragged; there was no trace of the clean-cut businessman he once was.

"Why did you break into my house, Uncle?" I demanded, lowering the stick in my hand.

"You changed the locks. I was hoping to find a place to rest, but I couldn't get in, so I had to break open the door," he said, not at all apologetically.

---

24 Thai Buddhists commonly keep an altar with the Buddha's statue inside the house, to which residents may pray, light incense, and make offerings. If a home is particularly religious—or just particularly large, like the Theerapanyakul family home—there may be an entire room dedicated to this.

"And why are you here, Uncle?" Chay asked, eyeing Uncle Thee warily.

"Aww…Chay, can't I miss the two of you…? By the way, are you two not staying here anymore? Did you move out or sell it? There's nothing left."

"What else do you want, Uncle? There's been nothing left here for ages," I said, staring at him in disgust.

"Heh… Of course. You already packed everything up to go live with the Major Clan. Both brothers—your lives must be quite comfortable. Mr. Korn treats you well, huh? Or, no, I should say Kinn and Kim treat you well… But, that's to be expected, since you've already sold your bodies to them…"

I scowled at Uncle Thee. He must've been keeping tabs on us the entire time he'd been gone—otherwise, how would he know all this?

"Uncle! What are you saying?!" Chay tried to lunge at Uncle Thee, but I held him back.

"Oh, did that hit a nerve? Your father and mother would be so proud. Both brothers know what's good for them, and they'll do whatever it takes to survive another day. You're doing all right for yourselves, huh? If you're gonna bag one, you might as well bag a rich one," Uncle Thee sneered.

I clenched my fists and took a deep breath to calm myself. "Still better than you, Uncle, stealing everything you can from us, even the last inheritance we had left!" My voice shook with rage. "You dare step foot in this place? Aren't you ashamed?!"

Uncle Thee rolled his eyes. "What? Kinn still hasn't told you…? I wonder why," he said with a mocking smile. He was clearly enjoying riling me up.

"What the hell are you talking about?" I demanded.

"You were never a smart kid, but I didn't think you were *this* stupid," he said, poking my forehead with his finger. I shook him off. "Be careful. The Major Clan will mess with your head… Last time, they gave me a huge wad of cash to act out a big scene in front of you, to trick you into believing I could take your father's last possession…"

My mind swam as my frustration grew. Fed up, I yanked Uncle Thee forward by his collar. "What are you saying?! Spit it out!"

"Tell your Major Clan buddies that my money's run out. Whatever secrets they want me to keep, they better quickly send me some cash, or I'll air *all* their dirty laundry." Uncle Thee bumped my shoulder on his way down the stairs, heading for the door.

My head was still reeling with unanswered questions; doubt began to creep into my mind. Even Chay looked confused and taken aback.

I grabbed Uncle Thee's arm. "Wait! What do you mean by that?" I asked.

He turned to face me with a sly grin. "Here! Give my regards to Korn… And if you want to know more, transfer some money to your dear old uncle. Five hundred thousand baht—no, you've got more now… A million, then. I promise I'll tell you everything: the circumstances of your parents' deaths and the sins of the Major Clan. It'll really make your skin crawl." He stuffed some sort of photo into my hand, and, with that, he hurried out of the house.

I carefully unfolded the scrunched-up photograph. I bit my lip, my heart plummeting to my feet as I took a closer look. This old photo was…

"Hia, that's Mr. Korn with our parents… And the child he's holding…" Chay looked at the photo and slowly turned to me.

The child in Mr. Korn's arms...was me.

[THE PRESENT]

"My love... Hey... My love!"

Kinn's voice startled me out of my thoughts. I quickly stuffed the photo back into my wallet.

"What were you daydreaming about, hmm?" Kinn flopped onto the bed and encircled his arms around my waist from behind me, pulling me into his embrace.

"You've finished showering?" I asked stupidly, when I could clearly see that Kinn was in his pajamas.

"Mm... What are you thinking about?" Kinn tugged me down so I was lying flat on my back.

"Nothing. Just glad Pete's back," I said, even if it was only a half truth.

"It's such a relief... When I saw Pete's grandparents, I felt so guilty. But now I'm so damn relieved." Kinn rolled onto his side and cuddled up closer to me, draping his arms and legs over me.

"It's all good now. My friend isn't dead, and...I don't want you to be so stressed. I'm worried about you," I said, staring into Kinn's eyes. He propped his head on his hand and stared back at me.

"What's all this about? Are you angling for a house or a car?" Kinn's other hand came up to gently stroke my cheek.

"And if I want a house *and* a car?"

Kinn leaned over to kiss my cheek. "I'll work hard and save every baht I make so I can buy you both."

"And if I want jewels? Silver and gold? Watches... What else is there?" I acted like I was thinking hard about it, but I couldn't help smiling when I saw Kinn looking at me fondly.

"Then I'll give you everything. If you want the moon and stars, I'll find a way to fetch them for you," Kinn teased, but he had an earnest look in his eyes—like he truly meant every word.

My heart skipped a beat. "You love me that much?" Even if doubt was starting to cloud my head, when I saw how sincere Kinn was, Uncle Thee seemed all the more untrustworthy. But...

"The sins of the Major Clan will really make your skin crawl."

I sighed. I couldn't get my uncle's words out of my head.

"I love you so, so much... Do you love me too?" Kinn asked, nipping at my lower lip. I slowly nodded in reply.

"Is there something you're not telling me?" I asked because I couldn't stop overthinking things. I hadn't even told Kinn about meeting Uncle Thee this afternoon because I still couldn't figure out what the hell my uncle had been trying to hint at. I wanted some time to get my thoughts in order and work out what I really wanted to know first. Uncle Thee could've just been talking out of his ass, but there could also be more to the story. I didn't want to make a big deal out of nothing...

"Why are you asking me that out of nowhere?"

"Just in case there's something you haven't told me," I said.

"Mm-hmm..." Kinn looked uneasy, like something had just popped into his head. "Actually, there is. But let me talk to Pete first."

"What's it got to do with Pete?"

"I'm not sure, but I'll tell you as soon as possible..."

"But I want to know now," I insisted. If it was about my parents' possible involvement with the Major Clan, I wanted to hear it from Kinn's mouth more than anyone else's. If anyone could help me understand it, it would be him.

"Go to sleep, my love..." Kinn quickly changed the subject. "I asked you what you wanted. Don't you want to know what I want?"

I frowned at him, but I couldn't resist asking him in return, "What do you want?"

"I want you…" Kinn burrowed his face into the slope of my neck and inhaled deeply, then started to suck a hickey into my skin.

"Kinn… Tell me what's going on first." I tried shoving at his chest, but that didn't work. He continued mouthing my skin all the way to my earlobe. "K-Kinn, that tickles," I gasped. His warm breath on my neck was making me lose my mind.

"Mmm…"

My mind went blank as he languidly pressed his soft lips against the same spot again and again…

"Kinn… Kinn!"

Kinn suddenly stopped kissing my neck. I was a little surprised when he paused there for longer than usual…then, his breathing evened out into a soft snore.

"Kinn…?"

I gently shook his arm and found that he had fallen asleep right on top of me. I rolled him off of me, then nuzzled into his chest, which was our usual sleeping position. He hugged me tighter. I knew Kinn had been exhausted lately, and that he'd had a lot on his mind, so it was no surprise that he'd dozed off so easily.

The more time we spent together, the more my love for Kinn deepened. Besides my little brother, I'd never worried about anyone's feelings or wanted to make someone feel at ease before. But today, I was worried for Kinn, and I wanted him near me always.

No matter what happened in the future, I wanted to remember his touch and the warmth of his love forever. I didn't want to lose anyone else.

Especially not Kinn… I can't lose him.

I woke up early. Maybe I'd gotten used to it from helping to host Pete's funeral—I'd been getting up to arrive at the temple by seven every day.

But that wasn't the only reason I opened my eyes at half past six: I couldn't find the man who'd held me all through the night. There was no trace of Kinn; he wasn't in the bathroom or his office.

I went to brush my teeth and planned to go out to find Kinn. In the morning, I usually woke to the sight of Kinn bustling around his room. I wondered what he was doing up so early this morning...

Arm passed me on the stairs. "You're up early. Is something going on?"

I greeted him with a nod. "Have you seen Kinn?"

"He walked past me on the way to Pete's room just now... What happened?"

"It's nothing. Where are you going?"

"Bringing the young master his hot milk. He's up early too. Said he was going down to find Pete. Pete's popular right now."

"Uh-huh." I waved goodbye to Arm and headed straight for Pete's room.

What business did Kinn have with Pete that was so urgent? He should have been letting Pete rest. Khun too—he was going to bother Pete the entire day, I just knew it.

"Did you get any sleep last night?" I heard Kinn ask Pete through the slightly open door. I was about to step inside...

"Not really," Pete replied. "I was thinking of going to the fitness room to work out."

"What were you worried about...? Is it Vegas?"

Pete didn't answer him.

"Pete... I'll ask you this candidly," Kinn said, lowering his voice. I froze mid-step. Kinn must've come down here early to speak with Pete because he didn't want anyone else to know about it. I had an idea what Kinn's suspicions were; I suspected the same thing.

"All right," Pete said.

"What did Vegas do to you?"

I stood by the door and listened to their conversation. I also wanted to know what Vegas had done. Pete had marks on him, but they weren't from a beating.

I'd heard stories about the Minor Clan's ruthlessness from Arm and Pol. If the Minor Clan caught anyone trying to take advantage of them, they wouldn't let that person leave alive. Their methods of killing were especially cruel...but Pete had managed to escape in one piece—which, if I understood things correctly, was incredibly unusual.

"He locked me up," Pete said.

"Where?"

"In his room."

"Did he hurt you?" Kinn pressed.

"At the beginning..."

"And after that?"

Pete went silent. I couldn't see his expression from where I stood outside the room, but the air was so stifling that I could feel it.

"Why didn't you contact me, Pete?"

"That day, when I sent everything to you, my phone ran out of power. I hid in the closet, and Vegas caught me... After that, there was no way I could contact you."

"Pete...I'm sorry," Kinn said. "You can be angry with me—hate me, even. Please know I am willing to take responsibility for everything that has happened. I will pay for the damages; just name your price. If there's anything else you want me to do, tell me. This was all a terrible misunderstanding. I thought you'd already gone home to visit your grandparents, and Khun thought you were still working for me. It was my mistake—I'm truly sorry."

"Why are you apologizing, Mr. Kinn? I understand. I'm just happy you guys didn't forget about me."

"You are like a brother to me, Pete. If there's anything you need, just tell me."

"You don't have to do anything, Mr. Kinn," said Pete. "But I might ask for a month's leave to go back home."

"Do you still want to work here?" Kinn asked. "If it's uncomfortable for you—"

"I can't leave Mr. Tankhun behind, Mr. Kinn. I never thought about stepping down from my position here, only...I might have to ask for some time away."

"I'm happy to do whatever it takes for you to feel comfortable here...because I was the reason Ve—"

"You don't have to worry about it, Mr. Kinn. I can sort myself out," Pete insisted.

"All right. Whenever you want to start your leave, just let Tankhun know... And please, forget about those terrible things. I understand what you've been through," Kinn said.

The way neither of them mentioned it outright made me certain about what Pete had gone through. *I've been there before, Pete. I know how agonizing it feels and how difficult it is to get past...*

"Oh... You're awake?" Kinn said, emerging from the room.

I stepped back and acted like I'd just arrived. I didn't know how torn up Pete was about this, or if he was comfortable with me knowing what he'd gone through, so I pretended to be obliviously walking by.

"Probably not," I said. "Did you have to ask?"

Kinn gave me a small smile. "Giving me sass so early in the morning."

"Porsche… You're up early," said Pete.

Now that I finally got a good look at Pete, I could see he was in bad shape. His eyes were swollen, and there were dark circles underneath, like he hadn't slept at all. It looked like he'd been crying a lot. It broke my heart to see him like this.

"Does your wrist still hurt?" I tried to sound normal, asking after his injury without focusing on the sorrow in his eyes.

"Not really. You want to go work out with me?" Pete asked. He was already wearing a long-sleeved tracksuit and fitted long pants.

"Sounds good. You should exercise. You're putting on weight, did you know that, Porsche? And you're studying sports science too! I'll leave him to you, Pete." Kinn ruffled my hair before he turned around and left.

I kicked the ground as he walked away. "Bastard!"

"Heh. It's good that you two made up." Pete beamed at me. "I'm happy for you." I suddenly realized that no matter how much gloom hung over Pete, he always had a smile to give.

"What about you? Are you okay?" I talked with him as we walked.

"I'm okay," he replied. I could tell something was weighing heavily on him just from the sound of his voice: He wasn't okay.

"That's good to hear." I didn't know how much I should say. I really wanted to comfort him, but I didn't know if he was miserable because he couldn't come to terms with what had happened, or if something else was on his mind.

When we got to the fitness room, Pete worked out hard, like he had a lot of pent-up emotions. He kept himself busy running on the treadmill and watching the gym's TV. He smiled and laughed as we talked about random things, but he was clearly trying to hide his pain.

I was half-heartedly lifting weights when I heard a grating voice: "Goood morning, everyone!"

I wanted to lift the rack and throw it at Tankhun's head.

"Good morning, Young Master. Did you sleep well last night?" Pete beamed at his young master, who, as soon as he laid eyes on Pete's face, rushed over and clung to the treadmill.

I looked at Tankhun in surprise—he was wearing workout clothes. Never in a million years had I seen him set foot in here. What was he up to?

"A little birdie told me you two were exercising to welcome a brand-new day, so I'm here to keep you company." Tankhun hopped on the treadmill adjacent to Pete's and turned it on. "Don't want you to get lonely."

"That's good, Young Master. Working out is good for your health." Pete reached over to set up the treadmill for Tankhun, who fumbled with the controls like a complete idiot.

I understood Khun—he was probably acting extra clingy right now because he was still shaken up by Pete's disappearance. *I mean, Pete's his favorite bodyguard!*

"What's everyone doing?" Chay poked his head in to greet us. It was unusual to see him up at this hour on a weekend, but he'd probably also gotten used to waking up early.

"Morning, Chay. Exercise?" Pete greeted him and waved my little brother inside.

Chay came over to me and sat down. "You're so fit. But you should be resting, P'Pete."

"I just wanted something to do," Pete said.

"Now that everyone's here... Tonight, tonight, tonight! Let's go to Madam Yok's! We're gonna celebrate your return. Sound good?" Tankhun said to Pete, then turned to raise his eyebrows at me.

"That's fine. I don't really want to stay in a...small, square room anyway," Pete said quietly.

"Please let me go with you. Please, please, please!" Chay begged, glancing between me and Khun.

"You're not old enough," I said. Chay scrunched up his nose. *When did you learn to pull faces like that, you little punk?*

"I'll allow it," Khun declared. "Who's going to tell me no? Chay, I'll allow you to go! Whoever stops Chay from going in, I'll go on a rampage. That'll show them." *Who taught you that violence is the secret to getting your way, you spoiled brat?!*

"Is that okay?" Chay snuck a glance at me. I rolled my eyes and shook my head.

"Yes, it is! Porsche, call Madam Yok right now. I'm reserving the whole bar!" Khun proclaimed. "Private party, no outsiders. And make sure there's a mic. I want karaoke."

I was on the floor, about to start my sit-ups, but I had to turn to Khun with an unimpressed stare. "Oh, is Madam Yok back from the afterlife?"

"Just light some incense to call her back," he said. "You take care of it."

"I'm not your butler!" I snapped, but I wasn't serious; I knew Khun couldn't help being a jackass.

"Just think of it as helping your husband's elder brother," Khun said with a cheerful smile. He looked happier than he'd been in days. Before Pete came back, Khun had cried nonstop—when his eyes were open, when they were closed, even when he was eating. I was astonished at how much he'd cried.

It was a good thing Pete was back; the atmosphere in the house was so much brighter now.

We spent the rest of our workout session doing our own thing. I messed around on my phone for a bit, then lifted some more weights. Chay sat on a yoga ball. Pete ran on the treadmill until he was swimming in sweat. Khun, however, was not so happy on his treadmill; his wide smile steadily got smaller until he was gasping for breath.

"Ah! Owww!" he shrieked and slumped down, the still-moving treadmill belt flinging him to the floor.

"Young Master! Young Master, what's wrong?"

"Cramp... I've got a cramp! Ow! It hurts!"

Pete hurriedly squatted down and massaged Khun's calf while Chay and I came over to sit down next to him.

"Stretch out your leg," I said, lifting his foot. I knew a thing or two about injuries from studying sports science.

"Ow! That hurts!" Tankhun wailed like he was dying.

"Young Master, you didn't stretch before running. And you rarely exercise—of course your muscles are tight," Pete said, still squeezing Tankhun's calf. I made sure his leg stayed stretched straight out.

"...Get me to Dr. Top! It hurts! Oww!"

"You're not dying, Khun, it's just a cramp," I scolded him. "Stop overreacting!" I'd heard enough out of him. *Before this, when your beloved Dr. Top came to the funeral, you completely ignored him! Now you're back to being head over heels?*

"Porsche! You keep defying me! Can't you understand that Dr. Top is my one true love?" Tankhun's pain seemed to have lessened somewhat because he'd started daydreaming.

"Can he still love you? Last I heard, he came to Pete's funeral and saw you pour fish maw soup all over Vegas's head. I think your precious P'Top was so shocked, he couldn't move." I'd blurted it out without thinking. Pete paused for a second, then acted like he didn't care about what I'd just said. "Shit," I muttered. *I'm sorry, I didn't mean it. I know you don't want to hear Vegas's name right now, but it just slipped out...*

"Yes, P'Top saw how fierce I am! I think he'll like a strong man who's ready to take on the world for him," Khun said, giggling.

Chay could barely hold back his laughter. He went to grab some massage oil and handed it to Pete. "If thinking that makes you happy, then you can keep on thinking it," he said.

"But that day, Vegas acted like he didn't know anything! I should've grabbed the pot and dumped the whole thing on him—such a shame! Instead of telling me my bodyguard wasn't dead, that motherfucker said nothing! Hmph! I must have my revenge," Khun declared. I knew he'd said it without thinking, but Pete went quiet, furiously massaging Khun's leg like he was forcing himself not to think about Vegas.

"But I'm so happy you survived and came back unscathed. Later, I'll take you to bathe in holy water to wash away your bad luck, since you miraculously survived," Khun rambled on. "Heh. Vegas. He's a psycho, did you know that?" I snuck a glance at Pete, who was starting to look uncomfortable.

"Psycho...how?" Chay asked. *And what's wrong with my little brother now? Why does he suddenly want to know?*

"There's so many stories to tell, I wouldn't be able to tell you all of them—even if I had ten years!" said Khun. "So let's just go with the latest one that my friend from university told me... Vegas is a pervert. If there's thirty gay guys in one major, Vegas has already slept with twenty of them!"

Pete froze. He stopped what he was doing and took a deep breath. "Keep massaging, Pete, it still hurts. Owww." Khun nudged Pete, who had closed his eyes in an effort to keep calm.

I was starting to wonder...was Pete a wreck because of what Vegas did to him, or was there more going on between them? His reaction was too telling—and it was all happening right in front of me.

"That many? What about the other ten?" Chay asked. I wanted to take off my shoe and slap my brother in the mouth with it.

"The other ten slept with Kinn. Hee hee." Khun gave me a teasing smile, the asshole.

"Fucking hell! Who?! When?!" I blurted, suddenly feeling mad at Kinn.

"The flames of jealousy sure burn hot," Khun snickered. "Heh. Ow. This happened a long time ago, so who knows if the rumors are true. Those guys might just be saying it to make themselves look good. Kinn's handsome; anyone would want a piece of that! But with Vegas...I'm sure the rumors are true." Khun turned toward a particularly nosy-looking Chay, itching to gossip.

"What, what? Spill!" Chay egged him on.

"A friend of mine said he slept with Vegas. He said that when they had sex, he had to beg for his life. Like this!" Khun clasped his hands and dragged out each word: "'No moooore... I'm scaaaared... Pleeease stop!'"

I did feel bad for Pete, who was hanging his head, but I couldn't stop myself from laughing. *Damn it!*

Chay was trying to hold in his laughter as well. "That bad, Phi?"

"'No moooore...' See? Can you believe it?! My friend can't look at long, hard objects anymore! He'll cry hysterically! Last I heard, he was afraid of a TV remote... Owww! Pete, be gentle."

Pete had inadvertently squeezed Khun's leg too hard. He quickly let go and apologized, "Sorry, Young Master."

"Massage it properly, it's still tight. Where was I? Chay! That's not all—Vegas fucked him until his eyes rolled back into his head! His pupils disappeared, and he was only left with the whites! His friends had to slap him for his eyes to go back to normal! Vegas really is a freak."

"That's enough, Khun. Stop talking about him," I warned, but Khun just clicked his tongue at me.

"Heh. His eyes rolled back into his head?" said Chay. "Isn't that a bit much, Phi?"

No one was listening to me. Chay was having too much fun with Khun's story, and Khun's descriptions were so graphic that I could picture them in my head.

"It's not an exaggeration. He said it happened last week, and I don't know if he's better yet. Look, his eyes were bulging out like this, and you could only see the whites... *Ow! Pete! That hurts! I must be bleeding by now—are you trying to kill me?*"

Pete let go of Khun's leg and bent his head apologetically. *This is getting weird.* I could sense a murderous aura coming from Pete. *Pete, don't tell me you couldn't accept what Vegas did to you, but you still felt something for him?*

"I think you should take a hot bath, Young Master. That might help," Pete said evenly. It made a chill run up my spine.

"Fine, okay," said Khun. "What about you, Chay? You ever had your eyes roll back into your head?"

Chay, laughing until he doubled over, immediately shook his head.

"What about you, Pete? Oh, wait, I can't ask you. You don't have a boyfriend like these two. Porsche?" Khun turned to me, so I lifted my foot, ready to kick him.

"Do you want *your* eyes to roll back?" I grumbled. "I'll hit you so hard, your eyes won't see what's coming, you bastard!" *If Pete's situation really is what I think it is, he must be fuming inside. You've done it now, Khun!*

"Excuse me," Pete said, and he turned around and strode out of the fitness room.

"What?! What's wrong with Pete? Was it something I said? Or does he not like the whites of people's eyes...? By the way, why do your eyes roll back? What makes that happen?"

"Call Top and ask him!" I got up from the floor and quickly followed after Pete.

"Oh, yes, P'Top is a doctor. He must know. Chay, bring me my phone, I'm going to call P'Top."

"B...better not. Ha ha."

"Pete! Are you okay?" I pulled Pete to a stop before he reached his room.

Pete turned to give me a small smile. "I'm okay. Why wouldn't I be?"

I reached into my pocket and pulled out my cigarettes. I handed one to Pete and kept one for myself. "Here... You'll feel better."

Pete held the cigarette in his mouth as I lit it for him.

"Shit, this is the best! I haven't smoked in so long," Pete said, rolling the cigarette between his fingers and staring at it longingly.

"...You shouldn't listen to Khun too much," I said. "You have to take everything he says with a grain of salt. A bucket of salt. You know how he is."

"Even if what the young master said is true, I don't care. Who Vegas fucks or where he goes to die is his business," Pete said, his voice shaking slightly.

I sighed. *How the hell did you end up catching feelings, Pete? Your mouth might be saying one thing, but your eyes don't lie.*

"Pete…you know you can tell me anything," I said.

He didn't reply.

"You can come to me about anything, Pete." I gently put my hand on his shoulder. "Even if I don't have any advice for you, I can still listen."

"Don't worry about it. I'll forget about it in a bit. He probably doesn't care, anyway."

Although we hadn't said it out loud, I could tell that Pete knew I'd seen through him. He probably didn't want to admit it.

"If it hurts to say it, maybe it's better not to say it at all," I said.

Pete's expression dulled; he looked lost in thought. I didn't want to make things worse for him, but I wanted him to come to terms with it.

"Heh… Ever since you became Kinn's husband, you're a lot more reasonable," Pete said, hiding his feelings behind a joke. "You're speaking like a human being now."

"Of course… Living with a lunatic like Tankhun, you've gotta have some logic," I said with a smile.

"Give me another one," Pete said. I reached into my pocket again for my pack of cigarettes. This morning, I'd been planning to go down the street to buy soy milk, so I had my wallet with me. But I'd completely forgotten about it, right up until my wallet fell out of my pocket.

"…Oh." Pete bent down to grab the open wallet. I saw him glance at the photo hastily stuffed inside of it. He furrowed his brow. "Here. This is yours."

I gave him another cigarette, snatching my wallet back and shoving it back into my pocket. I didn't know how much Pete had seen. Did he get a good look at the photo that I couldn't stop thinking about?

"Oh, right. Pete?"

"Hmm?" He raised an eyebrow at me as he took another drag of his smoke.

"If I wanted to know about the subsidiaries under the Major Clan's business...maybe ten years ago, who do I ask?" I knew I should tell at least one person, just in case, but I was still debating whether I should investigate this quietly by myself or if I should involve anyone else. I decided to test the waters with Pete.

"Hmm... P'Chan, of course," Pete said. "P'Chan knows everything about this place."

"What about you? Do you know anything about the subsidiaries?"

"I've only been officially working here for a few years." He blew the smoke from his mouth. "The only subsidiary I know well is the young master's chocolate factory."

"Mm-hmm. And the deed to my house—do you know anything about that?" I asked, remembering what Uncle Thee had said.

"Huh?" Pete turned to look at me, confused. "What's going on, Porsche?"

"It's..." *What do I do now? Should I ask for Pete's help so I can quickly find out if Uncle Thee was telling me the truth? I want proof, so that I can stay here without worry. If my parents were involved with the Major Clan...* "Pete! You have to help me!"

"Me? What do you mean, me?" Pete pointed at himself, looking close to tears.

"I don't trust anyone but you," I said.

"That's what Mr. Kinn said... Why don't you try trusting someone else—maybe Pol or Arm? Those two are trustworthy, believe me!"

Pete was clearly traumatized by Kinn sending him to the Minor Clan. *What do I do now?!*

"I promise I won't get you into trouble," I said.

"Mr. Kinn said the same thing to me. You two sure are made for each other."

It looked like Pete was gonna refuse no matter what. But I could guarantee that the subject I wanted his help in investigating wouldn't lead him to his death, like Kinn's nearly had.

I was silent for a while, considering my options. I still couldn't find a way to solve this. Where did I start? My parents? The house? How was it all connected? My parents had their own business importing luxury cars, so I'd guessed they might've been business partners or had some other involvement with the Major Clan. Starting with the subsidiary companies shouldn't be a difficult task.

"Fine! Damn it!" Pete exclaimed. He must have noticed I had gone quiet. "What is it? If I can help, I'll help."

"Really?"

"Really. You're my friend. What is this all about? I'll tell you up front, I won't break into anyone's house. Vegas was... Fuck!" Pete bit his lip hard, like he hadn't meant to say Vegas's name out loud.

I smirked and couldn't help but tease him, "I promise your eyes won't roll back into your head...heh."

"Shit, Porsche!"

Pete chased after me, and I scrambled to avoid his kicks. I hadn't meant to add insult to injury or mock Pete, but seeing his expression waver when he mentioned Vegas...I couldn't resist.

I only hoped that I could easily resolve this issue with the photo, and that it wouldn't affect the bonds I'd built here. I prayed that it wasn't what I thought it was. Maybe Mr. Korn and my parents had been friends in the past, or maybe they'd been business partners, and that was why they'd taken that photo together.

But if it *was* like that...did Mr. Korn really not remember me?

KINN PORSCHE

Vegas × Pete 10

VEGAS

ASEARING PAIN shot through my head as I came back to consciousness. I tried to open my eyes and focus, to make sense of what had happened, but I was still in a daze; my mind was completely blank.

"Hia...how are you feeling?"

My brother's voice drew my attention away from trying to piece together what had happened. I turned to see Macau clinging to my arm from next to the bed where I lay. These surroundings were strange. The softness of the bed and pillow, the unfamiliar throbbing in my head... It wasn't like every other morning. I'd finally opened my eyes to find that I was somewhere else.

"P'Top, P'Top! Hia's awake," Macau exclaimed. I was used to hearing noisy yelling every day, but not from Macau...

"Macau, can't you shut up? Hah! Your brother's fine, he just slipped and hit his head. He's not going to die. Why are you acting like such a pussy?" This voice was instantly recognizable, even though I couldn't see the speaker's face. It was a voice that always stabbed me right in the heart; the voice that only gave orders, the voice that berated me...the voice I least wanted to hear.

"Father! If you're not worried about hia, then you can go home. Nop and I can stay with him."

Pain pounded in my temples as Macau and my father started to argue.

"Macau!" Father shouted.

"If your new wife didn't need to see the doctor, you wouldn't even be here to see Hia," Macau muttered darkly, slamming a glass down. He poured out some water and handed it to me. "Hia, drink some water."

I sipped the water from a straw, my throat so dry that it hurt.

"It's good that he's finally awake," Father said, getting up from the sofa. "I'm going back to the office. Keep an eye on your brother, Macau."

Macau turned to glare at him as he left. As our father walked out the door, the doctor came in. I had so many questions: Why was I in the hospital? What had happened?

"Hello," the doctor said. "Let me take a look at you."

I turned to the other side. Nop was busy with the bedside switch, adjusting the bed to a sitting position. There was an IV drip attached to my arm.

The doctor slowly reached out to touch my head. As soon as he lifted the gauze off, a tingling pain shot through me. Images came flooding back. It was him...the man who occupied my thoughts: *Pete... Where are you?*

"Nop..." I turned to Nop, who startled and looked down at the floor, too scared to meet my eyes.

"Is Pete all right? Where's Pete?" I asked.

I couldn't sit still. The doctor pulled back, looking at Macau quizzically as I anxiously dove toward Nop. The pain I felt right now couldn't compare to the memory of Pete crying as he cursed and swore at me. His eyes full of hurt, his grievances—everything was still fresh in my mind.

Where was he? What was he doing? If I was in the hospital, was he still waiting for me in my room?

...No.

I didn't want to remember what happened next. I knew I was lying to myself.

Yes.

I didn't want to think about what happened after Pete hurled the chain at me. I could only hope that he was still there, still in that room. I was worried for him; usually, if I had business outside, Pete would call and ask me to come back. How long had I been out by now? Was he still waiting for me? Would he be angry with me?

Macau came to tug my hand off of Nop's arm. "Hia, hia, you have to calm down. What are you talking about?"

"Nop, answer me! Pete is still in my room, right?" There was only one answer I wanted. If I didn't hear Nop say it, I had no idea what I'd do.

"Hia! Hia, what are you talking about? Hia!" Macau held me back as I tried to get up from the bed.

"How did I get here, Macau?" I didn't even feel the pain in my head anymore. There was only the agony of losing Pete, engulfing my heart and driving me mad.

"You slipped and fell last night and hit your head on the floor," Macau explained, hugging me tightly. "We brought you to the hospital."

The doctor and nurse stood by, a little farther away. "Mr. Korawit, you shouldn't be moving," the doctor said.

I grabbed Nop by the collar of his shirt. "Nop...that's what you told Macau?"

"I didn't dare tell him the truth," he said quietly.

"Where's Pete?! Where is he?!" I raised my voice. I couldn't control myself. I was trapped on all sides. My heart dropped when I saw Nop's expression; he refused to answer me.

"Who? Hia, who's Pete?" Macau asked.

"Mr. Korawit, please calm down," the doctor said.

My temper flared, reaching its peak. *This* side of me hadn't come around for a long time, but I couldn't hold back anymore. I wanted to go on a rampage, to throw things, to explode the way I used to.

"Let go! Let me out! Where are my car keys? Get me my keys!" I yelled, yanking the IV out of my arm. Both the doctor and the nurse charged at me, but I didn't care. I threw them off and went straight for Nop, snatching my keys from his pocket.

"Mr. Vegas, please calm down," Nop said.

"Hia!" Macau cried out. "What are you doing?!"

"Mr. Korawit!"

The room descended into chaos. I didn't know where I found the strength, but I pushed everyone away, even the doctor trying to pull me back. Ignoring the astonished stares from the people walking by, I half walked, half jogged out of the room with blood dripping from my arm, leaving a macabre trail of red down the hallway.

I headed for the VIP parking lot and easily found my family's car, one of the few allowed to park in this section. I got in and locked all the doors.

"Mr. Vegas!" Nop and a few other bodyguards chased after me, but I stepped on the gas and sped off.

Along the way, I was confused and restless. I couldn't think, couldn't breathe; my chest was tight with the agony in my heart. I knew that Pete wasn't waiting for me at home like he always was, but I wanted to lie to myself. *For just once in my life, let me have some hope. When Pete is with me, I have hope...*

Pete had made me realize that there was always a way out of the darkness. He'd been through so much, yet he could still smile and live with it. He taught me to take control of my emotions. He showed me that even when faced with insurmountable odds, our outlook was a little sunnier if we looked on the bright side of things.

Pete's words of comfort had pulled me from my own stupidity and stubbornness. It was like his hand had reached out and pulled me out of the darkness. Just hearing the words *"It's all right"* reminded me not to lose myself again.

I used to think someone in his position shouldn't even be saying that to me—he was in a tight spot himself, after all—but just seeing his smile and the sincerity in his eyes...I'd finally felt *alive* again.

I would be devastated if he just walked out of my life.

Pete was my light in the darkness, my only smile. He was the only sincere thing I had. That hopeful gaze reassured me no matter how many times I saw it, but it was about to slowly fade away...

I grasped the steering wheel in terror, my hands shaking, so scared that I could barely breathe.

I tore through the gates so quickly that the security guard almost couldn't open them fast enough. I slammed on the brakes before storming out and rushing up to the second floor.

"Mr. Vegas!"

My men scattered in a panic and trailed after me, clearly shocked to see me in this state: the hospital gown, the blood on my arm, the wound on my head.

I didn't care. I only needed to know that in my room, in our own little safe haven, Pete was still sitting there with his mischievous expression.

I opened the glass door and called out his name:

"Pete!"

My heart raced in apprehension, which turned to dread when I was met with an empty room.

There was no cheerful voice to greet me with *"Are you back now?"* or a grumpy face complaining that he was hungry. Not anymore.

The room was still the same as it had been when he was here: Every item, every book, even the chain that I'd put on him so he'd be mine and mine alone lay there on the floor. The room still bore his mark; it was saturated with the scent of him.

Everything was so clear to me now. I had to face the truth. I slowly stepped inside and fell to the floor, reaching out to pick up the chain.

What have I done?

That day when I'd been hurting from my father's words, when I was wallowing in self-hatred over getting compared to *them* again, my anguish had been at its worst. I had suffered for so many years, and I'd felt like I was all alone. Then, Pete appeared…and now he was gone.

"Well…you still have Macau. He loves you very much, right?" Pete's words came back to me.

I'm sorry, Pete… I'm sorry…

"You're pessimistic," Pete had said. The images of us together were still imprinted in my heart.

"And you're naïve."

"That's none of your business."

"And what do you think about me?"

"You're a fucking asshole, stup—"

I smiled even as tears threatened to well up. On that first day, I'd chained him up because I'd wanted him to know who he was dealing with, and to find an entertaining way to get back at Kinn.

I hadn't thought someone like Pete existed in this world. I'd hurt him in so many ways; I'd hit him, beat him, forced myself on him. I was disgusted with myself—how could I have done something like that to someone like him? Today, I loathed myself even more.

Before this, Pete had been just another Major Clan bodyguard. He hadn't held any significance to me; he wasn't even someone I wanted to get to know. If anything, I'd thought he was a fool to tail me on Kinn's orders. When I went to the Major Clan's house, I saw him as just another one of their loyal dogs who greeted me with a smile. How could I have known that his smile would forever imprint itself in my memory?

Pete dictated my every feeling now. The longer we stayed together, the more he became my sanctuary. No matter what I went through, as soon as I stepped into my room, I felt at ease and more like myself than I could describe. I didn't have to put on a mask or pretend; I didn't need to shoulder any kind of hope. I could just be me.

In that time, just short of a month, it was like Pete had filled the emptiness inside me. I was his everything then. No matter what I did, wherever I was, Pete would care. Someone finally *cared* for me. Ever since the day my nanny abandoned me and my mother left this world, no one had ever asked after me, *Have you eaten, Vegas? What are you doing? Where are you? When will you be back?* Or even *Does it hurt? Was it your father? It's all right. It'll pass...*

There was no one to pull the blanket back over me when it fell or to pick out my clothes. When Pete came into my life and gave me a taste of what I'd been missing, I knew then that I hated myself, hated that I had to be alone. I liked myself when I was with him;

it was as if life had meaning again. Even when I knew he was doing things to annoy me, I could see in his eyes and feel in my heart that it was real.

I'd questioned what kind of person he was—how he could still smile after I'd hurt him so badly. I understood him now, though, after slowly absorbing some of his positivity. He made me see things in a new light. He'd showed me the way out after I'd been blind for so long. I'd chained him up and locked him in my room, but he'd still learned to live with it; he was kind to me when I was so cruel to him. He was the only one in my life who'd taught me what it meant to keep moving forward—to *want* to keep moving forward.

I began to look forward to hearing my phone ring. When the screen showed Nop's name, I'd get excited because I knew it was Pete calling to ask for his beloved Southern food.

"*Which dish tastes good...? It looks spicy.*"

"*Try it.*"

"*Fine.*"

"*Ugh! A small bite like that won't give you any flavor. Give it to me! Eat up.*"

The memory of him feeding me still hurt. Even when I knew he was just playing a trick, trying to find small ways to get back at me, the hope in his eyes while he waited to see what I thought of the food was clear. If I said it was delicious—or somewhat edible, even—he'd be so happy. If I said it wasn't, he'd be unable to hide his disappointment.

The way he tried to cheer me up...no one had ever done anything like that for me. Did he know that lately I'd been trying to please him because I wanted him to stay? At first, I'd thought locking Pete up was a fun little game, but my intentions began to change. I wanted him and only him. I wanted to keep him all to myself. I did everything I could to get him to want to stay with me, for him to want me the way I wanted him.

"*Vegas.*" I loved that chirpy voice he used to call my name when he wanted something, or if he just wanted to share a strange idea that popped into his head. It always put me at ease. Just like that, the weight of the world was lifted from my shoulders. Did he know that everything about him made me feel so content?

"*What now?*"

"*One day, you are camping with your friends, and you find a very beautiful rock. You stop to admire it for a little while, and once you look up, you find that all your friends are gone. What would you do in this situation?*

a. Proceed to go straight.

b. Leave the pathway to find a river.

c. Toss the stone and ask it to show you the way.

d. Cry for help."

I smiled at the memory. Sometimes Pete was childish, and other times, he was incredibly mature. Sometimes he liked to make a spoiled or petulant face that he probably wasn't even aware he was making.

"*Hmmm... I don't like camping.*"

"*It's a what-if scenario.*"

Like that time he made a fuss trying to get me to answer his questions. His talent at acting spoiled and begging for what he wanted had increased with every passing day he lived with me.

"*Uhh...but I wouldn't stop to look at a rock in the first place.*"

"*Ugh! What if you did?*"

The way he'd twist his mouth was so endearing. He played it off casually, but that little frown let me know when I displeased him. I loved it—he was like a little kitten begging for his owner's attention.

I didn't know when my tears had begun to fall. My heart squeezed tightly, aching and heavy, until I wanted to dig it out just so this would all be over. I had to face the emptiness on my own once again. I had to exist without Pete's lively spirit. His cheerful voice in the morning still echoed in my head like a knife twisting in my gut. Another memory slowly resurfaced, and it hurt so much that I wanted to die...

"*No, you bastard! No!*"

"*Oh, you're scared? Someone like you knows how to be scared? Heh...*"

"*Vegas... No... Don't do this! Let me go!*"

"*What? Where's the fearless Pete from before? What's this timid little thing in his place?*"

"*...You can beat me up, shoot me, kill me—do whatever you want. Just don't do this!*"

"*Heh...I told you already that I'm gonna kill you, but you have to suffer first... Oh, and I'm not doing this just to get back at Kinn. I know you're not that important. Even when you die, I doubt he'll be sad. You're just one of his stupid loyal dogs... And now, you're* my chew toy!"

Those terrible words that came out of my mouth... That day, everything I said had been for my own satisfaction, but now? It only left me with regret. It was because of me that everything ended up like this. I had wanted to hurt Pete, but now, it had all come circling back to hurt me instead, like a stone repeatedly hitting me in the chest. The sound of his voice and the fear in his eyes haunted me.

I clenched my fist around the chain, then flung it as far as I could. This was the pain and suffering that I'd personally handed to him. *That's enough. I know now. I know his fear.*

Was it really so horrible?

I'm sorry, I'm truly sorry.

I deserve this.

It was fitting that I had to face this pain because if I'd been Pete, I could never forgive what I'd done either. Now, I only wanted to tell him that I knew what I did was wrong. If he was angry with me, hated me, or wanted revenge, I wouldn't be surprised—I'd even let him do whatever he wanted to me.

He can berate me and hurt me as much as he pleases. I won't stop him. I'll only ask for one thing, just one thing, please... Just come back to me. Forgive my foolishness and the wicked things I've done...

I hastily changed into casual clothes and walked to the bathroom to splash some water on my face. Even the sight of his toothbrush made me feel another stab of heartache. No matter where I looked, I still saw Pete in every corner of this room.

"Am I so disgusting, Pete?"

"No..."

"I'm so tired."

The same words spun circles through my head: *I'm so tired right now, Pete... I'm so tired. I want to see your face. I want to hug you...*

Can you give me another chance?

I'd admit that I lost this game of ours. But I wanted Pete to win— I wanted him to win in every way. He'd won over my heart. He won when he made me feel things for him; he won when he managed to make me ache for him like this...

I wouldn't fight him anymore. If he came back, I'd give him more than he could ever want. I'd be proud to be the loser if he'd let this fool prove himself one last time...

What should I do?

I took a deep breath, feeling so disoriented. I wanted to see Pete's face. I wanted to apologize. I'd wronged him, but the last thing we'd argued about had all just been a misunderstanding: I wasn't seeing anyone else. I couldn't pay attention to anyone other than him. That situation with N'Yim wasn't what he'd thought at all. The fact that I came home late and left him all alone... I knew how lonely it was for him to be stuck in that little room; I'd wronged him. But I couldn't let him leave me after such a big misunderstanding...

That was why I decided to grab my keys and head out. No matter what, someone like Pete would run straight back to the Major Clan. I was certain of it.

I'm begging on my knees—just give me a chance. Just hear me out. I truly only have you in my heart, Pete.

I don't want you to misunderstand me. I don't want you to see me as a villain anymore... Can't you forget the Vegas from before? Let's start over. I promise I'll do my best this time.

As I drove, all I could think of was his face—his smile, his laugh, even his tears when he left me. I hated what had happened last night. I wouldn't be able to take it if he walked out of my life completely. I'd lost so many people; I couldn't bear to lose anyone else.

I parked next to the Major Clan's house, mulling over what I was going to say when I was face-to-face with Pete again. *How do I say I'm sorry for what I did I to you? What do I say?* I didn't know. I'd never been so terrified to see anyone before in my life.

"I don't want to go out! Why are you making me?!"

My heart fluttered nervously when I heard that familiar voice. It was the voice I'd so longed to hear, the voice I missed the most.

"We're just going out to get ice cream. What are you so afraid of?"

Pete had come out with Porsche, but I barely glanced at him. I only had eyes for one man. He wore casual clothes, all covered up. His expression was cheerful, but I knew he was hiding his pain. Without hesitation, I opened the car door and prepared to go up to him.

"Shit! I'm really scared, Porsche. I don't ever want to live like that again. Locked up in a room...it's torture."

I froze when I heard those words from Pete's mouth. My heart dropped when I saw how nervous he was. I quickly stepped behind a tree, my confidence plummeting.

Another guard—his name was Arm, if I recalled correctly—came up to loop his arms around both Pete and Porsche. "You don't have to be scared of anything—look who you're friends with! This is Porsche, the second young mistress of the Major Clan!"

"Nah," Pete said, shaking his head. Just seeing his face made me want to pull him into a hug.

"What now? Vegas can't do anything to you here."

When Arm mentioned my name, Pete covered his ears. What little confidence I had left completely vanished. My heart was so viciously stomped into the ground that I wanted to fall to my knees. *He must despise me.*

"Why did you have to say that? Go! The ice-cream cart is here. What do you want? My treat."

"Oooh! Pete, you're so dramatic. Even Mr. Kinn is afraid of Porsche, never mind Ve—"

Porsche turned to Arm. "Stop that!" Pete just looked at them blankly and marched up to the ice cream cart.

"So fierce, even with his friends. Hey, Pete! I want some too."

Porsche and Arm followed after him. I watched Pete's every move as he smiled and laughed with his friends. I couldn't tear my eyes away from his charm, not even for a second. It felt like I was falling for him again, over and over.

Ring, ring.

I saw Arm playing with the ice-cream cart's bell, but that startled Pete and made him jump.

"The fuck are you ringing that for?" Pete exclaimed, pounding Arm on the back. When I saw him like that, I felt guilt like I'd never felt before. *Can we ever go back to the way we were? No, can we start over? Why can't I see a way back...?*

"You're so jumpy. Khun's taking you to bathe in holy water soon. Just try to stay calm for now."

"Just watch my back. I'm scared," Pete said.

"Why? Is your ass...in danger?" Porsche said. He really was a menace. He got a kick for his teasing words.

Pete was having fun. He was happy with his friends; I began to wonder if I really should go up to him and turn that smile into fear. He was free, doing what he wanted to do, and he seemed happy. Should I really dredge up the past? It looked like he didn't want to remember. *He doesn't even want to hear my name...*

"I want the one with bread. And I was here first!"

"I ordered first. You're the slowpoke."

I sighed and watched Pete until he disappeared back into the house.

Maybe he really is better off without me.

The way he'd left me should have been enough of an answer. He didn't want me. Before, I would've done everything in my power to get him back, but now, I couldn't bear to destroy his smile or his happiness. Not anymore.

He was the one I loved.

I loved Pete from the bottom of my heart.

CHARACTER & NAME GUIDE

Characters

The identity of certain characters may be a spoiler; use this guide with caution on your first read of the novel.

MAIN CHARACTERS

'Kinn' Anakinn Theerapanyakul
GIVEN NAME: A-na-kinn
NICKNAME: Kinn
SURNAME: Thee-ra-pan-ya-kul

The second son and de facto heir of a notorious mafia family. Has a habit of getting rough with his partners.

'Porsche' Pachara Kittisawasd
GIVEN NAME: Pa-cha-ra
NICKNAME: Porsche
SURNAME: Kit-ti-sa-wasd

A normal college student who is extremely skilled at martial arts. Since their parents died, he takes care of his younger brother.

SUPPORTING CHARACTERS

'PORCHAY' PITCHAYA KITTISAWASD: Porsche's beloved younger brother.
UNCLE THEE: The younger brother of Porsche's late father. Has a severe gambling problem.
TEM AND JOM: Porsche's best friends and fellow university students.
MADAM YOK: Porsche's former employer and owner of the Root Club.

KORN THEERAPANYAKUL: Kinn's father and the current head of the main branch of the Theerapanyakul mafia family, aka the Major Clan.
'KHUN' TANKHUN THEERAPANYAKUL: Kinn's eldest brother.
'KIM' KIMHAN THEERAPANYAKUL: Kinn's youngest brother.
'VEGAS' KORAWIT THEERAPANYAKUL: The eldest son of the Minor Clan.
'MACAU': The youngest son of the Minor Clan.
ZEK-KANT: Korn's younger brother and head of the Minor Clan.

TAY AND TIME: Kinn's friends.

'BIG': Kinn's former lead bodyguard, before Porsche took over his position.
'PETE': Tankhun's lead bodyguard, who temporarily switched positions with Porsche.
'POL', 'P'JESS', AND 'ARM': Tankhun's other bodyguards.
'NONT': Kim's lead bodyguard.
'CHAN': Korn's secretary.

TAWAN: Kinn's ex-boyfriend.
MEK: Tawan's younger brother and a friend of Kinn's from high school.

Names Guide

Thai names follow the western pattern of a given name followed by a family name. Thais are also given a nickname, which is more commonly used when Thais refer to their family, friends, and close acquaintances in their daily life. Thai nicknames can be anything the parents find appealing, a nickname their friends prefer to call them, or even nonsensical words in foreign languages.

In Thailand, it is unusual for people to use someone's surname in casual conversation, unless specifically required. To formally refer to a person, given names are preferred.

Thai honorifics

P'/PHI (IPA pronunciation: /pʰiː˥/): A gender-neutral honorific term used to address older siblings, friends, and acquaintances. It can be used as a prefix (P'[name]), a pronoun, or informally used to address unknown people (e.g. store clerks, or shopkeepers).

N'/NONG (IPA pronunciation: /nɔːŋ˦/): Used to address younger people, in the same manner as "phi."

Teochew honorifics

The Thai Chinese are the largest minority group in Thailand, integrated through several waves of immigration. Of these, just over half are Teochew, from the Chaoshan region. Families with Teochew roots may still occasionally use the Teochew dialect, especially when referring to other family members. Some of the terms that appear in this novel are as follows:

HIA: Elder brother
BE: Older brother of one's father

ZEK: Younger brother of one's father
GOU: Older or younger sister of one's father
AGONG: Grandfather

Thai Dialects

The Thai language has four major regional dialects: Central, Northern, Northeastern, and Southern, corresponding to the major geographical/cultural regions.

CENTRAL THAI is the official language of the country, used in official settings, education, news reporting, and media. Most Thais are able to communicate in Central Thai, though those from the north, northeastern, and southern parts of the country typically also speak their regional dialect.

NORTHERN THAI (Kam Mueang) is considered soft and pleasant-sounding. It is derived from the language of the Lanna Kingdom (now part of northern Thailand).

NORTHEASTERN THAI (Isan) is heavily influenced by the Lao language. Although it is very similar to Central Thai, the difference in tonal patterns, vowel qualities, and common vocabulary can make Northeastern Thai challenging for people who only speak Central Thai.

SOUTHERN THAI (Pak Tai) is the fastest-spoken dialect. It has a more distinct intonation and sharp rhythm that lends it a melodic quality compared to Central Thai. Since the south of Thailand is close to Malaysia, the Southern dialect has influences from the Malay language and has several Malay loanwords.

The main dialect used by the characters of this novel is Central Thai. However, there are various instances of characters using other dialects, to show a character's roots or for comedic effect—for example, Pete and his family speak Southern Thai, as they come from the islands off the coast of Chumphon in the south. These instances of other dialects have been localized to other American English dialects/accents, which may not be an exact match, but the closest possible equivalent to preserve literary style.